McGILL

BY
GARY BARGATZE

Warfield

Happy Hollow

Hurricane Creek

Hollow Rock

Upcoming titles in the
Your Winding Daybreak Ways series

Cabedelo

Thunderwood

Babylon, A Human Requiem

*For more information about the series, visit the author's
website www.garybargatze.com*

McGILL

GARY BARGATZE

————————————

RIGOR HILL PRESS

For Katherine, who breathes life into stone

McGILL

1

d4 f5   g3 g6

As I SLOWLY circle the square, I concede, dear Catherine, you nailed it on two counts—chess and Brahms. The sleek, green cod atop the courthouse dome still rejects the biting wind and taunts my old garret window; but I ignore the copper insult suggesting I'm an amateur. I'd stipulated early on to all of you I don't always make winning moves. And as far as the music goes, again touché, a palpable hit, life does indeed rob us of so much more than death ever could.

The movers and shakers had finally drawn a line in the sand. They declared our fifth high school reunion would be held the last weekend in August just before I entered graduate school. I hadn't been back home since Dad made the difficult decision to leave Mom behind and accept a distinguished chair in physics on the Urbana campus. Mom's family became quite angry when Dad announced he was pulling up stakes. But even then I empathized with him. I had to acknowledge his decade-long struggle to get Mom the best care he could and his strong reluctance to commit her permanently to Our Lady of Hope.

Mom's mother, brother, and stepsister were well-intentioned. They just didn't understand the suffering. They weren't there with us twenty-four hours a day living in Mom's hell: the voices;

the screaming; the constant accusations; the Thorazine; the Haldol; the Stelazine; the depression; the constant restlessness; the medications to control the side effects; the shock therapy; the shuttling back and forth between the hospitals, clinics, and home; the overdose; and the deep slashing of wrists.

I had told Knox, Anderson, and Grimes I would meet them in the lobby around two o'clock Friday afternoon. The planning committee had fortuitously chosen the most appealing hotel in Louisville for our celebration. My parents and I used to eat in the hotel's elegant dining room after Mom finished a Sunday solo with the philharmonic. For me, these occasional trips to the grand hotel were dazzling visits to a mysterious, opulent castle. The long rectangular skylight transformed the lobby into a blinding gateway of luminosity, highlighting the soaring ceilings, the giant marble columns, and the colorful pioneer murals ringing the walls. I would flop down in one of the oversized velvet chairs and gaze at the gilded chandeliers and the white marble registration desk spanning the width of the room.

Even more exciting than the ambience and architecture were Dad's stories about the guests who had frequented the five-star establishment. No, it wasn't Taft, Wilson, Roosevelt, Truman, Fitzgerald, Tom and Daisy Buchanan, or Jay Gatsby who enthralled me. I only wanted to hear more tales about the bootlegging mobster, George Remus, and the legendary gangster, Al Capone. Dad would occasionally take me down the hall to the dark-paneled billiard room and let me peek into the alcove where Al played Texas hold'em. He pointed to the large mirror and explained the gangster had had it shipped in from Chicago so he could constantly watch his back.

But there was one Sunday afternoon in particular that I'll never forget. Dad tipped the bellman, and I received a VIP tour of the secret back room. My hotel guide pushed several oak panels to the side and revealed two hidden doors leading to secret passageways. He explained if the police raided the hotel, Al or George could disappear through one of the hidden corridors and escape into the streets. And for the tour's grand finale, the bellman allowed me to activate the spring-loaded doors, which outside guards could quickly lock if G-men were about to launch a raid.

As I reminisced, I heard a baritone shout my name from the bank of elevators to my right. I swung around, and there they were, the protective starting beef on the left side of our third-in-the-state varsity line. Since I was the second-string quarterback, I rarely got a chance to play when they were on the field. But I could guarantee you Knox would immediately bring up the one play I had tried to forget for more than six years.

I had repeatedly explained to our esteemed left guard that the 81 quick-pass is a bang-bang play. At the snap, the left end takes two steps forward and cuts to the right across the middle, and the quarterback takes two steps back, extends his body, locates the tight end out of the corner of his eye, and then fires a bullet. The play developed as planned; but as I was snapping my arm forward and releasing the ball, I saw my left end stumble. The only player within a mile of my pass was our rival's middle linebacker, who caught the ball and ran it in for a quick pick six.

When the three men approached, there were broad smiles and firm hugs all around. And as I predicted, the first thing out of

Knox's mouth was a humorously snide remark about "the play." "Still throwing those interceptions, huh, Taylor?" he asked.

I had spent the past five years preparing a humorous rejoinder and replied, "I hate reminding you, Knoxie, but very few quarterbacks throw touchdowns on the first play of their careers!"

These down-home jocks were my teenage antidotes to the rich profusion of classical music, derivatives and integrals of functions, and Ovid's elegiac love poems I had been steeped in since childhood. Knox's father was a successful building contractor, who pioneered open-air pedestrian shopping centers in the suburbs. Anderson's father had been in the Korean War, and when he returned home, he used his inheritance to purchase one of the first chain restaurant and motor lodge franchises in the South. And Grimes's dad had been the pastor of the New Canaan Lutheran Church for the past fifteen years.

While Knox and Anderson were outgoing, quick, and sometimes brusque, Grimes was a six-foot six-inch two-hundred-eighty-pound gentle giant who relished smashing into charging defensive tackles and blitzing linebackers. Compared to my other two teammates, Grimes was introverted and academically challenged. As we walked the two blocks over to the Market Street bus stop, I recalled a tenth-grade English assignment. We were supposed to draft a paper no longer than six pages describing our most important goal in life. I remember how hard we all worked on the project and what happened when Mr. Dugan returned our papers the following week.

He explained there was only one A and two A-minuses out of our class of twenty-five. When the bell rang at the end of the period, my three close teammates and I filed out into the crowded hallway.

"Hey, Knox, Anderson. What did you get?" I called.

"B-minus," Anderson replied.

"Ha! B-plus," said Knox with a smile, his head nodding.

"And you, Grimes?" I asked.

Grimes blushed. "A."

"What? Can we see what you wrote?" I asked. Grimes proudly handed me his essay, which I read out loud: "'My personal goal in life is to be loved.'"

"Huh. Good one, Grimes." Anderson and Knox both patted his shoulder. We were all quiet after that.

As we waited for the bus, I learned that Knox and Anderson were going to use their business degrees to follow in their fathers' footsteps in construction and the hotel management business. Grimes said that after high school he bounced around from one menial job to another until he finally found his calling as an assistant to a physical therapist in the local Veterans Hospital. He humorously explained how he had settled on his career: "I like working with people and always enjoyed lifting weights during training camp. I just exchanged the free weights for aging war heroes."

Our destination was the historic amusement park at the end of the Market Street line. We had spent many of our summers together there and thought it the ideal spot to celebrate our own personal reunion. The city landmark was much more than the penny arcade, the Rocket, the Comet, the Whip, and the Rock-O-Planes. It also featured a roller rink, holiday fireworks, and daily shows on the center stage near Gypsy Village, where we witnessed the waning acts of "high-class vaudeville," including the Juggling Mowatts, Snyder & Buckley, and the Marco Twins.

We exited the crowded bus directly in front of the majestic entrance. Knox said it was like going home again. There were the twin spires echoing the legendary thoroughbred track on the other side of town; the long, wide pavilion with thirteen columns; and the lighted harp hanging high above the entrance offering childhood promises of angelic happiness. Everything was made of wood covered with tens of coats of textured paint, simultaneously projecting a sense of freshness and of age. Our grandparents and parents had touched these layered surfaces; they had played here as children, met their husbands and wives here as adults, and brought their sons and daughters here to affirm a vital tradition.

The idyllic park was a sweet blend of sights, sounds, and smells: the soft beige gravel underfoot; the tree trunks painted white; the legions of dark green picnic tables under broad-striped canopies; fried chicken; cotton candy; popcorn; Dave "Baby" Cortez's "The Happy Organ"; the *pop, pop, pop* from the shooting gallery; the suspenseful *clickety-clack, clickety-clack* of the Comet slowly climbing the lift hill to the first peak of the coaster track; the piercing screams of crouching patrons hurtling down the far side of the first ninety-foot drop; and the ubiquitous, reassuring laughter of youthful innocence.

We decided to experience the park just as we had as teenagers. So we immediately headed over to the flashing penny arcade. Our favorite vending machines were still offering glossy pictures of cowboys and movie stars and naughty photographs of burlesque queens. Just three steps down we found the nickelodeons where we inserted tokens, turned the cranks, and watched some old silent movie scenes. While we passed on the Fishing Pond and Guess Your Weight, we did, however, stop to play the more manly games of Target Practice, Test Your Strength, and Spill the Milk.

I was happy for my old teammates but admittedly a bit jealous; at least one of them won a "valuable" prize at each of the challenging stops. Knox shot the lights out with his steady aim; Grimes slammed the heavy mallet down hard enough to ring the bell; and to my amazement, Anderson knocked over the pyramid of milk cans, which I had always sworn were either glued or nailed down to the wooden base. And they had a bucketload of prizes from which to choose: chalk-ware statues, straw hats, bamboo canes, Chinese finger cuffs, chimpanzees on sticks, and a variety of stuffed animals. So as we walked away from the penny arcade, Knox, Anderson, and Grimes proudly sported a pink giraffe, a green hippo, and a tangerine bear, respectively, tucked securely under one arm.

Our next stop was the hand-painted carousel, where we could stand to the side, listen to the calliope, and feel the gentle rush of wind as the carved horses, panthers, and gilded chariots raced around the gray wooden track. The average person might ask why we as teenagers or even as virile young adults would spend any time encamped near the old-fashioned carousel. But there was method to our madness. Every beautiful young woman entering the park would eventually gravitate to this spinning wooden magnet, ride the galloping beasts, and flash us alluring smiles.

We had learned early on it was ill-advised to eat or drink anything within two hours of embarking on the most challenging gauntlet of rides. We always warmed up on the Turnpike, where we zipped through the demanding hairpin turns in our miniature green-and-yellow Indy cars. We then graduated to the Whip, followed by the Rock-O-Planes, where we were locked in cages that simultaneously flipped us upside down and spun us around as the entire ride itself rotated like a giant Ferris wheel. We next scurried to the backseats of the Comet, where we could ride the harrowing mile while watching the wheels literally hover above the plunging track.

On the way over to our final stop of the evening at the Fun House, we paused at the Tunnel of Love, and I did something I had never done before. Anderson egged me on. "Andrew, I dare you to stick your arm in the water up to your elbow."

"Oh yeah? Watch this, Ray!" I blurted as I rolled up both my sleeves and thrust both my arms into the churning waters. It was a brave act. As children, we had always been warned to keep our hands inside the boats because there were large poisonous snakes lurking in the depths below.

So after proving my manhood to my cohorts, we rushed over to the Fun House, paid the ticket taker, and passed through the turnstiles into the darkened vestibule. Two eight-foot-tall animated mannequins welcomed us with boisterous, sinister laughter. These giant greeters had dark brown hair, rosy cheeks, and front teeth missing on both the top and bottom rows. Knox and I reluctantly admitted Sam and Sue had truly frightened us as youngsters and suggested their menacing laughter still had a certain disturbing creepiness about it even today.

Beyond the vestibule we entered the labyrinthine Maze of Mirrors, which distorted our bodies into countless shapes—tall and skinny in this one, short and fat in the next, oblate, wavy, and elliptical in the three that followed. According to Anderson, the combined effect of Sam and Sue's mad laughter, the disfigured images projected along the mirrored maze, and the extensive electrical wiring strategically placed throughout the hall to shock the neophyte and the forgetful alike, was that of a nightmare voyage into a madman's mind undergoing shock therapy. I knew my mother's long-standing medical history had been forgotten as he made his cutting observation, and I opted not to remind him.

So as we entered the Fun House proper, we had four objectives: don't grab an electrified rail even if we are falling; don't rest on any of the wired benches no matter how inviting; experience the Devil Slide, the Sugar Bowl, the Angel Slide, the Wheel of Joy, and the Barrel of Fun at least once; and position ourselves near a mischievous rogue who controlled an abundant supply of compressed air. For whatever reason, ladies never seemed to dress properly for a visit to the Fun House. First, you would hear the loud hissing of air being forced up through small holes in the floor; next, the men yelling and whistling; and then, a few seconds later, the screams as the young women realized the backs of their summer dresses had been raised up over their heads. As Knox observed, women wearing dresses in the Fun House were at the operator's mercy, and thankfully he was always unmerciful.

I met all my Fun House objectives except one. I had no problem with the Angel Slide, which descended at a moderate forty-five-degree angle; but the Devil Slide was a different story. I got to the top of the slide, looked down the near-vertical drop, remembered back to seventh grade and my best friend's severely broken arm, and slowly descended the stairs to loud caterwauls of derision.

Once the good-natured ribbing abated, I recommended we leave the park and relive a memory across the street at the Dairy Mart. This family-owned, one-of-a-kind establishment was known far and wide for its cherry shakes, the kind with thick, creamy ice cream and hundreds of monstrous pieces of natural red fruit guaranteed to clog even the most expansive straw.

Knox eased up to the window to order for all of us. "Four of the usual, Mrs. Miller."

The owner's wife peered through the window, shook her head, and replied, "Well, look what the cat's drug in. . . . Is that really you, Knoxie? Long time no see. Not since you boys raised that regional trophy and finished third in the state that year."

Knox smiled and replied teasingly, "Yeah, Mrs. Miller, been away at school learning the ways of the world. But don't you worry, I'm back now, joining my dad's business. I'll be a regular again haunting your place all season long."

"Large cherry shakes, Knoxie?"

"You remembered!"

"How could the team's favorite booster forget?" She paused and looked intently at Knox. "So really good to see you again, Knoxie," she said.

"Same here, Mrs. Miller."

As she turned away from the window, she shouted back over her shoulder, "Four large cherries coming right up!"

We got our milkshakes, caught the last bus of the night, and headed back downtown to the hotel. As we rode along past familiar schools and neighborhoods, I looked over at the three footballers squeezed together on a side seat and wondered aloud, "Man, do you really think it was worth it?"

"Worth what?" Grimes asked.

"The headaches from trying to suck these cherries up through the straw. If I had a do-over, I'd opt for a pint of bluegrass bourbon."

Knox chimed in, "Man, oh man, I wish I had thought of that."

Anderson flashed a Cheshire cat smile, reached into his back pocket, and whipped out a silver flask. "Well, whaddaya know? The genius among us did just that." He raised the pint and added, "Cheers, anyone?"

2

Bg2 Bg7   Nc3 Nf6

I WASN'T LOOKING forward to Saturday except for the lunch at Armando's. The conversation at the formal reunion Saturday evening would most likely be a mile wide and an inch deep. I had arranged a respectable weekend wake-up call for nine o'clock, but I couldn't sleep past six. The hallway noise was different from that at home, motorcycles were already roaring through the streets, and annoying sunlight beamed through a thin crack in the curtains next to my bed.

I untangled myself from the sheets, canceled my wake-up call, and turned on the radio for some quiet rock and roll. I didn't want to go downstairs for breakfast. I'd surely meet some of my old classmates, who'd either try impressing me with their budding careers or insist on reminiscing about our glorious lost past on and off the field. It was just too early in the morning to layer on the veneer, so I splurged and ordered up room service that would rival the beignet at the Café Du Monde: real southern French toast with fresh white bread soaked in eggs and milk, browned in a hot skillet, and topped with a generous coating of powdered sugar and freshly ground cinnamon. After that delicious meal, I spent the rest of the morning reading and preparing for the day ahead.

At one o'clock the fun was supposed to begin. I walked down

the back stairs to an inconspicuous side door off the main lobby. Knox, who always had his watch set fifteen minutes ahead, was already standing there. I surveyed the room and asked, "No Anderson? No Grimes?"

He shrugged. "What else is new, Andy?"

I punched him lightly on the biceps and joked, "Not your underwear, Knoxie."

Just as he was about to throttle me, Grimes and Anderson appeared. While the gentle giant was wearing the same rumpled clothes he had worn the day before, Anderson was sporting a stunning escort he had engaged sometime during the night. She smiled seductively at us, pressed up against Anderson as if to say, "Eat your heart out, boys," and then whispered in his ear, "See you again later tonight, Ray."

As we watched her make a memorable exit, Knox mumbled, "I'd like to have that swing on my front porch."

"Yeah, me too," I chimed in. I turned to Anderson and said, "Must have set you back a pretty penny, Ray."

Anderson smiled, shook his head, and responded, "No worries on the money front, gentlemen. Fully deductible."

"Deductible?" Knox asked.

"A business expense. Marketing. Attracting new customers to our hotels. She'll recommend our properties to her clientele when they call in for appointments."

I shook my head and turned to Knox. "Sure looks like I'm headed into the wrong line of work, Knoxie."

He nodded and shot back, "Yeah, me too, Andy! Riding that thoroughbred would be a whole lot more satisfying than driving nails into two-by-fours."

We exited the hotel and ambled up Fourth Avenue to Market Street where Armando's had been serving its devoted patrons for almost a century. As we passed through the heavy oak doors and pierced the thick clouds of tobacco smoke, I immediately sensed I was home again in a place I had always treasured. We had even come here for lunch after Grandpa's funeral, not because it was the family's idea but because Grandpa had demanded it in his will.

Nothing had changed. The waiters in their long white aprons still shouted orders above the boisterous din and glided along the tile floor balancing multiple dishes on their young, muscular arms. The bartender stood behind the twenty-foot-long carved masterpiece pouring beer after perfect beer from the taps touting local brews like Fehr's, Falls City, Sterling, and Oertels 92.

Businessmen, policemen, judges, politicians, stockyard workers, and weekend shoppers squeezed in around the small wood and wrought-iron parlor tables to marvel at the fleur-de-lis-stamped ceiling; to enjoy the heirloom posters advertising everything from bygone prize fights to Roaring Twenties burlesque shows; and especially to savor Armando's specialty, the rolled oyster, a baseball-sized delicacy of four oysters wrapped up in a thick cracker-crumb batter and deep fried to a crusty, succulent golden brown.

We had been lucky enough to get a table after just a few minutes' wait and enthusiastically placed our orders. As we inhaled our feast of oysters, bean soup, and beer, a handsome middle-aged fellow with his hair parted down the middle approached our table, introduced himself as the owner, and asked if everything had been prepared to our satisfaction. After enthusiastically declaring in unison the food was outstanding, we former jocks immediately reached for our fountain pens and asked for autographs. The proprietor was the "Sizzling Southpaw" from Memphis who'd struck out Babe Ruth three times in one game.

"Thanks for the autographs," the star-struck Knox said.

"Yeah, I hope Armando's is around for another hundred years!" Anderson chimed in.

The restaurateur replied humorously, "No worries there. I don't plan on retirin' or closin' up shop any time soon. And I hope you young fellas will keep comin' around, especially after ya turn eighty-one."

The four of us looked at each other and shrugged.

"Why eighty-one?" I probed.

The owner smiled slyly and replied, "'Cause ya get a free meal."

"A free meal?" Grimes asked.

"Yeah, we have a standin' offer of a free meal to customers over eighty who show up for supper with their mothers on their arm."

"Well, that's one offer you'll never have to honor," I said jokingly.

As the restaurateur disappeared into the swirling crowd, he responded good-naturedly, "Nice to think so, but we've already given away two free meals so far this year!"

"Great fellow, huh?" Grimes said.

"Not every day you get to jaw with a living, breathing legend," Anderson added.

Knox winked at me, raised his mug, and offered a toast: "To the Sizzling Southpaw . . . and to Ray's sizzling business expense!"

We all roared, "Hear, hear!"

When we got back to the hotel, I stopped by the front desk and asked the concierge to place a wake-up call for seven o'clock in the evening. I wanted to burn off some of the local beer and, to be honest, postpone the inevitable as long as I could. So I managed to enjoy several hours of sound sleep that afternoon; but when the telephone blared at seven sharp, I immediately lapsed into a surly mood. I had to reach down deep to roll out of bed, stumble through the artificial darkness, and stand motionless in the momentary comfort of a pulsating shower.

The primary reason I'd returned to Louisville was to spend time with Knox, Anderson, and Grimes. I had nothing against any of my former classmates. They had never done anything to me. They were intelligent, down-to-earth folk from middle-class families with a strong, positive will to succeed. If I were to be up front about the dysfunction, I'd confess most of the onus lay on me. Contrary to popular belief, I was shy, avoided large parties, and never looked forward to superficial conversations about the weather or how or where folks spent their last vacation. I rode the elevator down to the lobby silently preparing for the onslaught.

As I passed the hotel bar and reluctantly entered the teeming hall, I discovered the reunion planning committee had put a lot of thought into the layout of the decorated space. They had pushed back the accordion dividers between two adjoining conference rooms, positioned the attractive buffet table and the obligatory open bar at the center of the enlarged room, and placed the oversized dining tables in concentric rings around the abundant food and colorful umbrella drinks.

But as usual, the event participants frustrated the well-intentioned attempts at social engineering. The four corners of the large space appeared to be magnets. Attendees approached the buffet table and bar only long enough to refresh their glasses and refill their plates. And instead of gravitating to the linen-covered tables ringing the food and drinks, attendees returned to the ongoing conversations at their respective corners of the room.

On closer observation, however, I realized each of the rapt crowds actually encircled one of my former classmates holding audience in the corner. This quartet of charismatic luminaries had several things in common: they were all young men; they had all starred on our highly ranked varsity football team; and they had all continued their sports careers at highly respected universities.

But to be fair, they also had remarkable qualities beyond their good looks and superior skills on the gridiron. Brown, our starting quarterback for three years, finished his degree at Rutgers and cofounded an enterprise near Trenton refurbishing old passenger cars for the Pennsylvania Railroad. Our lightning-fast running back, Sullivan, attended Michigan and joined the navy after graduation with a realistic goal of becoming a top gun pilot. Thompson, our bludgeoning fullback, completed his bachelor's at Vanderbilt and had just finished his first grueling year at the highly touted University of Louisville Medical School. And our crushing, first-string, all-state middle linebacker, Roberts, suffered through three competitive but losing seasons at Indiana, which he had chosen because of its superior music program. I learned he had just finished his first year at Julliard, where he was studying composition for his master of music degree.

Although sweat beaded on my forehead at the thought of it, I determined to mingle further with my former classmates. I paused to consider which group to join.

Ever since my early years, I dreaded the family announcement I was being dragged to another public event or party, where I'd have to make small talk with the adults and, God forbid, with the little monsters in attendance. But to my surprise, once I was in the thick of battle, I usually found myself enjoying the folks attending the various compulsory social functions. This year's reunion was no exception. I have to admit I had a good time. I believe, however, I owe my positive perceptions to a strategy I employed throughout the evening. I decided to converse only with classmates hovering at the fringes of the four rhythmic crowds. My unscientific sampling upon arrival had indicated the farther I moved from the center of the four masses, the more likely I was to engage a pleasant, enlightened person in an increasingly meaningful conversation.

And that's where I found Catherine Lynch, circulating in one of the outer bands of Thompson's galaxy. During our senior year, she and I had been lab partners in an experimental physics course using plywood, rubber bands, paper clips, and glue to mount sophisticated exercises illustrating complex physical theories. She was intelligent, attractive, and most of all, caring. I never asked her out or revealed how I really felt about her. There was an intervening variable: Anderson. They had dated off and on throughout high school. They were the ideal couple confirming that opposites attract. He was a football hero; she a salutatorian. And Anderson had repeatedly confided to Grimes and me he would marry her someday.

During their senior year they both enrolled at Tedrow State, where Anderson would play tackle for the Thundering Herd and would work part-time in the library. But as usual, life, reality, circumstances, fate—call it what you will—stepped in and spoiled paradise.

Catherine at eighteen was the oldest of four children; the youngest was ten. Catherine's father was a pleasant, industrious salesman whose territory encompassed roughly the entire western halves of both Kentucky and Tennessee, and her mother was a loving, steadfast wife who doted on her children. While everyone else in the family was the picture of health, Catherine's mother had experienced heart palpitations most of her adult life. During the summer after Catherine's graduation, her mother developed a blood clot, which lodged in her brain. The symptoms came on lightning fast—first the severe headache, next the blurred vision, and then the paralysis on the right side of her body. The good news was Catherine's mother beat the odds and survived; the bad news was she now slurred her speech, was blind in her right eye, and no longer had the mental capacity to adequately take care of herself and her children.

Since Catherine's father had to travel to make a living, the obvious solution was for Catherine to stay home, care for her mother, and become mom to her younger brothers and sisters. Anderson left for school in the fall, and their relationship slowly eroded from passion to distant friendship. During this trip home for the reunion, I saw them speak only once briefly in the hotel lobby; and Anderson never mentioned Catherine or her family when we were hanging out much of Friday night and Saturday afternoon.

While standing in line to refresh our drinks, I asked Catherine, "How's your father doing? Staying busy traveling?"

She nodded. "He'll never change. Feels guilty when he's home relaxing. Thinks he should be out there every minute of every day earning more for the family."

"Your brothers and sisters okay?"

"Yeah, but they've all gotten to that age where they think they know more than everybody else. Most of the time now it's like hitting your head against the wall trying to get them to do anything."

"How's your mother? Is she making any progress?" I asked empathetically.

She shook her head and began tearing up.

I instinctively grasped her arm and led her out of the hall. I found a bench at the far end of the main concourse and motioned for her to sit down. I took a seat beside her and whispered, "I'm sorry, Catherine. I didn't mean to upset you."

"Nothing you did, Andrew. It's just the accumulation of things over a whole lot of years and . . . and we didn't really have a choice with Mom." Catherine lowered her head and paused.

"A choice?" I asked.

"Yeah, about locking her away. We didn't have a choice. She was bedridden, confused. And despite bathing and turning her several times a day, she still got gaping bedsores on her hips and heels. She needed care twenty-four hours a day, seven days a week, and there wasn't any way we could provide it ourselves."

Without sharing the details of my mother's history, I still spoke with some conviction: "Believe me, Catherine, you and your father did the right thing. You can now begin thinking about yourself and get on with your life. Seeing that your brothers and sisters are older and spending more time away from home, perhaps you can think about taking some courses at one of the local colleges or universities."

"I . . . I don't know."

"I don't mean a full load. Just a couple of courses, things you're interested in, to help you get back into the swing of things."

She looked up and gazed into my eyes. "How long you here for?"

"Through tomorrow, and then I'm headed south to begin graduate school."

She appeared disappointed, as if she were losing an ally.

Trying to pull our conversation up out of a spiral, I said encouragingly, "Even though I'm away, there's no reason we can't correspond and talk regularly." I reached into my pocket and pulled out a notepad and pen. "Here, let's exchange addresses and telephone numbers. What do you say?"

She nodded. "I'd like that. You sure you'll have the time?"

I smiled. "Believe me, I'll make the time for you." I reached over and turned her head toward me. "And I have one other suggestion."

"What's that?" she asked.

"We stick together the rest of the evening."

She gave a weak smile and whispered, "I wouldn't have it any other way."

I lay awake until near dawn replaying what might have been, what was, and what perhaps could be. I didn't know how I really felt about Catherine. Was it sympathy? Nostalgia? Admiration? Empathy? Physical attraction? Platonic love? Or perhaps even lasting affection? But what I did know was Catherine had demonstrated unspeakable courage. She had bravely accepted what had come her way. And she had sacrificed for the good of her family deftly playing the terrible hand she'd been dealt.

Having fallen asleep around five o'clock, I felt the Sunday morning wake-up call was the unkindest cut of all. I crawled out of bed, showered and shaved, packed my bag, and then headed down to the hotel café to join Knox, Anderson, and Grimes for a farewell breakfast.

As we put away multiple buffet plates of smokehouse bacon, hash browns, and buttered grits, we relived the past forty-eight hours and enthusiastically began planning our next sidebar reunion five years hence. When the restaurant became crowded with late risers demanding tables, we reluctantly adjourned to the lobby, where Grimes and I said so long to Anderson and Knox, gave them both strong bear hugs, and then waved good-bye as we pulled out of the hotel circle into the light morning traffic.

I had earlier asked Grimes if I could sleep over Sunday evening at the parsonage. There were several reasons I wanted to stay with him and his family: it would save me money; Grimes worked downtown near the train station where I needed to go the next day; and the parsonage was east of the city in the direction of Our Lady of Hope. I had told Grimes I wanted to visit my mother before hopping the train Monday morning. He agreed to drop me off Sunday afternoon and pick me up several hours later.

As we approached the wrought-iron gates fronting the stately institutional grounds, we noticed clusters of patients and nurses scattered all about the lush green lawn. The patients were all seated in antique wheelchairs, the wooden ones with wicker seats, large front wheels, and tall, slanted backs that you see in the movies. Everyone was wearing white; and the frail patients wore thick, heavy robes and had woolen blankets either draped over their shoulders or folded neatly across their thin, quivering knees.

We drove up the tree-lined driveway to the imposing front entrance of the five-story brick building. Grimes let me out, said he would be back at four o'clock, and respectfully wished my mother well.

After I signed in at the front desk, the administrative aide telephoned for an escort to accompany me to my mother's room. As we waited for the guard to appear, the middle-aged lady tried making small talk, saying something about enjoying the good days now before the winter weather set in. I slowly nodded my head in agreement.

My mind was miles away. I was worried about seeing Mom for the first time in years. What would I say to her? How would she look? Would she recognize me? Did she know it was her birthday? Would she mention the concert? Had she improved? Would she ask me about Dad? And then the loud jingling of the approaching key ring yanked me back to the affable aide and the anteroom. The dark gray uniform appeared in the hallway and motioned for me to follow him. We moved through two sets of locked, windowless, heavy steel doors to a small bank of secured elevators. The old man searched his ring of keys, misfired twice, and finally managed to open the defiant elevator doors.

We rode up to the top floor, the one closest to heaven where Mom and the hopeless fight their incurable demons every day. We exited the elevator, turned to the right, and walked down a short hallway to another secured door, which, unlike the others, had a small shatterproof window to observe the ward. After unlocking the door, we stepped into a long corridor with the patients' rooms on our right and a series of tall windows to the left. The walls and ceiling were semigloss white and reflected a surprising amount of late-August light filtering through the black wrought-iron window grills. It was the bright tunnel the dying see as they cautiously pass through on their way to the other side.

An elderly woman in a light blue hospital gown sat under one of the windows rocking back and forth and trying to count her illusory fives and tens. A tall, thin, wrinkled old man in his mideighties approached us with his arms outstretched and demanded we take the phantom child he held so he could rush back into the house to save others. The guard spoke quietly with the old fellow, gently turned him around, and sent him back down the corridor in the opposite direction screaming for someone to take the baby from his arms.

The guard explained the confused old man had been the Pleasant Valley fire chief, who only days before retirement broke down after failing to save five children from the upper bedrooms of a turn-of-the-century Victorian tinderbox. Eyewitnesses and firefighters alike tried to reassure the chief he had done all he could. Everyone thought he would recover with time, but his condition worsened. Nothing helped; so here he was, decades later, still trying to right a wrong, remove an indelible stain, and perform daily penance for his self-decreed failure.

There was something extremely unsettling in that thickness of white air. It was not the challenged inmates wandering the hallways speaking to their pasts. I suspect it had something to do with the randomness associated with the place. We usually lead rational lives. We believe things will happen within accepted limits. But here, at any moment, a plaintive wail could flood the corridor and destroy those few rare moments of restorative peace.

My escort gently tapped my arm, guided me halfway down the corridor, and then stopped under the large windows across the hall from my mother's room. The door was open. She was sitting motionless on the side of the bed with her hands folded and her head bowed. The guard apologized in advance. "Sad to say, ah, your mother's behavior has taken an odd turn and become more noticeable over the past few years. She doesn't have much to say anymore. She spends most of her time just humming an unknown melody. When the music reaches a certain point, she stops suddenly, gives a deep bow, and then immediately starts the melody over again from the top."

I shook my head, flashed a knowing smile, and asked, "Would you please come back for me in about half an hour?"

The guard nodded and replied, "No problem. Half an hour it is. See you soon." He then turned and walked back toward the elevators. I remained standing across the corridor from Mom's room. She appeared to be napping. I wanted to let her rest a little while longer.

I understood exactly what the guard was saying. I had never heard Mom humming the concerto, but I knew the circumstances that drove her current behavior. All was right with the world. I was twelve years old. We were going to Mom's Sunday afternoon performance, and then we were all headed over to Al's hotel for the bounteous buffet dinner. The orchestra typically opened with a short contemporary work followed by a concerto with a special guest artist. And after intermission, the players usually concluded the concert with an expansive romantic or classical symphony.

Several times a year, however, the various principal chairs of the orchestra would solo in the concerto instead of a visiting virtuoso. During the forties, Mom had the unique honor of being one of only three female concertmasters in an American orchestra. It was now her time in the rotation to solo, and she had chosen her favorite work, Sibelius's compelling Violin Concerto in D Minor.

I once asked Mom why she favored the Sibelius over the Beethoven, Mendelssohn, or Tchaikovsky. By way of explanation, she described the second of three tours the orchestra had taken to Europe, which included stops in Copenhagen, Stockholm, and Helsinki. "During the orchestra's final weekend stopover in the Finnish capital, I visited the Ateneum Art Museum on Kaivokatu Street near the Central Station. I saw an exhibition of Nordic painters including Gallen-Kallela, Sibelius's close friend.

"In fact, Sibelius appeared in two of Gallen-Kallela's exhibited works, a sketch, *Kajustaflan*, and the later mystical painting *Satu*, which the composer had loaned to the Ateneum for this special exhibition. But it was not the portraits that moved me. It was Gallen-Kallela's Finnish landscapes that helped me understand Sibelius and interpret his rare, rhythmic music. You see, hanging to the right of the *Kajustaflan* sketch was the hauntingly beautiful oil on canvas *Lake Keitele*, which depicted soft, reflective light shimmering on the silvery waters and evoked strong feelings of silence . . . solitude . . . profound loneliness.

"Next to the lake masterpiece was Gallen-Kallela's even more compelling oil, *Imatra in Winter*. The artist portrayed the Imatra Rapids during the coldest months of the year and captured the tension between the free-flowing waters and the static, frozen landscape bordering the roiling stream. And to the right of the dramatic *Imatra* was the oil on canvas *The Great Black Woodpecker*, which provided me the greatest insight into the most powerful emotions coursing through Sibelius's major works. The terrain around Lake Paanajärvi was stark, and the only living thing in the landscape was the large ebony bird with crimson crown perched at the top of a blighted, celadon birch. The museum guide explained the great black woodpecker was Gallen-Kallela's symbol of freedom and loneliness, and the bird's brilliant crown was 'the cry of an individual's life in the silence of the wilderness.'"

I've forgotten the contemporary piece the orchestra played to open the concert, perhaps a Blacher, Dello Joio, or Ibert composition. But I do remember the house lights coming up to remove the Steinway, expand the orchestra, and allow late arrivals to be seated. As the house lights dimmed again, the audience quieted and focused on the door at stage right. Thirty seconds later the door swung open. The applause swelled. Mom stepped out into the brilliant light with her violin and moved to the left of the conductor's podium. The long-haired, graying maestro, who had followed closely behind Mom, mounted the dais, turned to the audience, and bowed deeply, acknowledging the enthusiastic ovation. After Mom quietly tuned the orchestra, she turned and gazed into our third-row seats. I never knew whether she actually saw us seated there at the dimming edge of her distant light.

Mom was stunning in the shining silence. Her long, auburn hair cascaded down over her black brocade cheongsam with flame-red dragons and piping. The elegant formal gown was ankle-length with a mandarin collar and slits up both sides toward the thigh. But only Dad and I understood the poignant intersection between the crimson crown, the flying dragon, and Sibelius's lonely quest in D.

The bocate baton rose and fell in 2/2 time. The *Allegro moderato* had begun with the quiet, haunting oscillations of the first and second violins. We all sensed the ice, the bleakness, and the Nordic interplay of white on white. Three and one-half bars of rest and then the lone, pensive voice spoke out *dolce ed espressivo* in the silence of the wilderness. Eight minutes into the riveting interpretation, Mom played Sibelius's own virtuosic cadenza perfectly; it had been drilled into her fingers at fifteen.

And then there was the daunting coda near the end of the movement written *allegro molto vivace*. Mom said there was no way to play it absolutely cleanly and accurately at that demanding tempo. She said it was just too awkward, jumping from the G to the E string in a sixteenth of a second—from first to twelfth position, impossible. But Mom threaded the needle. She slowed just enough to be accurate without violating the spirit of Sibelius's severe requirement.

After the novice applause, deferred coughs, and complimentary murmuring subsided, Mom briefly retuned and then signaled she was ready to begin the lyrical *Adagio di molto*. The aging maestro lifted his right arm and gracefully eased the clarinets, oboes, and timpani into the syncopated introductory measures of some of the most beautiful, contemplative pages Sibelius ever penned. Mom entered at the sixth bar on the G string playing the sonorous melody broadly and creating a tension between the pulsating accompaniment and her forceful, expansive main theme. Seven minutes into the *Adagio*, Mom and the orchestra finished weaving their expressive strands and reached the evocative coda announcing the beginning of the end—*crescendo*, then *tutta forza*, *mezzo piano*, and finally, *pianissimo*. . . .

Those final notes were Mom's farewell. At that moment a thick, permanent curtain fell between her and the rest of us. Instead of preparing to play the pyrotechnic *Allegro*, Mom lowered the loaned Amati to her side, bowed deeply, and then left the stage. After several moments of murmured speculation, the managing director appeared and announced Mom had fallen ill and couldn't continue. He then asked for the house lights so the stunned audience could take a needed twenty-minute intermission before embarking on the concluding work, the Mahler *Titan*.

When Dad heard Mom was ill, he jumped up and told me to follow closely behind him. We rushed backstage to the green room, where we found her sitting on a large sofa with her head in her hands, sobbing and speaking irrationally about having had her fingers crushed in a wire fence. As Dad approached the sofa, the concerned staff backed away and explained they had already telephoned for the house physician, who lived in a walk-up only three blocks away.

The doctor arrived within fifteen minutes, assessed

Mom's condition, and asked us to join him in the managing director's office down the hall. He said his cursory examination indicated Mom was either suffering from extreme exhaustion or had experienced a complete breakdown. He suggested Dad temporarily commit Mom to the asylum, where doctors could conduct a thorough examination and run batteries of tests to reach a definitive diagnosis. Dad concurred; asked the stage manager to call an ambulance; and then rode out with Mom to Our Lady of Hope for the first of her many visits there "to rest."

The old woman continued rocking under the window, and about every thirty seconds or so, she randomly shouted "ten," "five," or "dollars." The fire chief approached again; and having learned an appropriate response from my experienced guide, I effectively turned the outstretched arms around and sent them off questing toward the other end of the long hallway.

I then moved across the corridor and entered Mom's room. She was still napping. I gently stroked her hair, which had turned stone gray and was drawn back into a small, tight bun. She began to stir, and I responded with, "Happy birthday, Mom." She opened her eyes, briefly stared through me, and then slowly turned away. I asked her how she was doing. She didn't answer. I told her who I was, and she didn't react. I explained I was leaving for graduate school. She didn't reply. I asked her about Grandma, her brother, and her stepsister. She still didn't respond.

After a few moments, Mom sat up straight at the edge of her metal bed and began speaking in a distressed, childlike voice: "But, Father, Betty called me names. . . . She deserved to have her fingers pinched in the fence. . . . No, Father, please don't. . . . Father, you're hurting my fingers. Stop! Please stop! I won't do it again. . . . I'll tell Betty I'm sorry I squeezed her fingers in the fence."

And then the voice changed to a slightly older pitch, and all I could do was watch as she played out another scene. "Father will be here shortly for my lesson. . . . Sit up straight toward the front of the chair. Place my left foot just a bit forward. Shoulder rest in position. Relax my hand. . . . Slightly turn my wrist to the left, and now let the fingers gently curve over the top of my bow stick. Place my left elbow under the center of the violin. Keep my wrist gently rounded. Don't rest my wrist against the neck. Now tune. . . My A string's slightly flat. Tune again. . . . Perfect.

"Good afternoon, Father. Yes, I've practiced every day. Here's the 'Bourrée' from the *Fireworks*. How's that, Father? I'm sorry! I know I missed some notes. I didn't reach across the fingerboard. Father, I try so hard not to pancake, but my wrist hurts. I know it makes it hard to vibrato. . . . Okay, I'll try the 'Bourrée' again. Father, I'm really trying hard to keep my fingers boxed. I'll start again. Father, please, that hurts! You're squeezing my fingers! Please stop! Please stop! I won't do it again!"

Mom's voice trailed off, and she began crying. I sat down beside her on the edge of the bed, put my arm around her trembling, thinning shoulders, and pulled her close to my side. I tried comforting her by whispering that everything would be okay. When the intense anxiety lessened, she rested her head on my shoulder and made a calm, heartbreaking request. "Son, please take me home with you. It's so lonely here. They've all forgotten me. Please take me home." I didn't reply. I didn't know what to say. I just turned my face toward her, lightly kissed the crown of her head, and began gently stroking her shoulder and arm.

The guide reappeared under the luminous windows across the corridor from Mom's room. I pulled her closer to me and explained visiting hours were over and I'd have to leave. I eased out of our embrace, slowly moved to the hallway door, and looked back at Mom for a final time. "I love you. Thanks for everything you've done for me. I'll never forget."

Mom sat up straight again. She lifted her head above the audience and stared into the brilliant slants of light beaming down over my corduroyed shoulder. She cleared her throat, counted off three and a half measures of rest, and then began humming the hypnotic *Allegro moderato* in the momentary silence of her white-on-white ward.

3

Bg5 Nc6 Qd2 d6

THE WIPERS COULDN'T handle the remnants of the hurricane slowly spiraling northward from the ravaged Mississippi coast. Strong waves of water forced us to stop twice under railroad viaducts until the horizontal rain slowed and Grimes could keep his '51 coupe firmly on the road. The streets were relatively clear of traffic. Most citizens had heeded the mayor's advice to stay off the roads unless it was absolutely necessary to travel. Thank God Grimes had a serious work ethic and my train wasn't scheduled to leave until eleven o'clock or I would have been wearing out my welcome at the New Canaan parsonage.

But give Grimes all the credit. We got to Union Station with fifteen minutes to spare. When we pulled up to the front entrance, I told Grimes to stay in the car out of the driving rain. I gave him a big bear hug, grabbed my suitcases from the backseat, and then ran up under the broad iron canopy sheltering the north sidewalk. As Grimes drove off, I rushed into the building and up to the counter. "One-way coach to Warfield via Nashville, please."

"That'll be forty-three one way," the agent said. "And . . . I'm sorry but she'll be about an hour late because of the weather. We'll start boarding around ten minutes of noon."

"No worries," I replied. "It'll give me time to walk around the depot and reminisce."

I fell in love with trains the Christmas my next-door neighbor, Harry, received his Santa Fe American Flyer and I got my Lionel freight with the 2458 double-door box car. From that fortuitous day on, I never declined an offer to visit the majestic Tenth Street Depot, smell the smoky air, and experience the rumble of the arriving and departing trains. So I really looked forward to the ride down to Warfield that day and the opportunity to walk within the walls of two architectural masterpieces: the Louisville Union Station and the tour de force in Nashville, which I'd heard so much about when Dad returned home from a scientific forum in the Music City.

These imposing structures accommodated the wealthy. Sarah Bernhardt and Mae West performed under the barreled vaulting. The atria welcomed the mighty who bent history. Roosevelt, Eisenhower, and Truman spoke here. And these vast spaces embraced the linear scale of human emotion, from the highest joy to the deepest despair, and included the everyday humdrum between the extremes. The masses moved through the touchstones daily on their way to conduct business, begin a new life, or lose one at the hands of young, reluctant strangers in distant lands. And many went there to pray for the callow recruits and the flag-draped warriors crossing paths and exchanging hallowed whispers in the comforting light of the luminous rose windows.

I checked the large Seth Thomas on the paneled wall above the ticket counter. I still had fifteen minutes to kill before the *Humming Bird* was scheduled to arrive. I sat down on one of the worn cuneiform benches at the rear of the station. I closed my eyes and replayed the lively, one-way conversation we'd had Sunday evening at the holy residence. As mothers are wont to do, Mrs. Grimes raised a sensitive issue at the dinner table ostensibly (albeit perversely) to publicly admonish her wayward son and perhaps garner a twofer, counseling me on the iniquitous ways of the world.

"There's no use denying it, son. Just fess up that you bought it."

"I'll swear on a stack of Bibles I didn't buy it! I borrowed it from one of the patients at the VA. He's an avid reader of modern fiction."

The "it" in question was Nabokov's newly published account of the Humbert-Haze affair. Mrs. Grimes had found the smoking gun wedged between the mattress and box springs while changing Grimes's "soiled" sheets. But the longer the amusing, uncomfortable encounter continued, the more I became convinced Grimes had never cracked the book. The true literary expert here was the inestimable Mrs. Grimes, who cast her lot with the betrayed and humiliated widow, Charlotte.

Over the course of an hour, Mrs. Grimes intermittently treated us to every important element of what summed to a detailed plot outline: Ramsdale, the sunbather, the diary, the accident, summer camp, the Enchanted Hunters, Beardsley, *The Hunted Enchanters*, Quilty, Rita, the deaf veteran, *The Confessions of a White Widowed Male*, and Christmas Day 1952. When Mrs. Grimes presented her bottom line that Humbert was a depraved miscreant, Poe's imp reared his ugly head in me. "The impulse increased to a wish, the wish to a desire, and the desire to an uncontrollable longing." I blurted out an alternative, heretical interpretation—the precocious child had preyed upon the vulnerable Humbert. God, you could have heard a pin drop. Everyone stared into his or her bread pudding, but I believe I detected an ally, a knowing smile emanating from the parson's chair.

Mrs. Grimes slowly lifted her head and in the voice of the Almighty boomed the arrival of the southbound to "Nashvull." I had risen, grabbed my suitcases, and taken several steps before I realized I wasn't pushing back from the Grimes's table but unconsciously rushing toward the station exit. I walked out onto the platform between two streamlined trains: one, a Pennsylvania passenger decked out in brick-red Tuscan with gold-leaf lettering, and a second, my sleek, seven-car *Humming Bird* with dark blue sides, silver roof, and gold script announcing the storied names of *Duncan Hines*, *Royal Canal*, *Boston Club*, and the *Alabama Pine*.

After an unauthorized tour of the first-class accommodations, I found a row of empty seats toward the front of the second coach car. I stowed my large suitcases in the open overhead rack, dropped Henry James's *The Golden Bowl* and my bag lunch onto the aisle seat, and then sat down next to the window. The conductor in his dark blue uniform and cap with gold band and lettering made a round-trip through the coaches before signaling to the engineer we were ready to leave the station. I heard a distant "All aboard!" behind me; two short blasts on the horn; a crescendo of diesel rumbling; the snap and hiss of air brakes releasing; and then the anticipated clanking as the couplings engaged.

As the streamliner cleared the long shed, I sensed a decisive break with the past. I felt the ancient fear of my heart once again beating alone. Admittedly, I still had friends back home, but Mom and Dad were both gone. Dad was in Urbana deservedly beginning a new career and resurrecting an earlier life with an understanding younger colleague, Sonya, who taught music theory in the graduate school. And Mom? She sat alone on the edge of her hospital bed staring out into the brilliant floodlights trying hopelessly to complete the redemptive journey from the D-minor wilderness to Gabrieli's ennobling key of glory.

As in the Sibelius, Mom never really allowed herself to experience the harmonic joys of pulsating tempos, double stops, and long spicatto runs. From the earliest years she lived her life in a minor key. I've always wondered where and when the limitless, limiting fear began. Was she born with a predisposition? Or was the anxiety the inevitable outcome of Grandfather's old-school way of imposing discipline and retribution for perceived failures?

Mom had told me several times about Betty and the fence; and that childhood trauma predated anything I'd ever heard. But the intense angst must have really begun the day Grandfather dismissed the "third greatest violin pedagogue in the world" and assumed responsibility for instructing his teenage "quasi-prodigy" himself. On many occasions, Mom recounted the grueling sessions: her initial errors, his brusque behavior, her more serious mistakes, his frustrated shouting, her tearful screams, his growing aloofness, her imploring for another chance, his theatrical disengagement, and her slide again and again from guarded hope into numbing despair.

After one of these discouraging encounters, it would take Mom several days to begin healing, gather enough strength to reenter the practice room, and resolutely try again. The tortured sessions always ended in disillusionment and dejection. Since she never heard a word of praise for her hard work, Mom's compulsion to please Grandfather grew stronger and more debilitating as the months passed. The downward spiral continued until Grandfather suffered a coronary and died facedown on the practice room floor.

Mom never spoke about how she really felt at Grandfather's passing. Was she relieved knowing the demeaning sessions were over? Did she believe her unintentional lapses caused her father's sudden fatal attack? Did she feel disappointment, realizing her taskmaster would never see her seated in a major metropolitan orchestra? Did she later feel vindication following bravura performances of the Prokofiev and the Brahms? Did she believe her futile, exhausting attempts to please him caused or exacerbated the serious breakdowns she suffered later in life?

While she never mentioned regrets or displayed resentment about her childhood years, her behavior often bore the scars of those distant practice sessions—spontaneous episodes of crying, disengagement from Dad and friends, pacing during the night, loss of concentration, and disturbing speculation about a peaceful afterlife. Over time, these alarming symptoms morphed into the uncontrollable maelstrom that ultimately separated her from us and imposed a blinding loneliness that only the gods could ever know.

4

h4 e6   O-O-O h6

IT WAS ALSO raining here the day the earth grabbed Floyd and wouldn't let go. For fifteen days in early '25, Barren County, Kentucky, became the center of the universe. Floyd Collins, the spelunker who became trapped in Sand Cave when a boulder crushed his ankle, was the third largest media event in the years between the two great wars. After the cub reporter, "Skeets," arrived and began his forays into the cave, twenty thousand Fords idled here and hundreds of thousands listened for updates on their new RCAs.

What had been a compelling human story rapidly devolved into a toxic blend of lucrative media circus and vapid soap opera. Fifty reporters from twenty major newspapers, film crews from seven respected motion-picture studios, three detachments of soldiers, zoologists, geologists, anthropologists, Mrs. Blaine's surgeon, fortunetellers, impostors, pickpockets, and lost children twisted a narrow dirt road into an epic, full-length, ten-mile backup.

Bluegrass vaudeville further deteriorated into grassroots commerce. Advantageously positioned vendors feverishly worked portable grills supplying ravenous sojourners from sixteen states with succulent hot dogs, pulled-pork sandwiches, and thick, potent, all-day joe. And sad to say, the substantial profit and revenue stream outlived "The Greatest Cave Explorer the World Had Ever Known." As the story goes, after "Skeets" won the Pulitzer, Floyd's family sold their property to an entrepreneur, who installed Floyd in a glass-top casket and charged hefty admissions to enjoy the ghoulish show. Several years later an industrious kidnapper stole Floyd, failed to cash in on his daring necrotic enterprise, and eventually dumped yesterday's hero in a muddy field minus his storied leg, which the interloper retained as a potentially profitable souvenir.

As the *Humming Bird* slowly pulled away from the Horse Cave depot, I scurried over to the empty seats on the other side of the car. I wanted to see what the better angels had erected to honor their ill-fated Floyd. The seasoned conductor, who had met Lindbergh here and witnessed the colossal hubbub around this very station, had warned me earlier to keep a sharp eye out for the tobacco barn just beyond the flashing lights on the fabled Dixie Highway. And like clockwork, no more than twenty yards beyond the large black barn, there it was: a one-hundred-and-fifty-foot-high tribute built of river rock gracefully disappearing into a dense gray layer of lingering, low-hanging clouds.

I could truly empathize with the Collins family. Dad and I had experienced a similar fate when Mom suffered her onstage breakdown. For several days after the story broke, the press handled our situation discreetly; but then the competitive juices began flowing. The photographers and reporters became increasingly more aggressive, camped out in our driveway and on neighborhood lawns, and swarmed anyone trying to enter or leave our modest home. Whenever we left for church or the hospital, we reluctantly became the lead car in an unofficial press pool motorcade. The reports in the newspapers, magazines, and on air became even more sensational and salacious as the weeks passed into long, painful months.

First, there was the unsubstantiated account of Dad's torrid affair with a university colleague. Then it was Mom's turn to be slandered with unfounded stories about her abrupt rejection by a young cellist in the philharmonic. The absurdity only subsided after Dad sought and won a restraining order to prevent the blatant trespassing and a strong F-4 tornado ripped through the eastern section of town, braiding steel beams, exploding houses, and killing fifty-three. On the front pages, the new tragedy had replaced the old.

Thirty minutes after leaving Horse Cave, the *Humming Bird* rolled through Bowling Green. We were now a little more than halfway to Nashville. So far, so good. Despite the heavy rain and gale-force winds, we'd made good time, and there was a decent chance I'd make my Nashville connection with the *City of Memphis*. Since I couldn't afford the haute cuisine in his dining car, I honored Bowling Green's favorite son, Duncan Hines, by scarfing down the thick, piquant pimento cheese sandwich Mrs. Grimes had so graciously prepared for me even after our contretemps over Dolores Haze's culpability. I guess there's still something to be said for Christianity.

I finished my pimento on white and picked up my worn copy of James's novel, *The Golden Bowl*, and resumed reading:

> They had been alone that evening—alone as
> a party of six, and four of them, after dinner,

under suggestion not to be resisted, sat down to "bridge" in the smoking-room . . . with the game forming itself, as had often happened before, of Mr. Verver with Mrs. Assingham for partner and of the Prince with Mrs. Verver.

As Adam Verver's daughter, Maggie, watched the serious and silent foursome from the far corner of the clouded room, she finally understood she could destroy everyone at the table with a single sentence and that every relationship, including her own, now relied solely on her restraint. And only moments later out on the terrace, Maggie came to another realization: she didn't want to destroy but to gain a satisfying, complex retribution through self-discipline and resilient love. The maturing ingénue now saw the endgame through a more sophisticated, ancient prism: chess.

You see, early in the match, Maggie and her father had a distinct advantage. She was the only daughter of this wealthy American financier. But through questionable marriages to Charlotte and the Italian Prince, respectively, Mr. Verver and Maggie had inadvertently ceded their power to the clandestine lovers. Old World knowledge had overtaken New World wealth. The smiling, scheming couple quietly announced, "Check!" But Maggie counterattacked; and with growing insight of the adulterous affair, she methodically set about clearing the board and stealthily separating the furtive pair for good.

As we reached the first yard switches outside Nashville, our car began rocking abruptly from side to side. It was perfect timing. Maggie had deftly pinned, skewered, undermined, and gained control of the center. Because of her moves after that night of bridge, Maggie's father was now leading his adulterous bride, Charlotte, around by a silken tether—"Mrs. Verver's straight neck had certainly not slipped it; nor had the other end of the long cord . . . disengaged its smaller loop from the hooked thumb . . . her husband kept out of sight." For Maggie, a delicately engineered and undetected revenge was sweet. Charlotte was now being led away forever, to America, from the only man she'd ever really loved. And Maggie smiled and announced, "Checkmate!"

Nearing the terminal, the conductor hurried through our car shouting the good news: Nashville dispatch had held the Atlanta and Memphis trains so we could make our connections. When the train finally stopped, I jumped up, pulled my large suitcases down from the open rack, and lunged for the exit. A uniformed attendant was standing at the bottom of the coach steps repeating in a loud, bass voice, "The *Dixie Flyer* to Atlanta is on track seven; the *City of Memphis* is on track five; the *Dixie Flyer* to Atlanta is on track seven. . . ."

I rushed toward the depot, rounded the *Royal Canal*, scurried over to track five, and ran up the platform toward the red, silver, and blue coaches of the Nashville, Chattanooga & St. Louis Railway. I entered the first coach I came to after passing the observation and the diner-lounge cars. Since the first coach was relatively full of tired, frustrated folks who had been waiting for us for more than an hour, I moved on to the less-crowded middle car, stowed my suitcases in the overhead, and collapsed into a window seat on the left-hand side of the aisle.

I remembered the phrases my maternal grandmother employed when assessing daily outcomes to events. She would say, "There's good news and there's bad news" and "On the one hand" and "on the other hand." Well, there was good news and bad news today. On the one hand, I had successfully connected with the last train to Warfield; but on the other, I'd have to continue relying on Dad's fading recollections of Nashville's Tenth Street Station, since I never had a chance to enter the iconic building.

A last-minute arrival made his way up the aisle and placed his tan valise and double-gusset briefcase in the open rack above the seats. He sat down next to me and mumbled some thanks to God that the train was really late today. The tall, distinguished fellow with dark hair swept back from his broad forehead then opened our conversation. "Man, I'm sure glad that ordeal's over!"

"Ordeal? What ordeal's that?" I asked half-heartedly.

"The interviews. Been interviewing all day at Vanderbilt for an opening in the History Department and now, thankfully, I'm headed back home to my family in Memphis."

Again, there was good news and bad news. On the one hand, the professorial candidate was arguably a spellbinding and knowledgeable storyteller as he spun tales describing every historical event of the past four hundred years occurring within fifty miles of our rail bed. But on the other hand, my conflicted head began hurting early on in his soliloquy, trying to absorb all the facts while attempting to devise novel ways of succumbing to sleep without closing my eyes. The poor man was running on adrenaline. The last nugget I remembered before my mind completely numbed was his recounting of the chaos at Dutchman's Bend about five miles from Nashville near the Harding Road.

Our contemporary Herodotus began, "It was forty years ago this last July two Nashville, Chattanooga & St. Louis passenger trains, the No. 1 from Memphis and the No. 4 from Nashville, collided head-on here along this sharp, steep-graded curve. The two iron horses traveling at least sixty miles per hour crashed into each other, reared up, and toppled to the sides of the twisted track and splintered ties. The force of the powerful impact drove the Nashville-bound heavyweight baggage car back through the fragile wooden Madison coaches; telescoped the lounge car; and flipped the last two passenger coaches in the air. The dead and dying lay in the cornfields on both sides of the tracks.

"A fellow I ran into some years ago, who worked feverishly for hours helping free people from the collapsed lounge car, told me few of the bodies were in any condition to be viewed by friends who wanted to pay their respects at the mortuary. While some of the bodies were completely cut in two, others were crushed into a sickening pink pulp. The only good news here—in almost every case, death was instantaneous. There was no evidence of prolonged suffering.

"But how could this have happened? How could one hundred twenty passengers and crewmen be killed and fifty-seven gravely injured? What caused this worst railway disaster in American history? Well, we'll probably never really know for sure, but experts have speculated it had something to do with the engineer on the No. 4 from Nashville. Either he received wrong instructions, raced past the warning signal, or tried beating the delayed No. 1 to the switch at Harding Station, which was several hundred yards from the scene of the crash.

"But you know what gives me the cold chills about

the tragedy at Dutchman's Bend is the arbitrary nature of determining who lived and who died. Was it fate or the gods who made Mr. Fordham arrive late, fail to find a seat in the desirable front cars, and force him to be seated at the very rear of the No. 4 train, where he escaped death and serious injury? Was it fate or the gods who made the politic Mr. Daniels stay behind in a rear passenger car to finish hearing a humorous story one of his friends was telling, while his less polite companions left early for the lounge car and suffered a cruel rendezvous with death? Was it fate or the gods who killed Private Bynum before he ever had a chance to prove his bravery on the battlefields of France, dying here instead at Dutchman's Bend woven into the twisted steel with an unmailed letter to his mother in his torn uniform pocket promising 'I am going to get out of this all right. . . . When you hear from me next I will be over the seas'?"

He droned on story after story until we reached the Hotel Halbrook in the small, rural railroad town of Dickson, where he trailed off like an antique mantel clock; and before I knew it, his chin was securely resting on his slowly rising and falling chest. With so much riding on his crucial, all-day interviews, he'd stockpiled an enormous reservoir of energy, which he'd finally depleted as we rolled to a stop at the quaint, single-story, brick depot with its freshly painted red tin roof and seashell white trim around the windows and doors.

Thank God my new friend had fallen asleep. I was becoming increasingly anxious as we approached Dickson. My father had told me to begin looking out for the rock crusher on the right-hand side of the tracks west of town, which would signal we were closing in on the old homestead. I didn't want to be rude to my historian, but I did want to see a little of my own heritage as we passed the antebellum farm midway between Dickson and Warfield.

As Dad had predicted, our train began slowing as we neared the industrial rail sidings packed with long lines of open-top hoppers poised to enter the limestone amphitheater and be loaded with hundreds of tons of riprap and gravel. Because they'd lost so much time with the tropical storm, the truckers and operators were now working overtime to meet the late-summer demand before construction all but ceased during the winter. Their oversized blue-and-silver dump trucks, excavators, and front-end loaders swerved in, around, beneath, and out of the steel maze of tall towers, crushers, conveyors, and stationary vibrating screens.

Dad had also told me to watch for an old, abandoned one-room schoolhouse on the left-hand side once the train had cleared the crusher and the westward sidings. We were still traveling very slowly; and then, no more than a minute or two later, there it was, the shell of a decaying one-room structure, marking the eastern boundary of the bicentennial family farm. There were large holes in the rough-hewn pine walls. The mossy roof had partially collapsed. The front steps were missing. And tangles of thriving blackberry vine choked the fieldstone foundation. Out near the barbed-wire fence bordering the highway, a faded wooden marker announcing "Miss Owings School" stood between the last two of a series of six white-on-red signs, with the one on my right displaying the long-anticipated punch line, "Before the hearse," and the other to my left touting the celebrated sponsor, "Burma Shave."

But the rest of the farm looked no worse for wear. To the south beyond the tall, tasseled corn, I could see a six-room, two-story, white clapboard farmhouse with black-shuttered windows, wrap-around porch, three brick chimneys, and a gray tinplate roof with only hints of early rust. Directly behind the farmhouse there were two small, primitive log buildings. And fifty yards west of the house stood a tool shed, a six-stall stable, and a massive red barn with a host of lightning rods running lengthwise along its shingled peak.

I made a mental note to let Dad know his relatives had gotten into the advertising business big time. Besides the series of humorous Burma Shave signs running the length of the farm's frontage, a hand-painted ad on the side of the stable recommended that travelers "CHEW MAIL POUCH TOBACCO, TREAT YOURSELF TO THE BEST," and another large, hand-painted sign in brilliant white block letters on the charcoal roof of the antique barn encouraged everyone to "SEE ROCK CITY."

After passing the entry gate, the train accelerated. It would now be only a matter of minutes until we reached the Warfield Depot. We stayed at top speed for only two minutes or so before slowing and entering a gentle, sweeping curve. The *City of Memphis* diesel fired off two short warning blasts announcing our imminent arrival. I looked out the window on my left and saw a highway sign indicating historic Graves Bend was only a mile south of town. Dad had told me the immediate area around Warfield was the "hornet's nest" of guerrilla resistance in Union-occupied Tennessee. He said two thousand horsemen, loosely associated with the Confederate army, "entertained" forty thousand Federal troops there for more than three years.

Many of the rebel cavalry who died during the war or passed on later of old age received the community's highest honor: burial at the hallowed guerrilla stronghold, Graves Bend, on the wide, meandering Duck River.

As the engineer lightly applied the brakes a final time, the conductor moved quickly through our car announcing, "This is Warfield, Warfield station." I jumped up, stuffed Henry James in my back pocket, retrieved my suitcases from the overhead rack, and quickly exited at the front of the car. I made my way through the depot to the street-side exit and hailed one of the ubiquitous yellow cabs waiting on call for the slightest signal from the harried traveler's hand. After piling my suitcases into the wide trunk of the old Studebaker, I climbed into the backseat and said, "McGill, 920 West Main Street."

"In the center of town, right?"

I looked at him quizzically and replied, "I don't think I can help you with that one. Never been there before."

As he pulled out into heavy traffic, he swiveled around and said lightheartedly, "Well, don't ya worry. We'll figure it out. I'll get ya there in no time. No more than thirty minutes for sure 'cause we'll be takin' the back roads known only to me . . . and God."

About fifteen minutes into our harrowing all-over-the-road ride, I concluded his turning around to ask questions was his modus operandi when communicating with passengers. Up to that point, three oncoming cars had stridently blown their horns, first out of sheer panic and then out of adrenaline-fortified anger at having swerved to avoid head-on mayhem. But almost miraculously, after our third near miss, my distracted daredevil slowed and became a well-informed guide, highlighting the forgotten, unmarked sites of minor skirmishes and Confederate encampments, which were now slowly surrendering to a determined underbrush.

But the driver saved the crown jewel for last. He slowed to a crawl, thrust his bare arm out the open window into the dusk, and pointed toward a two-story, white frame house with a large front porch partially hidden by a number of evergreens and overgrown lilacs. He announced with an agreeable, understated provincial pride, "The outlaw Jesse James used to live here. Two of his four children are buried in the lot behind the house at the bottom of the hill."

I leaned toward the window to get a better look. "Wow, I didn't know that. Now I've got one on my dad. I'm sure he would've said something if he'd known about the place. You see, he's really into telling rare stories about outlaws—you know, like George Remus and Al Capone."

Convinced my genuine surprise demanded significantly more detail, the cabbie pulled over to the side of the road, thankfully flipped the meter flag up to stop the charges, and began telling the circuitous story of the legendary son of a wandering minister from a neighboring state. And his fifteen-minute description of Jesse's thirty-four-year, thirty-four-mile arc from Kearney to Saint Joe, Missouri, eerily rivaled his driving. It was all over the place.

Early on in the narrative I devised a strategy to manage his progressive digressions of dependent clauses within independent, stand-alone, sidebar tales. I'd focus solely on his datelines and his headlines: Missouri, Little Dixie, Slave Owner, Martial

Law, Insurgents, Bloody Bill, Centralia, Wounded, Zee, Sheets, Kansas City Fair, Rock Island, Pinkerton, Zerelda, Northfield, Nashville, Mr. Howard, Nolan Hotel, Big Bottom, Link Farm, Red Fox, Gould, Montgomery, Killen, Glendale, Saint Joseph, Ford, Assassination, Charged, Sentenced, Pardoned, Legend, Museum, and Eleven Movies to Date.

He finished with a poignant flourish. After quoting a distraught mother's bitter epitaph for a betrayed son, the driver abruptly ended his picaresque tale, reset the meter flag, and pulled out onto the highway without ever looking back or checking his rearview mirror. As we rode along now in a more contractual, conventional silence, I acknowledged that on the one hand, my guide had effectively anticipated every conceivable question I might have ever had about the plot, the desperado, and his hapless victims. But on the other hand, he never drove down into the darkened, murky depths of why. Why did Jesse start shooting to avenge Bloody Bill's death without first confirming the bank cashier was indeed the Major Sam Cox who had earlier killed Jesse's "brother"? Why did the Swede emigrant from halfway around the world fail to understand the frustrated gunman's simple command to get out of the way? And why did a New England lad leave Concord; join the Woodworth Rifles; survive Chickasaw Bayou, Champion Hill, and Vicksburg; overcome dysentery; marry and quickly become a widower; join the bank at Northfield; and then have his fear, hope, love, sadness, and joy splattered across a nondescript back wall from point-blank range, and all of this for a meager take of $26.70?

After squeezing the padded door handle and holding my breath again for another fifteen minutes, we finally weaved our way into the lighted outskirts of McGill; population: 28,003, elevation: 275 feet. At the first flashing intersection, we took a right onto a wet, reflective East Main Street, where flickering red and yellow neon signs pitched tattoos, billiards, and whiskey by the drink. As we continued westward toward the courthouse square, the storefronts and street lamps brightened enough to where we could actually read the addresses posted on the two-story brick and limestone façades lining both sides of Main. My guide reminded me—odd to the left and even to the right. After moving into the nine hundred block, we began spontaneously shouting out in unison the addresses in a reverse countdown: 914, 916, 918, and then—voilà!—there it was, 920 posted on a large, rectangular blue-and-white sign.

The driver pulled into a large space between two Ford pickups, flipped the meter flag up, and diplomatically reported the damage. After pocketing the hefty fare plus generous tip, he leaped out of the taxi, opened my door, and then raced toward the trunk for my bags. That's when I did something I'd never done before. I shook the cabbie's hand, sincerely thanked him for the entertaining local color, and wished him good health and good luck. As I slowly turned away, I silently thanked God for getting me from Warfield to McGill in one piece and then began walking up a few doors from my new apartment to 940 West Main where my new landlord had earlier instructed me to pick up the keys.

Professor Emeritus McMasters still played life the way he had always instructed his undergraduates to play the famous board game—spend your fifteen hundred dollars quickly to snap up as many properties, railroads, and utilities as possible. By constantly collecting rent and piling on the houses and hotels, you slowly and inexorably bleed your competitors into a glorious submission. Only months after moving to McGill, the perceptive, young academic had already developed a unique, profitable vision of the commercial properties comprising the four corners of McGill's quaint, sleepy courthouse square; the businesses would be extremely valuable investments in developing a lucrative real estate empire "supplementing" a modest professorial income.

When I reached 940, I discovered the professor lived in a second-floor apartment above McGill's only hardware store. I climbed the narrow stairs next to the storefront filled with rakes, denim jackets, and seeds for fall planting. I turned left and then knocked on the solid mahogany door at the far end of a dimly lit hallway. A tall, thin, balding, mustachioed fellow cautiously opened the door. I smiled broadly and extended my hand. "Professor McMasters?"

"Yes."

"I'm Andrew Taylor, sir. I've come to pick up the key to the apartment at 920."

"Yes, yes, of course. Nice to see you. Come on in. Take a seat in the parlor here. I'll fetch the key." He took several steps and turned around. "I'm sorry, Andrew. Would you like a cup of English breakfast tea? I drink it all day. I find it much milder than most of the other teas."

"Oh, no, sir. Thank you for the offer. But drinking anything with caffeine after five o'clock and I'll be pacing the floor all night."

The professor smiled and then resumed his journey over to

a large Tuscan floor-to-ceiling cabinet. He opened both doors, revealing row upon row of numbered keys rivaling the collection that hung on the dank walls of the Cárcel de Sevilla at the height of King Philip's Inquisition. As he handed me the key, he said, "Well, if I can't interest you in tea, could I offer you some soup and a sandwich?"

"Oh, I'm tempted, Professor, but I want to get settled in and then get some good sleep tonight. I've got a big meeting in the morning with my graduate school adviser."

He nodded understandingly. "I know, I know. Even after all these years I still remember those first days on a new campus eagerly anticipating teaching my first undergraduate courses and taking on the challenges of a demanding graduate school curriculum."

He showed me to the door, shook my hand warmly, more as a friend than as a property owner, and said, "Well, if not tonight, then let's get together for dinner here one evening early in the semester. What do you say?"

"Once I get my crazy schedule worked out, I'll give you a call and take you up on your offer. You have my word on it."

I quickly descended the stairs, turned left, and walked back up Main Street in the cool, residual mist of the retreating storm. When I reached the blue-and-white address sign, I realized I, too, would be living above a business just like Professor McMasters and ninety-five percent of his apartment clientele. The outside light above the red-on-white storefront sign had either burned out or had inadvertently never been turned on; but there was enough ambient light from the street lamps and adjoining businesses to read "Hudson's Pharmacy" and "Prescriptions

While You Wait." And just below these first two lines were the words "Fountain Drinks" and "Luncheonette" in a slightly smaller font. I briefly tried staring into the store through the plate-glass window, but the small security light behind the lunch counter was no match for the stronger glare coming from the passing automobiles and the powerful floodlights illuminating the courthouse grounds across the street.

I walked to the far side of the storefront, opened the door to the stairwell leading to the apartments on the second floor, and rushed up the steps in anticipation of finally entering my first off-campus apartment. I turned left at the top of the stairs and began looking for the telltale signs of my scholar's garret: an old-fashioned office door with a frosted window on the left-hand side of the corridor.

Professor McMasters had earlier explained he'd just finished converting an old dentist's office into what would be my two-room furnished residence hopefully for the remainder of my academic career. After passing two doors on the right, I stood before an antique masterwork with features worthy of installation at any prestigious school of design: a rich, darkly stained mahogany frame; a thick, frosted windowpane comprising the full upper half of the vintage door; and a brilliant, wide-faceted octagon crystal knob. I turned the key, groped for the switch plate on the inside wall, and finally flipped on the lights. While the appliances and tufted carpeting appeared new, the furniture obviously had endured a previous life, bearing many signs of subtle scarring.

I dead-bolted the door and deposited my suitcases between the micro closet and the tag-sale chest of drawers. As I surveyed the furniture and appliances in the front room and the kitchen located at the rear of the apartment, I quickly concluded the living space was appointed in what interior designers would diplomatically call "retro-eclectic." Besides an oak dresser near the closet door, the home inventory included a beige contemporary sectional sofa bed; a faux Chippendale red wing arm chair; a diminutive crème de menthe Art Deco bookcase with three curved shelves connected on one end by a vertical dowel; two small, miraculously matching Queen Anne end tables; a rustic maple desk with dark brown colonial Windsor chair; a turquoise electric range with four burners, full-function clock, and lots of chrome; a six-foot-high, white, wooden kitchen cupboard; a five-foot-high Philco refrigerator and freezer; a round dinette table with a blue laminate top, ribbed aluminum edge, and double chrome legs; and three heavily padded, vinyl, red-and-white kitchen chairs rescued from some permanently shuttered ice-cream parlor down the block. After finishing the cursory, inaugural tour, I immediately christened my new humble residence "Rainbow Row."

The long, winding day had finally caught up with me. I fished around at the bottom of my suitcases and found my ebony Big Ben with the excruciating alarm, long, sweeping hands, and luminous ivory numbers. I pulled the sofa sleeper out into a bed, set reveille for seven, turned off the lights, collapsed onto the lumpy mattress, and wedged one of the thick, abrasive cushions under my head. I closed my eyes and began replaying the day in random order, but my brief interaction with Professor McMasters returned repeatedly.

I definitely planned to take him up on his sincere offer for dinner at his place sometime soon. In his apartment he had multiple floor-to-ceiling bookcases in the front living room crammed with hundreds of inviting leather-bound volumes. And in an adjoining room I could see even wider cabinets loaded with even more hardbacks and at least six full shelves of long-play vinyls. While my landlord's extensive collection of music and books was a strong motivation to foster his friendship, I really did want to hear about the professor's stellar career and his fifty-plus years of unbroken success investing in off-campus ventures.

I pulled the covers up around my shoulders. After another fifteen minutes of restless planning, my tired mind finally succumbed to the darkness and to the hypnotic ticking of my clock.

5

Bf4 Bd7   e4 fxe4

Unfortunately, Mr. Feisty bested my Big Ben by more than an hour. The Crawfords' prized, free-range countertenor chose Hudson's Pharmacy for his warm-up space that morning. After the deep-breathing and lip-roll exercises, the silver-laced bantam unleashed arpeggios worthy of Dellar preparing for the *Leçons des Ténèbres*—scale after scale, three octaves of each from A through G including sharps and flats. I tried rolling down into the valley, covering my face with the sofa cushion, and willing myself back to sleep. But once I'm awake, I might as well get up and stop fighting the inevitable. Otherwise, everything just gets magnified: annoying incidental sounds, regrets for what I did and didn't do, and the anxious anticipation of a multitude of promises I still had to keep before I could sleep again.

I scaled the heights, swung my feet over the side of the bed, and hesitantly eased into a freezing shower. After repeatedly pressing my crumpled blazer beneath a small damp towel, I opened the kitchen drapes to assess the dawning view atop Rainbow Row. Given the central location of my apartment only three short blocks from campus, I considered the professor's charges reasonable, but the impact of that first glimpse out the front window at the back of my garret drove my appraisal from "equitable" to at least "misdemeanor theft" on my part.

The vista was stunning with clusters of tapered spires and glazed domes rising nobly above the newly burnished crowns of ancient trees. And in the foreground of that terracotta panorama, a large copper fish swam inexorably toward me, suspended permanently above the courthouse dome in a cloudless, cerulean September-morning sea.

To be fair, Mr. Feisty had actually done me a favor. I would now have time to stop by the student union for a coffee and a powdered jelly doughnut before the nine o'clock appointment with my graduate school adviser. Since this was a special day, I trimmed my deep auburn beard, tied an impeccable Windsor, brushed the lightly padded shoulders of my navy jacket, and double-checked the breast pocket for my favorite antique fountain pen. I took one final look in the mirror, ran my fingers back through my hair, grabbed a spiral-bound notebook, hurried down the stairs, and headed west on Main toward the Pantheon campus.

As I walked along in the early autumnal chill, I could feel the tingling and the tension building in my shoulders and arms. It was not the negative type of nervousness—the fear of failing at something important—but a strong sense of anticipation and a determination to focus squarely on the challenge at hand. I was now back in the high school baseball regionals. The legendary Pee Wee Reese had walked over from his house on an off day to watch us play. We were down by one in our last at-bat. The bases were loaded with two out. The count was 3–2. I stepped out, used my Louisville Slugger to knock the mud off my spikes, stepped back into the box, and squarely planted my back foot. As Conley began his full windup, I focused on one thing and one thing only—picking the ball up as it left the lanky pitcher's gifted right hand sixty feet six inches away.

Nervous? Absolutely. Afraid of failure? No. Focused? As never before. Successful? Well again, there was good news and bad news. The good news: I located the pitch as it left Conley's hand and even managed to pick up the rotation. He had the balls to throw me a curve on 3–2 with the bases loaded. The bad news: I got wood on his curveball but fouled it back into the catcher's mitt, and the state all-star managed to hold on to the ball. It was one of those rare moments when success and failure are inextricably fused and the bittersweet memory of just being there among the blessed few participating in something very special only enriches with time and never fades with age.

I passed Professor McMasters's apartment and stopped for the traffic light at the intersection with Forrest Avenue. I fortuitously looked down the busy cross street and discovered a railroad viaduct used by local freights. For a brief moment, I forgot the stress and serious tenor of the day. I laughed aloud. A courageous, crazy, or drunk wag with a flair for model trains had skillfully climbed over the side of the trestle and painted L-I-O-N-E-L in large white block letters between the vertical steel ribs of the highly visible overpass. McGill's pedestrians, pets, automobiles, trucks, buildings, and trees had all magically shrunk and become part of an animated model railway landscape.

After crossing Forrest and then the next intersection at Beauregard, I began catching glimpses of the massive Haldeman Arch, which had served as an iconic gateway to the Pantheon campus for almost a century. I walked the final block up Main to the entrance, where the street doglegs south three blocks and then turns east again, creating the western and southern boundaries of one of the most highly respected private universities in the South.

I approached the storied arch and followed Professor McMasters's detailed instructions to a tee: place the right hand over the word "Fidelis," carved in the right support pillar; place the same hand across the heart; and then touch the Latin inscription again. Giving me a wink, the professor assured me that following this long-held tradition of ceremoniously swearing allegiance to a new *alma mater studiorum* would significantly increase my chances of academic success at this highly competitive institution.

I walked beneath the arch and viewed the old quadrangle for the first time. It was right out of central casting. I checked my campus guide and determined the student union was just off the northeast corner of the quadrangle behind Harris Hall. I was hungry; I hadn't eaten anything since Mrs. Grimes's pimento cheese on white yesterday afternoon on the *Humming Bird*.

I started following one of the shortcut paths the pioneer faculty and students had spontaneously etched during the early years. As I moved between the terraced, emerald pond and the beds of roses, poppies, and hyacinths, I felt a quiet exhilaration. I was home again now after almost five years of wandering about in a foreign land. I'd truly enjoyed my undergraduate days on the East Coast, but I always experienced a nagging disquiet. I couldn't believe it; I had even begun to miss the syrupy veneer of everyone's "Good to see you" and the restaurateurs' "Ya come again, ya here."

I wasn't homesick while out East. With everything that was going on with Mom, I was admittedly relieved to be away for a while. But I felt hollow, unanchored and exiled from all that I'd known and trusted while growing up in the casual elegance of a relaxed southern metropolis—a common heritage, the importance of family, the suffering, the patience, the perseverance, the courage, the faith, the earned reward, the afterlife, the warm greetings, the embraces, the smiles, and the slight, healing touches of discerning friends and empathetic strangers. I walked a little lighter, stood a little taller, now that I was back home in my beloved South.

The wooded northeast trail I'd chosen became increasingly more secluded and eventually ended at the back of the castellated student union near a relatively hidden but truly remarkable arched entrance of cedar timbers and hand-forged hinges. As I opened the heavy doors and entered the fortress, I briefly imagined Catherine de Medici inviting me to Château Chaumont to hear her acclaimed seer, Nostradamus, announce his latest prophecies.

While I'd actually stepped into a twentieth-century reading room with blue upholstered chairs, heavy oak desks, and small, decorative table lamps, the dominant structural features of the interior allowed me to continue the vision of visiting Europe during the Renaissance. There were two massive, working fireplaces on either end of the lofty hall. The towering walls were constructed of large, quarried blocks. And thick, darkly stained ceiling beams rested against large stone arches majestically supporting the impressive vaulted roof.

But the architectural touchstones of the imposing chamber were the eight long, rectangular stained-glass windows, four on either side of the room, depicting important scenes from *Sir Gawain and the Green Knight*: the New Year's Day feast at King Arthur's court; Sir Gawain's bargain with the Green Knight; the mysterious Knight's beheading; the restoration of the Knight's head; the accidental meeting at Bertilak de Hautdesert's castle; Lady Bertilak's temptations of Sir Gawain; the combatants' follow-up meeting at the Green Chapel; and Sir Gawain's long, pensive ride back to Camelot wearing a green sash in knightly shame.

I moved to the other end of the elegant space, turned for a moment to revel in the breathtaking transformation of poetry into artistic glass, and then passed through a Romanesque archway into a startlingly bright, stainless flurry of contemporary breakfast commerce. I picked up a napkin and plastic tray at the beginning of the cafeteria line and moved along quickly, focusing solely on my immediate objectives of strong black coffee and a freshly powdered raspberry jelly doughnut.

I checked my watch. Fifteen minutes until nine o'clock. It was perfect planning and execution. I'd still have plenty of time to finish breakfast and stroll over to the English Department in Redman Hall, where I'd finally meet the highly acclaimed American Renaissance scholar, J. Alfred Wagner. Since I'd never seen him and had only corresponded with him twice over the past summer, I didn't know what to expect regarding his appearance, his personality, and most of all, his plans for my future as a scholar and undergraduate lecturer. The tone of his two brief letters was what I'd call "business professional," and his enclosed recommendations about course work were both unsurprising and according to Hoyle.

After entering the ivied brick building, I checked the directory at the bottom of the marble staircase and then climbed the steps to the top floor, timing my arrival at room 311 for nine o'clock sharp. Five, four, three, two, one, and knock. Doctor Wagner shouted from inside, "It's unlocked. Come on in."

I cautiously pushed the door open and discovered my renowned graduate adviser sitting behind a large oak desk that occupied half the available space in his surprisingly limited on-site office. Open books and stacks of annotated typewritten pages were strewn everywhere about the room: on the tall bookcases lining the side walls, on the wide windowsills behind the professor's desk, and on the squares of faux marble linoleum tile running the length of the room.

It would have been easy to mistake this highly respected academic's office for a grossly underfunded, amateur reenactment of the last days of Pompeii. Thick, heavy clouds of rum-soaked cigar smoke wafted through the air, as fine, gray particles settled out and floated down across the scholarly landscape, adding new thin layers of residue to the substantial strata already coating every flat surface in the room. As I negotiated the winding narrow space between the sacred mounds of scholarship, Doctor Wagner rose from his chair, removed the smoldering cigar stub from between his clenched teeth, and extended his hand. "Mr. Taylor, I presume?"

I extended my hand. "Yes, Professor. It's nice to meet you."

He carefully cleared the only chair reserved for infrequent visitors and then motioned for me to sit down. "Here, take a seat. Sorry for the chaos, but I'm putting the finishing touches on an article for the *American Scholar*."

"If I may ask, sir, the topic?"

"The state of Poe studies." He paused reflectively and added, "It's frustrating."

"Frustrating?"

"Seeing all the Poe scholarship add up to so little. He began life as an orphan, and he's continued an orphan . . . a scholarly and critical orphan."

The professor was ruggedly handsome, appeared to be about five feet six inches tall, and had a surprisingly muscular build for a fellow in his forties, with light blue eyes and gray hair that he wore in a crew cut reminiscent of military recruiting posters. But for me, his most memorable features were his highly starched, button-down oxford dress shirt with the sleeves rolled up to the elbows and his butterfly bowtie with just the right amount of hand-tied asymmetry to proudly certify the neckwear was not a clip-on but the real deal.

After reviewing the required administrative protocol related to my becoming an instructor and doctoral candidate, Doctor Wagner and I launched into a substantive discussion of my formidable responsibilities for the fall semester.

"I'm pleased to see you've accepted my advice about your initial course work. Let's see. . . . Shakespeare: The Early Plays, American Literature to 1800, and An Introduction to Graduate Studies."

I nodded and replied, "It looked like a nice overview of graduate work. By the way, I couldn't tell if you'd be teaching the Intro to Grad Studies. The instructors' names weren't listed on the sheet I had. I assumed you would be, since you developed the course. . . ."

He smiled slyly. "I wouldn't miss it for the world. I get a great deal of pleasure whipping you newbies into shape, transforming you from students into scholars. It's a wide gulf to bridge, but somebody's got to do it."

"I look forward to it, sir."

He laughed aloud and said, "I'd withhold judgment if I were you, Mr. Taylor. Something you need to know about me up front, something personal. I've always set the bar high for myself. Unlike many of my colleagues, I like to get down in the trenches, get my hands dirty. Helps me to stay current and keep in close contact with my students. So I stay busy—real busy—teaching graduate and undergraduate courses, mentoring doctoral candidates, and conducting research about the American Renaissance, Hawthorne, Emerson, Melville, Poe, Thoreau. . . .

"So, fair warning, Mr. Taylor, I'm going to make similar demands of your time, your creativity, your intellect. Just so you know, I've reviewed your transcript and read the three undergraduate recommendations, and I want to push you, stretch you, help you find your limits. So I've decided to have you lead the only advanced English composition course offered this fall and also teach a 200-level course in the development of the English novel beginning with Defoe, Richardson, Fielding, and Sterne. You think you're up for it, Mr. Taylor?"

"I'll give it my best shot, sir." In truth I was filled with trepidation, but what else could I say?

He smiled slyly again. "I'm so convinced you're up to the challenge, I've decided to make your life even more interesting."

"More interesting?" I asked haltingly.

"Yes. More interesting than you could ever imagine. I'd

like to see you adopt an experimental approach to teaching the advanced composition course."

"Experimental, sir?" My trepidation was turning to excitement.

"Well, here's the method to my madness. The fifteen students who qualified for the advanced course excelled on their composition tests. They've all declared English as their major. And they indicated to their advisers they were open to a unique approach to instruction."

"How would the advanced course work, sir?"

"Fair question. You'll meet with the undergraduates only once during the semester."

"Only once the whole semester?"

"That's right, only once. The first day of scheduled classes. During that meeting, you'll explain the unique process, your expectations, their deliverables, and your grading criteria. And at the end of that one and only class, you'll give each of the students a personalized assignment. They'll then spend the next week drafting an essay based on their unique topics. After the seven days, they'll deposit their completed papers in your internal mailbox in the English Department's administrative office.

"One week after dropping off their essays, they'll return to the English Department to check their own internal mailboxes. There they'll find your helpful feedback on their previous assignments, brief notes describing their next unique topics for compositions due the following week, and a model essay illustrating the specific rhetorical principle currently under review."

My mind immediately began racing at the possibilities.

"Thank you so much for the opportunity, sir. I believe the students will immediately become engaged in the approach. They'll have so much autonomy."

The professor rose from his chair and walked over to a standing antique coat rack at the back of his crowded space. He opened a tan canvas satchel hanging from one of the four decorative hooks and pulled out a book and some papers. As he handed the materials to me, I asked, "What do we have here?"

"Well, you've got the recommended reference work associated with the English novel course, the detailed syllabi for the courses you'll teach, and a typewritten page of possible topics for the experienced enrollees in the advanced composition course."

When the professor paused and glanced down at his watch, I sensed he was signaling our meeting was over. I stood up, confidently extended my hand, and then slowly navigated my way to the door. As I descended the two flights of stairs to the ground floor, a number of thoughts and emotions raced through my mind: relief that the meeting went well; personal pride that this highly respected professor valued my accomplishments and potential; a strong determination to overcome even the slightest negative thoughts or doubts I might have had about succeeding either as an instructor or as a graduate student; and a firm resolve to immediately begin serious preparations for the undergraduate courses I'd launch early the next week.

Before our appointment, Doctor Wagner was a renowned scholar, an intellectual demigod who deserved homage on the scale somewhere between adulation and outright worship. But after the meeting, I no longer felt deification was in order. The professor was a human being, a mere mortal, who should be highly respected for his scholarly successes and, perhaps more importantly, admired for his leadership skills and his ability to raise the students' level of play well beyond what they thought they were capable of achieving.

During our discussion, I began realizing the wiry professor shared many characteristics with strong political and military leaders. He was positive, passionate, engaged, demanding, creative, intelligent, a risk-taker, humorous (albeit entertaining a somewhat acerbic, wry, satirical wit), a doer, an active listener, and a leader by example. You could tell he was not a nose-in-everything, hands-on-everything, bureaucratic control freak. He'd set direction, provide instruction, and then step out of the way. But as he assured me during our conversation, he'd always be there to support me.

But one thing I knew for sure: transforming resolution into "Wagnerian" action required an immediate foray into the stacks of the university library. I checked my student guide and determined the Dunn Memorial was in the southwest corner of the quadrangle next to the law school. I located another of the student-etched paths running diagonally across the campus from northeast to southwest, which I affectionately and interchangeably named for now and forever, the "Pythagorean," the "Hypotenuse," and the "C-squared" trail. Contrary to what I'd always told Dad about Euclidean geometry, I'd finally found a real-time application for the discipline. I had literally stepped into a theorem and begun solving for c.

When I reached the seven-story limestone building, I rushed up the impressive staircase two steps at a time and entered a large foyer serving as a temporary exhibit room for manuscripts, first editions, and illustrated texts from the library's rare-book collection. I passed through the thick, wooden doors and entered an enormous rectangular space with seven tiers of decorative wrought-iron balconies containing the extensive stacks. These balconies surrounded an elegant reading room featuring at least ten rows of long, lightly stained desks and carrels; polished-brass reading lamps; an ivory marble floor with ebony inlay; and twenty-four fluted Doric columns soaring almost a hundred feet into the air to a barrel-vaulted ceiling crowned with a massive, translucent Tiffany-style skylight. The effect was enough to stop me in my tracks while I took in my opulent surroundings.

Since there were a number of folks sitting at the long tables near the card catalog, I angled off to my right toward several unoccupied carrels in the quiet stacks beneath the ornate second-floor balcony. I sat down, retrieved the advanced composition syllabus from my coat pocket, and opened my notebook to the first blank page beyond the extensive dictation I'd just taken during my conversation with Doctor Wagner. Staring down at a blank page while feeling the pressure to deliver can cut one of two ways. It can scare the hell out of you and cause the brain to freeze, or it can excite you because you now have an opportunity to challenge others and express your theories on the infinite creativity of literary scholarship. And I knew now I was up for that challenge.

Because Doctor Wagner and I were dealing with "the dark side of the moon," the syllabus was sketchy at best and offered few clues concerning where to begin. Between the introductory paragraphs describing the course concept and process and the concluding administrative paragraphs related to grading and attendance, Maestro Wagner had penned few notes in the syllabus for this four-month concerto. Everything between the opening bars and the finale had been marked "cadenza." And it was now my job to craft the solo part comprising the primary thrust of the overall work.

So where to begin? Dad had always taught me to first define primary goals and their subsets before undertaking any significant project. I reflected for a few minutes and then began writing:

ADVANCED COMPOSITION: COURSE GOALS

A. Introducing rhetorical principles cumulatively from the simple concrete to the complex and writing at least one composition of:

> 1. Description
>
> 2. Definition
>
> 3. Classification
>
> 4. Comparison and Contrast
>
> 5. Problem Solving
>
> 6. Analysis
>
> 7. Research
>
> 8. Argument and Persuasion

B. Using standard grammar, spelling, and punctuation. (See style sheet for abbreviations, capitalization and spelling, hyphenation, italics and quotation marks, numbers and dates, seriation, quotations, citations, etc.)

C. Reading at least one model essay for each composition assignment.

D. Effectively organizing and structuring each assignment.

E. Increasing vocabulary by reading challenging texts.

F. Simulating the process of working with unseen editors a continent away.

By formulating the primary goals and subsets, I was simultaneously developing the structure for the advanced course. So the next task was to select model essays for the eight assignments exemplifying how specific works have been organized and why their particular organizations serve their writers' key objectives well. According to the newly established game plan, the first model essay would have to be descriptive and brief, since we'd both read and discuss the paper during our first and only class.

I can now understand why I so quickly settled on a passage from Melville's *Moby-Dick* for the first model essay. I'd just finished reading the behemoth in my final undergraduate honors course and the day I planned this class, a copy was fortuitously sitting on a nearby cart filled with books ready for reshelving. But serendipity played an even greater role in my choosing chapter sixty for the first model passage of the course.

While reading the masterwork the previous spring, I plowed through the minute description of the harpoon line, simply adding the passage to the plethora of chapters already describing everything you always wanted to know about whaling but never knew to ask. But as I began thumbing through the text that day at the library, the book spontaneously cracked open to "Chapter LX: The Line." In a mystical way, the chapter chose me; I didn't select the chapter.

I began reading the initial paragraphs and immediately

decided this brief passage would be an outstanding example of descriptive writing. But little did I know at the time where these mere ten paragraphs would later lead us during our extended free-flowing discussion on my inauguration day.

I next flipped back through the earlier pages of my notebook to discover any Wagnerian predilections related to the remaining seven model selections. Confidentially, in a bottom-line analysis of the chosen works, the final score was young, inexperienced graduate student 5 and the world-renowned literary scholar 2. Oh, the manifest hubris of it all! Well, the elite seven authors chosen to illustrate effective exposition, argument, and persuasion included Woolf, Huxley, Jarrell, Fiedler, Baldwin, Sartre, and, of course, in honor of my old hometown's hostelry, F. Scott Fitzgerald. And the subject matter for the chosen few ranged from Pascal to patrons, from mental breakdowns to the German occupation, and from intellect to "the most terrible and improbable of all human creations, beauty itself."

With the planning for the advanced composition course now under control, I turned my attention to the rise of the English novel. I reviewed the professor's syllabus for the 200-level course and read the opening chapters of the recommended reference. Unlike the structure for the advanced composition course, the flow there would be much more straightforward. It made a lot of sense to teach chronologically with emphasis on the two main directions the novel took during its formative years, internally toward the individual character and externally toward the broad, picaresque sweep of contemporary society. Defoe, Richardson, Fielding, Sterne, Smollett, Austen, and James made the cut; and the range of engaging, enjoyable characters would doubtless include a thief, a hypocrite, a transgressor, a digresser, a virtuous footman, a foundling, an irascible hypochondriac, a self-deceiving snob, and a balding innocent abroad.

I just knew this was going to be serious fun. The amount of reading alone would be daunting. Now add to that challenge several primary objectives, for example, (1) accurately defining the novel, (2) describing the spontaneous adoption of realism by significantly disparate authors, and (3) identifying favorable literary and social conditions promoting the development of a new fictional form, and now you have a formidable task, falling somewhere on the scale between Herculean and Sisyphean and worthy of depiction among the monumental frescoes in the Lesche at Delphi.

On concluding my work, I was spent and hungry. I had toiled straight through the afternoon without a break. The game plan now would be to check out a reserved copy of Moll, the lovable whore who was five times a wife; find a tasty soup and sandwich shop; head back to Rainbow Row on the courthouse square; and then begin tackling Defoe. As I left the library that day, I felt relaxed and admittedly pleased with my accomplishments. One thing I'd learned while an undergraduate—focused preparation builds confidence, which, in turn, leads to acknowledged success. I knew I was confronting challenges unlike any I had ever faced before, but I was determined to enter the graduate student–junior instructor fray both joyfully prepared and resolutely unafraid. *Laissez les bons temps rouler.*

I exited the quadrangle through the storied arch and began walking west on Main. I remembered seeing a hole-in-the-wall restaurant somewhere along the way. As I approached the Beauregard intersection, I noticed something that I hadn't spotted while strolling over to campus that morning. I guess I had been too distracted thinking about my impending interview to detect the life cycle symbolism now staring me in the face.

Beginning on the northeast corner and moving counterclockwise as if unwinding a life, you first see the Medical Arts Building overflowing with family doctors and specialists. On the northwest corner, you hear the sirens screaming into the emergency lanes at the McGill General Hospital. Next, you read on the southwest side of the intersection, "J. Patrick & Sons Mortuary, Serving the County for Over 100 Years." And completing the ironic juxtaposition of service establishments surrounding the bustling intersection, you find colorful bouquets and elaborate floral arrangements for all occasions in Solley's storefront on the southeast corner of Beauregard and Main.

While waiting for the light to change at this metaphorically charged crossroad, I discovered the Two-Way Café literally surrounding Solley's across the way. Contrary to campus lore, the etymology of the moniker was not rooted in sex but in the uninspired, literal reality that there were actually two entrances to the eatery, one on Beauregard for the full-service bar and the other on Main leading to the more formal dining room.

I crossed the street and entered the Two-Way via Beauregard and vaulted up onto one of the wooden Windsor stools scattered along the length of the ornately carved mahogany bar. The cacophonous room was moderately dark, humid, and more than half-filled with loyal patrons seriously intent on unwinding around a dozen or so primitive red oak tables and chairs. In contrast, the back bar was well lit with multicolored floodlights reflecting, refracting, flashing, and angling off the sixty or so bottles and crystal decanters of Dickel, Maker's, Daniel's, and Beam lining the top shelf against the paneled back wall. But the undisputed showcase here was the four-by-six-foot heirloom mirror with a stunning antique mottled-copper frame and a highly detailed etching of Confederate General P. G. T. Beauregard on horseback, with sword drawn above his head, leading his attacking forces into ferocious battle at nearby Shiloh almost one hundred burnished years ago to the day.

After polishing the decades of lacquer in front of me, the middle-aged barkeeper drawled his welcome, proffered a menu, and queried, "What'll it be?"

I smiled and jokingly responded, "A big, frosty draft and a little time to check this huge bill of fare."

You see, it was a monster of a bar menu. There were over a hundred items listed randomly in serious need of Melvil Dewey's decimal system—two-way, three-way, four-way, and five-way chili; authentic southern barbecued chicken, ribs, and beef; deep-fried turkey; fried catfish, shrimp, and oysters; ten different overstuffed sandwich platters; mammoth hamburgers and cheeseburgers; homemade fries, hushpuppies, baked potato salad, fried okra, collard greens, and black-eyed peas; chess, key lime, and pecan pies; and a "one-hundred-dollar" German chocolate cake.

Several minutes later the bartender circled back and asked with a chuckle, "Make it one of each?"

I laughed aloud and replied, "I'm hungry, but not that hungry. So why don't we make it a fried catfish sandwich with catsup on white and a 'crater-size' bowl of your 'volcanic' five-way chili with spaghetti, shredded cheddar, chopped onion, dark kidney beans, and some crisp oyster crackers on the side."

"Got it! Will be up in a jiffy."

I dug into that chili as soon as it arrived. And sad to say, I didn't stop with the entrées. I splurged with a Dixie-generous piece of the moist, coconut-laden dark chocolate cake and a half a pot of potent coffee extract, which had probably been simmering on a back burner since late morning or early afternoon. With my youthful agility significantly diminished by my sins of the past hour, I slowly eased myself down from the elevated bar stool and began listing toward the Main Street door, which would put me at least fifty paces closer to home sweet home.

As I ambled west on Main between Beauregard and Forrest, I stopped briefly to inspect the eclectic memorabilia deviously displayed in the modest storefront of the Off Again, On Again, Gone Again antique shop. The crafty merchant, Finnegan, had done his job well. He'd conjured up my suppressed, unarticulated emotional need for a "rarely used" 1950s Magnavox Stereophonic High Fidelity Micromatic console featuring a turntable, a radio, and a storage bin full of mostly classical and operatic LPs.

Unfortunately, the store was closed for the evening, but you could bet your bottom dollar I'd be down there early in the morning negotiating long before Mr. Feisty began his deep-breathing and lip-roll exercises. So what to do in the interim to counter my frustration? I'd hurry home, undress, and jump into bed with Moll, the penitent whore.

6

Nxe4 Nd5   Ne2 Qe7

"Now that everyone's finished reading the first model 'essay,' let's discuss what Melville was trying to achieve with these ten brief paragraphs totaling about fifteen hundred words. How would you classify the overall chapter? Does it compare and contrast? Does it present an argument and try to persuade? Does it attempt to solve a problem?"

Everyone sat silently, heads shaking.

"Well, if it's none of these things, then what does the chapter try to do? Anyone like to take a shot at it? . . . I see a hand there. According to my seating chart, you're . . . you're Jim. Right?"

"Yes, Mr. Taylor. It's Jim."

"So, Jim, what does the chapter try to do?"

"Like a lot of *Moby-Dick* I think Melville's trying to add heft, veris . . . veris . . ."

"Verisimilitude. Go on, Jim."

"So basically I think he's, ah, describing a harpoon line in minute detail."

"All right, Jim. Thank you. So does everyone agree then that the chapter basically describes a harpoon line?"

Everyone remained silent looking at his or her fellow classmates quizzically.

"Well, let's test Jim's idea by taking a closer look at the first seven paragraphs. So the first four of the seven address which of the useful *who, what, where, when, why,* and *how* analytic questions?"

Everyone spoke up confidently in unison: "The *what* question."

"That's right. The first four paragraphs answer the *what* question—*What* is the rope made of? *What* does it look like? *What* do you do with it? And the next three paragraphs of the first seven address which other analytic question?" I paused to let the students catch up. "Good, I see a hand there. And according to my seating chart it must be, ah, Bill. So, Bill, the next three paragraphs answer which of the analytical questions?"

"I'd say they answer the *where* question, Mr. Taylor."

"That's right, Bill. *Where* is the overall line stowed before use? *Where* is the lower end of the line with the loop placed? *Where* is the upper end of the line moved before lowering the boat for the chase? So based on these seven paragraphs alone, wouldn't we have to agree then, using Jim's terminology, Melville is basically describing a harpoon line?"

Everyone nodded in agreement.

"And based on our analyses so far, wouldn't we classify the chapter as a descriptive essay?"

Everyone mumbled, "Uh-huh."

I scratched my head for effect and asked, "So why would Melville include seven paragraphs describing harpoon lines and where they're stowed? Perhaps Jim was on to something. Does everyone agree with Jim that Melville included the seven paragraphs to add heft, gravitas, and . . . and verisimilitude to the novel? If so, what does the descriptive weight add to the reader's experience? . . . Anyone have an idea? Anyone?" I paused again, this time for a little longer. I was heartened to see the students pondering the question I had posed. And then recognition set in.

"I see a hand at the back of the room. My seating chart says . . . says . . . it must be Donna. So, Donna, what do you think the descriptive weight adds to the reader's experience?"

"I believe it allows the reader to become a part of the action, become a sailor on the *Pequod* alongside Ishmael, Starbuck, and Ahab."

"Very good, Donna. And I'd suggest your insight brings us to another observation. Did anyone notice a style change in moving from paragraph seven to paragraphs eight through ten?

"I see a hand there. It's Brad, correct?"

"Yes, Mr. Taylor. I'm Brad."

"Did you see a style change moving from the first seven paragraphs to the last three?"

"Yes, sir, but I think Melville may have made a mistake moving from the third person to the second."

"Does everyone agree with Brad that Melville made a mistake here shifting pronouns from the third person—for example, 'harpooner,' 'everyman,' 'seaman'—to the second person, 'you'? Is it possible this literary giant made six blunders in the ninth paragraph, using *you* over and over again? Or could this approach have been intentional?"

About three-fourths of the class was nodding their belief Melville changed the pronouns intentionally.

"And what about the change in tone between the penultimate and last paragraphs? Note the diction and the vowels in the last two sentences of paragraph nine vis-à-vis the vowels in paragraph ten. Melville uses light, staccato vowels, what we call front vowels (*a*, *e*, and *i*) in paragraph nine; but in the tenth paragraph, he chooses back vowels (*o* and *u*), which add an aura of gloom, seriousness, and heaviness to the tone. So does anyone have an idea what Melville is trying to accomplish in the last three paragraphs?"

Everyone looked around for answers.

"In reality, isn't Melville moving from the objective to the subjective?"

Silence.

"So what's the subject matter of the last three paragraphs?"

Still silence all around.

"There are clues here. . . . You notice he's now employing threatening, ominous words and phrases, for example, 'twisting and writhing,' 'perilous contortions,' 'deadliest snakes,' 'hangman's nooses,' and 'make the very marrow in his bones to quiver in him like a shaken jelly.' Does everyone agree that's a far cry from the objective description of the harpoon line in the opening paragraphs?"

All heads nodded in unison.

"So any ideas what Melville's up to here?"

Silence. Some of the class was looking down while others glanced over at their peers.

"Okay then, let's explicate the final paragraph for clues. The first sentence is pretty long:

> Again: as the profound calm which only appar-
> ently precedes and prophesies of the storm, is
> perhaps more awful than the storm itself; for,

indeed, the calm is but the wrapper and envelope of the storm; and contains it in itself, as the
seemingly harmless rifle holds the fatal powder,
and the ball, and the explosion; so the graceful repose of the line, as it silently serpentines
about the oarsmen before being brought into
actual play—this is a thing which carries more
of true terror than any other aspect of this dangerous affair.

"What's Melville saying here? I see a hand there. My chart says
it's . . . it's Doug. So, Doug, what's he saying here?"

"I think Melville's describing the danger built into the line."

"Very good, Doug! Yes, Melville's describing the inherent
mortal threat pervading every golden fiber of the rope. And do
y'all sense the correlation between the diction in this sentence
and the overall structure of the essay? Here are some hints: 'calm
before the storm,' 'wrapper,' and 'envelope.' In essence, aren't the
first seven paragraphs the 'calm before the storm,' the 'wrapper,'
and the 'envelope' preceding or hiding the stormy, awful truths
following in the final paragraphs of the chapter?"

I read on:

But why say more? All men live enveloped in
whale-lines. All are born with halters round
their necks; but it is only when caught in the
swift, sudden turn of death, that mortals real-
ize the silent, subtle, ever-present perils of life.
And if you be a philosopher, though seated in

the whale-boat, you would not at heart feel one
whit more of terror, than though seated before
your evening fire with a poker, and not a harpoon, by your side.

"You see what Melville's driving at here? He observes so
poignantly we're all metaphorically in the same boat with the
seamen—fearing, hoping, despairing, laughing, crying, and
ignoring the inevitable that we're all enmeshed in 'whale-lines'
and, ironically, calmly living out our lives while waiting to die.
So in these ten brief descriptive paragraphs, Melville skillfully
foreshadows what will happen to the questing sailors, while
simultaneously reminding us of our own mortality. That's his
courage here. That's his genius.

"Let's step back now and place *Moby-Dick* in the context of
Melville's overall work. His travelogues and sea yarns—*Typee*,
Omoo, *Mardi*, *Redburn*, and *White Jacket*—they're the 'wrapper,'
the 'envelope,' and the 'calm before the storm.' Except for
Mardi, where Melville tentatively stuck his philosophical toe in
the water and paid the price, he kept his personal fears, doubts,
and existential fury to himself. But with *Moby-Dick*, he rips away
the 'envelope' and the 'wrapper,' and we now confront the storm
head-on.

"Responding to Hawthorne's feedback about the novel,
Melville wrote to his friend indicating he was relieved Hawthorne
had grasped the demonic undertow lurking beneath the poetic
narrative:

A sense of unspeakable security is in me this

moment, on account of your understanding the book. I have written a wicked book, and feel spotless as the lamb. Ineffable sociabilities are in me. I would sit down and dine with you and all the gods in old Rome's Pantheon. It is a strange feeling—no hopefulness is in it, no despair.

"And what did Hawthorne understand? He realized Melville had wrestled with the angels and had elegantly captured the ambiguities of the human condition. Ahab's quest for certitude had become our quest; his rage, our rage. In chapter forty-one he writes:

All that most maddens and torments; all that stirs up the lees of things; all truth with malice in it; all that cracks the sinews and cakes the brain; all the subtle demonisms of life and thought; all evil, to crazy Ahab, were visibly personified, and made practically assailable in Moby Dick. He piled upon the whale's white hump the sum of all the general rage and hate felt by his whole race from Adam down; and then, as if his chest had been a mortar, he burst his hot heart's shell upon it.

I paused, surveyed the room, and then concluded, "Are there any questions?"

The students shook their heads.

"Well, time's up for the day and also for the semester. . . . This is the only time I'll see you unless you have a pressing question and make an appointment. Please don't forget to pick up your individual assignments on the table next to the door. Your descriptive essays are due a week from today. Please deposit them in my internal mailbox in the English Department. The following week, check your internal mailboxes. You'll find feedback on your descriptive exercises, a copy of the next model essay, and your personal assignments for your definition essays due a week after that. So work hard, probe the depths, and most of all, have fun!"

After picking up their first assignments at the door, several of the students approached the lectern either to continue the classroom discussion or to clarify minor points about their individual projects. I spent about fifteen minutes reassuring, listening, and responding before diplomatically disengaging from this highly laudable but narrowing circle of undergraduate high achievers. I apologized and explained I had an important one o'clock appointment over at Redman Hall across the quadrangle, and I just couldn't be late for the meeting.

I want to emphasize here I tactfully extricated myself from this coterie of ambitious freshmen. I didn't want to dampen their enthusiasm, and I didn't want to lie. I just rounded the rough edges a bit. I did indeed have to be at Redman Hall at one o'clock sharp, but my "appointment" was actually my first encounter with a graduate school seminar—not just any colloquium, but the first lecture by the legendary creator of the literary research course itself, the dapper, cigar-chewing J. Alfred Wagner.

Our bow-tied General Patton surged into the classroom about ten minutes after one o'clock with his signature rum-soaked stub firmly secured at the right side of his mouth. He placed his stack of spiral notebooks and miscellaneous papers on the lighted speaker's stand; removed his dark brown sport coat; rolled up his oxford sleeves to the elbows; and then slowly gazed about the cenacle at the twelve burgeoning graduate scholars eagerly anticipating his recitation of the good news.

And the master didn't disappoint. With a confident, polished, understated flourish, he removed the dark, dormant cigar from his clenched teeth and then projected his holy, resonant voice out in waves above the excitable heads of his duly sworn disciples: "In the introduction to his *Problems and Methods of Literary History*, written some forty years ago, Morize captured the essence, the value, if you will, of serious, disciplined literary studies:

> A love of precision joined to aspirations toward general ideas; respect for historical facts, and warm appreciation of beautiful writings; minuteness in research, and breadth of view; finesse in analysis; strictness in criticism; penetration in aesthetic judgments; lastly, exacting loyalty toward oneself, toward facts, toward the ideas and the men studied—these are a few of the valuable qualities that, thoroughly understood and thoroughly carried out, literary studies tend to develop.

"Our introductory course will focus on the use of specialized reference materials, research methods, and textual studies, especially textual criticism and bibliographical description. Our seminar will provide a hands-on introduction to both scholarly theory and practice. There will be no tests. You will be evaluated solely on how well you perform on your personalized exercises, which will give you practical experience in collecting targeted information, assessing evidence, drawing conclusions, and drafting scholarly papers and articles.

"The exercises will introduce you to the primary bibliographies and reference works in use today; encourage you to detect and correct textual errors; and force you to challenge the evidence and authority for long and widely held scholarly assertions. And to add a bit of spice to the course, for some of the advanced exercises you will be required to visit our rare-book library to edit original manuscripts and relevant correspondence." He paused, smiled, and asked lightheartedly, "Now honestly, does it get any better than that?"

My classmates and I nodded and laughed aloud.

"Are there any questions? Okay then, if there are none, please stop by the desk here and pick up your first exercises, which will introduce you to highly useful bibliographies and effective reference materials. Since your investigations could be time-consuming, your brief reports will be due ten days from today, at the end of our Thursday seminar. There will be no class in the interim. By the way, my hours are posted on the bulletin board outside my office door, if you believe it's necessary to chat." As the students picked up their assignments and began to leave, he called out, "Good luck. I'll see you on the twentieth."

I picked up my sealed assignment but didn't open it until I got over to the library, where I had planned to finish reading *Moll Flanders* and begin preparing my opening remarks for the course on the rise of the English novel. But before I could continue reading Defoe, I had to satisfy my intense curiosity about J. Alfred's exercise. I pulled the addressed envelope from my jacket, tore open the sealed flap, and began reading.

I was relieved. It was a simple, factual, straightforward question of determining a specific date for two events. The note referred to "Newsreel 57" of Dos Passos's novel, *The Big Money*, which is part of his trilogy, *U. S. A.* Dos Passos used actual newspaper and magazine headlines to anchor his work both in time and space. "Newsreel 57" includes the headlines, "Queen Sleeps as Train Departs" and "Coolidge Urges Advertising." After throwing me one clue, that the queen in question was Marie of Rumania, J. Alfred asked three simple questions: "Where was the queen? Where was Coolidge? And what was the exact date for the two headlines?"

Forget Defoe, forget Moll, and forget the English novel. I was now on a mission to quickly resolve the mysteries. First things first. To make big headlines in the major newspapers I assumed Coolidge was president of the United States at the time he urged advertising. So based on this assumption, I had to know when Coolidge was president. And thanks to my undergraduate honors history class I knew the answer. He succeeded Harding in 1923; was reelected in 1924; and served until March 1929, when Hoover took over.

Since I knew nothing about Queen Marie of Rumania, I immediately bolted for the reading room and specifically for the

Documents Information Desk, where I could access untold reels of archival information, including old newspapers and magazines. But wait. First I'd have to know something about the queen. So over to the reading room wall and the bank of encyclopedias. I had it! She was born October 29, 1875, and died July 18, 1938. But there was absolutely nothing in the article about sleeping on a train.

Well, so far so good. I'd narrowed the date down to a seven-year period, 1923–1929, when Coolidge was president. Now to the Documents Information Desk where I explained to the librarian I needed to review the contemporaneous accounts of President Coolidge they had on microfilm. She said I could do that; but if I preferred, I could go up to the top floor in the stacks and research the bound volumes of the *New York Times* back to the 1890s. So forget the high-tech approach; I was off to the stacks! As I rushed off, she advised me to first consult the *New York Times Index*, which lists every article back to 1913.

Following the librarian's advice, I discovered several good leads about Coolidge in the *Times Index*. I then rushed up to the seventh floor of the stacks and located the bound volume containing the October 1926 newspapers. I could smell success. It wouldn't be long now, and I'd be back with the amiable whore.

Okay, I had three papers to check. Nothing relevant in the October 21 edition, so I moved on. Nothing in the October 25 paper about Coolidge and advertising.

At that point I became sidetracked. I'd discovered a compelling story—Harry Houdini, the master magician, had arrived at the Garrick Theater in Detroit, Michigan, with a fever of 104 degrees. The doctors thought it was acute appendicitis, but the show had to go on. Houdini took the stage. He fainted during the performance, rallied, and continued to wild applause. After the show, attendants rushed him to Detroit's Grace Hospital. And that was the end of the report. Curious about the conclusion, I moved on to the next day, the day after, and then the day after that. Houdini was still hospitalized, and his condition had worsened. I checked the October 29 paper. He was now reportedly in critical condition. What did the October 30 edition say? He was "clinging to life." The October 31 paper? Houdini was still alive but gravely ill. And the November 1 edition? Oh no! The paper reported Harry Houdini had died of peritonitis from a ruptured appendix on Halloween at the age of fifty-two. Reading each succeeding account in the newspapers created an immediacy and intensity I had never felt while researching historical events. I'd been transported back to room 401 at 1:26 p.m. and watched the doctors pounding on the magician's chest. But then the magic ended. There was no escape this time. All was silence.

I sat back in my chair and took several deep breaths. My pulse had quickened. Understandably so. I'd just watched a man die a painful death.

Where was I? Okay. I had checked the October 25 paper, and there was nothing reported about Coolidge and advertising. Let's go back now to the October 26 edition. Anything there? No. So let's move on then to the October 27 paper. Still nothing. How about the October 28 *Times*? Hallelujah! The paper reported President Coolidge gave a speech on the twenty-seventh to the American Association of Advertising Agencies, Washington, DC.

Now it would be easy. Find something in the October 28

edition about the queen of Rumania sleeping on a train on the twenty-seventh, and it's game, set, match! So I scoured the newspaper and found a story about the queen. What did it say? Dateline Canada. Wednesday, October 27—The Queen's train arrived in Montreal. She visited City Hall. She toured *La Presse*, Montreal's leading newspaper. And she worshipped at a Romanian church.

The queen then attended a luncheon in her honor with the mayor and three hundred guests. Next, she visited Montreal College and, ironically, McGill University, where the presidents received her and gave her a tour of their libraries. Afterward she visited the Romanian consul of Montreal, where they hosted a dinner in her honor. She finished the night with a performance of the *Barber of Seville*.

Damn! Damn! Damn! There was nothing about sleeping on a train! J. Alfred, you magnificent bastard! Okay, I took a deep breath; and it was back to the drawing board, back to the *Times Index* for the first references about the queen around this time. Aha, there! The October 19 paper indicated she'd just arrived in New York the day before. Now I was headed back upstairs to the stacks to continue the mission. Any mention of sleeping on a train on October 19? Nothing. October 20? Still nothing. October 21? No. October 22? Still no references to sleeping on a train. October 23? Again, nothing. From the nineteenth on, there'd been plenty of articles about her visit and even some mentioning train rides, but nothing about sleeping. The October 24 paper? Nothing.

On to the October 25 edition. Wait . . . this could be promising. The paper said that on Sunday, the twenty-fourth, the queen attended Calvary Church in New York; ate lunch in the ball-room at the Biltmore; attended an impressive reception at the Plaza Hotel given by the Newspaper Alliance of America (that's ironic—just as with the president, another newspaper function); appeared at a Hungarian friend's art exhibit and purchased a painting for her daughter; attended a dinner that evening given by Mrs. Oliver Harriman at Mrs. Harry Black's Plaza apartment; went to the Metropolitan Opera to enjoy a ballet illustrating one of the queen's original fairy tales, *The Story of Lily*; and afterward, *boarded her special train that would become her home for the next few weeks.*

Okay, she'd had a really long day; it was night, and she was now on the train, which would serve as her home for some time. Close, but no cigar. I kept on reading. What did the October 26 paper say about her October 25 activities? *The Queen's train arrived at West Point in the morning.* General Merck B. Stewart, commander of West Point Academy, welcomed her. After reviewing the cadets on the parade ground, she boarded her train and made additional stops at Albany, Utica, and Syracuse, where she greeted well-wishers from her observation car. The queen's train reached Buffalo at eight p.m., where she attended a banquet at the Statler Hotel. So it's not a real stretch to infer Marie, Queen of Rumania, slept on the train the night of October 24!

So there was good news and bad news. I continued checking the papers up through October 28, which was the edition reporting Coolidge's speech on advertising. But there was nothing remotely close to reporting she was sleeping as her train departed a station. Well, the good news: I was relatively sure I knew when the queen slept on the train: October 24, which happened to be the same night the great Houdini checked into Detroit's Grace Hospital with a high fever. The bad news: The queen appeared to have slept on the train on the twenty-fourth, while Coolidge urged advertising on the twenty-seventh.

The dates didn't jibe, and J. Alfred wanted to know the *exact* date the two events supposedly happened. Now that was a problem. What to do? Well, I could either describe all the steps of my extensive investigation and simply report I couldn't find the exact date, or I could grow a pair, so to speak; report the assumption of an exact date was inaccurate; and assert there was never an exact date. To be or not to be, that was the question. Whether 'tis nobler . . . I decided to table a decision for now. I had plenty of time to decide my fate. I'd get back to my immediate concerns—Moll Flanders and the rise of the novel.

For the next ten days, I played Eliot's Prufrock: "Do I dare disturb the universe? In a minute there is time for decisions and revisions, which a minute will reverse." So on that cursed, moonless night preceding judgment day, I put pen to paper and declared boldly, "THERE WAS NOT AN EXACT DATE; THE WRITTEN QUESTION CONTAINED INACCURACIES."

After suffering through a sleepless night and a distracted morning, I attended class that following afternoon. At the end of his lengthy lecture on selective English and American bibliographies, of which admittedly I remembered very little, Professor Wagner instructed us to deposit our papers on the side desk near the lectern. I waited until all the other students had dropped off their work and left the room before I approached the desk, forced a dubious smile, and dropped my bombshell onto the stack of homework.

Trying to get a read on which way this might go, I made a leading, spontaneous remark about the possibility there was no exact date. The professor immediately fired off a smile worthy of Iago and asked what I'd learned from the exercise. I thought very carefully for a moment and then responded, "Don't believe everything you read in print." He simply replied, "Bingo! I think you've just begun paying your dues."

Well, that wasn't the end of his professorial chicanery. It was only the beginning. A month later J. Alfred assigned each of us a unique sonnet from Robert Lowell's collection of forty-two short poems, *Lord Weary's Castle*, and asked us to explicate our assigned works for the following week's class. To my relief, I learned my assignment was a simple, straightforward sonnet, "Concord," which contained many very familiar references.

Concord? I had visited the rude bridge, the Old Manse, and Sleepy Hollow Cemetery during the summer months between my sophomore and junior years of college. I'd read Thoreau's journals. I knew about Ephraim Bull, the Concord grape, the transcendental forest fire, and Thoreau's amputated toe.

In fact, I remembered watching the cemetery warden climb Authors' Ridge with a small headstone in tow. He passed the grave sites of Bronson and Louisa May Alcott, Nathaniel Hawthorne, and Emerson (the one with the giant, jagged, nonconforming boulder for a marker). He stopped at the Thoreau family plot and planted the simple, foot-high marker in a preexisting hole. The warden then retraced his steps down the ivied slopes toward his green Chevy pickup truck. As he passed by, he turned to explain he continually had to replace the tiny "Henry" headstones because Thoreau devotees were requisitioning them and then proudly displaying the markers as distinctive bookends in the paneled libraries of their well-appointed homes.

And King Philip? That same summer I'd also visited the very cave on Talcott Mountain where Chief Metacomet had watched the settlements burn before finally being quartered, beheaded, and strung up among the boughs of familiar evergreen trees.

I reread the poem more carefully now, stopping after each of the four sentences to mine the textured phrases for any hidden meaning. The first six lines were relatively easy to interpret— hordes were visiting the Minute Man statue and the Walden woods to recapture their lost past. But the diction was troubling: "dry sticks," "fished-out perch," and the double entendre related to the church belfry "ringing out" the hanging Jesus. Had formal religion "wrung out" the healing, redemptive powers of the initial message? Could a spiritual husk compete with the vast powers of capitalist wealth and industry?

Now back for another double entendre, "This Church is Concord." Wasn't the hidden meaning there "conquered"? Hadn't everything been radically changed as Heraclitus had predicted about the water in the stream? Where was the lost tradition these visitors sought? Where was the fervent spirituality of the past? Where was the early innocence of the lonely woodsman and his painted partner with a primitive bow? Everything had been cruelly reduced to a death dance of ancient anguished screams.

Again, I was placed in the position of climbing out on the proverbial limb. The title of the poem denoted harmony, but the negatively charged nouns and verbs connoted an unsettling disquiet and dissonance. The intellectual undertow here was powerful and threatening. Why would Lowell brand his poem

"Concord"? Was it simply because the sonnet was literally grounded in the historic village? Or was it because he wanted to emphasize what Concord had been in the past? The machine had now overtaken the American Adam; and the "dry sticks" of the past and the "whited spindling arms" of the crucifix could never reclaim the inspired innocence lost to the omnivorous mercantile beast.

When I handed in the assignment the next week, I employed my previous modus operandi—I waited until everyone else had left the classroom before dropping my provocative paper onto the pile and offering the professor a tentative rationale for my thesis. "Well, it appears there's considerable discord in Concord." J. Alfred looked up, removed the cigar from his mouth, and said, "That's pretty damn good, kid. Pretty damn good."

For the final assignment of the introductory course, the tide appeared to have turned. The professor seemed to have let up on me and now put the screws to several of my respected cohorts. After receiving our last assignments, six of us marched en masse over to the rare-book reading room to assess what J. Alfred had in store. This last project required us to edit and annotate an original manuscript archived among the rare books.

We submitted our requests for the manuscripts, and the library assistant retrieved each of our assigned documents one request at a time. Since my manuscript was last on the assistant's list, I had a chance to determine the types of challenges awaiting my classmates. The good news was they'd be editing correspondence from famous writers to relatively well-known recipients. The bad news was the letters were written in an unintelligible scrawl, packed with abbreviations and rich in fairly obscure allusions requiring many hours of tedious research to unravel the mysterious entries.

I finally received my manuscript, slowly opened the manila file folder, and breathed an enormous sigh of relief. It was correspondence running to four pages from Alfred Lord Tennyson's older brother, Frederick, to a fellow named H. G. Coxhead. I scanned the manuscript; it was entirely intelligible and as legible as the proverbial handwriting on the wall. After convincing the professor of my research abilities during the earlier exercises, I believed J. Alfred had now finally dialed back the heat and applied it elsewhere.

I began reading the document more carefully in an attempt to discover any serious challenges. The letter was written from Saint Ewold's on the Isle of Jersey in August 1888 and contained references to routine personal matters; descriptions of pastoral life off the Normandy coast; the political situation in Great Britain with specific comments about several current politicians; his own publishing activities; and discussions of his younger brother's attempts to persuade the American actress Mary Anderson to produce his musical collaboration with Arthur Sullivan about Robin Hood, Maid Marian, and the merry band. Frederick also alluded to the progress he was making on his next volume of poetry, tentatively called *The Isles of Greece*, and actually quoted passages from the work:

> And in short nights of Summer, as we lay
> Together in one bed, we sang and gazed
> Up to the stars, that seemed to tremble to us,
> Thrilling back the keen pulses of our song
> With gushes of sweet light and throbs of fire.

It was not until I'd already left the library that a serious question sprang from my roiling subconscious: what do I really know about the recipient of Frederick's clearly and legibly written four-page missive? Who was this H. G. Coxhead? Had J. Alfred done it to me again? Not to worry; I was certain Coxhead's identity would be exposed soon after consulting the library's extensive biographical information on almost every living being who had ever walked the planet.

Besides, I had plenty of time to research this slight mystery. My paper wasn't due for two weeks. And believe me, beginning early the next morning I was back in the rare-book reading room closely reviewing more than fourteen hundred items in the Frederick Tennyson collection the university had acquired over the past decade—his letters; manuscripts of both long, narrative poems and brief, philosophical sonnets; family photographs; publishers' contracts; a coat of arms; and the most interesting but disturbing item of all, Frederick's actual death mask. Here I was rummaging through this minor poet's effects, while he literally stared up at me from the desktop, observing my every move and recording every audible, whispered comment I made privately to myself.

I next checked every other conceivable source I could imagine, including three hundred additional archived manuscripts related to the Tennyson family—for example, all of their correspondence and a few early poems by Lord Tennyson himself. The theory was H. G. Coxhead would surely appear in at least one of the immediate family's personal or business letters to recipients scattered from Italy to the Isle of Jersey. But the bottom line here was this: all the intensive exploration was a monumental time sink, a totally unproductive dry hole. The longer the mystery remained unresolved, the more weight I gave to the theory that J. Alfred had really done it to me this time.

The two weeks of term papers and final exams passed quickly, and judgment day was nigh at hand. Continually distracted by this secretive Coxhead, I finally completed J. Alfred's assignment from hell several hours before the final class was to convene. I took a quick shower, dressed, and rushed off to at least the humiliation of the public stocks or perhaps even worse, execution on the failed scholar's gallows. Class began and ended. I don't remember anything; it was all a blur. I'd nervously dreaded but couldn't wait for the hour to end so I could implement my honed approach of gaining an advanced read on the final judgment and sentencing.

After everyone had left the room, I approached the lectern, dropped my comprehensive, incomplete paper on the mountain of hopeful A's, and genuinely thanked the professor for the instructive, hands-on, albeit adrenaline-depleting course. I then initiated step two—alluding to the enigmatic letter recipient, H. G. Coxhead. The professor's attention became much more focused; he quickly removed the dark stub from the corner of his mouth and asked what I'd learned.

I lowered my head and apologized for the glaring gap in my scholarship. I admitted I didn't have a clue about the identity of this mysterious H. G. Coxhead. The professor paused, put his hand on my shoulder, and expressed his disappointment that I hadn't shed any light on a mystery that he and my predecessors had left unsolved for more than five years. *Aha!* J. Alfred smiled broadly and said he'd enjoyed having me in class. Again, the adrenaline surged. I shook his hand nervously, thanked him repeatedly, and made a quick, I-don't-want-to-know-anything-else exit from center stage.

While that final assignment was both challenging and rewarding, it was actually the earlier classroom trauma related to Queen Marie, Houdini, Coolidge, and the train that caused the highest angst and yet the greatest joy. Perhaps it was because it was the first time I'd matched wits with a champion and proudly left the ring a bit bloodied but unbowed. I'd gained valuable experience during the encounter and had perfected a process to determine my fate long before receiving the professor's written feedback.

So after basking in the professor's kudos for bravely positing "never believe everything you read in print," I floated out of Redman Hall that glorious September afternoon, sailed above the scenic quadrangle, and finally touched down gently in front of Hudson's Pharmacy, the home of tall, tasty fountain drinks and a five-star luncheonette. Without question it was time for an enormous, supercaloric academic reward.

After inhaling a seven-out-of-ten cherry shake, I climbed the dark stairs to Rainbow Row, unlocked the door, and discovered two unexpected envelopes lying on the floor. Anna, the lady hired to clean the lobbies and hallways of McMasters's real estate empire, enjoyed retrieving our letters from the downstairs box, reviewing the addressers and addressees, and then sliding the correspondence under our respective doors, all, of course, in the name of doing us the favor of expediting our mail.

I dropped my notebooks on the sofa bed, carried the letters back to the kitchen table, and read the face of the first envelope.

It had obviously never been mailed. The only writing on it was my first initial and last name. I opened the unsealed flap, removed the small folded page, and began reading.

The letter was actually an invitation to attend a Halloween soiree at Professor McMasters's apartment at the end of October. The occasion was twofold: to celebrate All Hallows' Eve and to warmly welcome new faculty members to the English Department. I'd heard something about this celebrated tradition while visiting the faculty lounge during my first week on campus. Despite having taught economics in the business school for decades, Professor Emeritus McMasters had an unusually strong affinity for literature, for those who create it and for those who teach it. The letter instructed me to complete the RSVP and deposit it in McMasters's mailbox within the next ten days.

The invitation demanded a public performance, and I hesitated to complete the RSVP. Would it be like all the other similar outings I detested? No, not with Professor McMasters at the helm. I enthusiastically completed the card and propped it up against the tall wooden peppermill as a reminder to return it to the professor the following day. I then picked up the second envelope and read the return address. There were no real clues on the face of the pale blue envelope divulging the identity of the addresser—no last name or even initials—only the postmark and the return address, both indicating the correspondence had been mailed from my old hometown.

Intrigued, I whipped the single page from the envelope and began reading. It was from Catherine. She was writing to thank me again for my kind words while attending the class reunion at the end of the previous month. She said she'd thought a great deal about what I'd advised and was seriously thinking of gently declaring her independence from the family, resuming her education, and beginning to live her own life again. She closed the brief note with a sincere, upbeat request to keep her posted on my graduate adventures here at Pantheon.

The letter immediately compelled me to again question my true feelings for her. Was it just some form of sympathy knowing what she had suffered over the past five years? Had I gained a deeper respect for her endless sacrifices? Was it a longing for a shared past in the same school and comfortable, easygoing hometown? Was it sensing the potent combination of her abeyant sexuality and an engaging mind? Or was it an honest love that could be shared for a lifetime? Something buried between the paragraphs, between the lines, something in the tone of the letter said call her and encourage her to visit McGill.

I've concluded life is sequential but never truly linear. We inexplicably revel one day in frenetic, euphoric highs and the next suffer debilitating, unspeakable lows. Unpredictability is the insidious constant the devious genius imbedded in the organic formulae. Do we really ever act independently or do we simply react to the reactions of others? One day I was alone, anxious, and somewhat depressed that I might fail my first test with Dr. Wagner. I couldn't reconcile the damn immutable dates. But the next, I knew I had succeeded and I had received at least one, if not two unsolicited invitations to the dance.

7

c4 Nb6   c5 dxc5

I'D BURNED THROUGH all my change when the operator interrupted our conversation again to tell me the time was up. But the call had lasted long enough for me to dance around the question; for Catherine to pause and then graciously accept; and for the two of us to make arrangements for her first visit the following weekend. I slowly placed the receiver back on the hook and stood for several glorious minutes staring at my incredulous smile in the polished chrome of the payphone casing. It was now almost ten minutes past closing, and the tired, sensitive pharmacist finally cleared his throat to gently suspend my reverie. I quickly turned, apologized, and hurried out the door into a swirling starry night over the Rhône.

A basic phenomenon we learn early in life is that excited anticipation of favorable, upcoming events positively affects our attitudes toward the rest of our agenda regardless of how tedious the impending activities might be. My goal was to stay at least one assignment ahead of my challenging class in the English novel course. I'd just finished *Moll Flanders* and had begun reading the first few pages of Samuel Richardson's *Pamela; or, Virtue Rewarded*. "Transitional culture shock" didn't come close to effectively describing the sensation of moving abruptly from a picaresque, "blue-collar morality tale" containing premarital sex, incest, adultery, prostitution, divorce, and thievery to an epistolary guide instructing the nouveau riche in both letter writing and virtuous behavior where the watchwords were piety, innocence, virtue, virginity, loyalty, dignity, sweetness, and humility.

But the forthcoming weekend with Catherine inspired an acceptable, if not stellar, alternative approach to teaching Richardson's inexhaustible sermon—emphasizing the author's resolution of novelistic problems Defoe had left unresolved, especially the strengthening of plot by moving from an erratic, episodic story line to one focused solely on a single courtship. So Richardson's focused design eliminated Defoe's shortcomings of abrupt transitions, numerous repetitions, and loose ends.

Despite reinforcing my resolve, I must confess I hit the wall again, after having read only the next fifty pages of *Pamela*. Since it wasn't very late, I thought I should finish reviewing the last of the descriptive essays for the advanced composition course. I'd promised to have feedback in the students' mailboxes by the next Monday; and to be totally honest, I also wanted to clear the decks so I could spend as much time with Catherine as possible. After having read the majority of the descriptive pieces, I was impressed with the quality of the work they'd delivered.

The assignment was straightforward on the face of it but with something of a twist. Each student had received a short, descriptive lyric with his or her instructions. I asked them to read their poems, to analyze them, but not to include any explication in their essays. I instructed them, however, to use the tone, imagery, and themes of the poems to inspire an original descriptive essay drawn from their own personal experiences.

I'd intentionally postponed reading Donna's essay until the end of the grading process. Since she'd made several insightful observations about Melville's work, I suspected she'd perform well on the assignment; and I wanted to end my first review with a flourish. But her composition far exceeded my expectations. I'd given her Ezra Pound's two-line, single metaphor poem, "In a Station of the Metro," in which the poet compares the apparition of faces in a Parisian subway to spring blossoms stuck to a dark, wet branch following a storm.

As instructed, Donna began her essay with a detailed description of a bustling metropolitan train station with its imposing stone exterior, richly paneled waiting room, large marble columns, majestic circular stained-glass windows, massive dark oak ticket counter, and thick, decorative doors leading to the shed protecting passengers boarding the outbound trains. She then depicted the weary travelers patiently suffering on the hard, straight-backed benches; standing in the long, glacial lines at the ticket counter; or desperately weaving their way through the overcrowded waiting room toward the last-call express.

Her paragraphs progressively narrowed until the focus was solely on a woman in her late thirties, standing near the main entrance and holding the hand of a young girl wearing a pale yellow princess dress with a white collar and short puffed sleeves. Donna then transitioned dramatically from the impersonal to the personal. She revealed her mother took her to the station every year on the anniversary of her father's disappearance to ritually search for him among the detached, uncaring crowds. On April 1, when Donna was less than a year old, her father boarded the morning commuter and had been playing the cruel joke on mother and child ever since.

The aperture narrowed even more. The focus was now solely on her mother's repetitive, lonely life "measured out in coffee spoons." She'd rise early every weekday morning; ensure Donna had a good breakfast before heading off to school; catch a sweaty metro bus ten stops from the city center; ride a monastic elevator up the sterile office tower; and perform her invisible backroom clerical job "adequately" in a bureaucratic, pinstripe world.

The weekends and the evenings were the hardest. After her husband left, there were two gentlemen callers who eased themselves briefly into her life but stayed only long enough to fall back in love with their conventional, comfortable pasts and then say they were so sorry. The second scoundrel disappeared on her forty-second birthday, and that was the last time she baked a cake, made a desperate wish, and blew out the lying, flickering, candy-striped candles.

Donna's essay was well beyond her years and infused both with pathos and lightning. The literary allusions to the works of Williams, Miller, and Eliot added unrelenting poignancy; but the incisive quotations from one of Jarrell's unpublished poems, "The Woman at the Washington Zoo," transformed Donna's essay from an academic exercise to a publishable work of art.

Almost a year before, she'd read in *The Nashville Tennessean* Jarrell was returning to his alma mater for a poetry reading during his tenure as consultant in poetry to the Library of Congress. Jarrell spent most of that memorable night reciting lyrics from his earlier published poems, "Cinderella," "The End of the Rainbow," and "Seele im Raum." But near the close of the evening, he read several recent unpublished works. "The Woman at the Washington Zoo" in particular was memorable for two significant reasons: Jarrell spent a great deal of time explaining the creative process that produced the poem, and more importantly, he'd chosen a lonely, aging narrator to describe a numbing, isolated life, which so closely tracked her mother's own feelings and experiences.

Fragments, lines, and phrases from that extraordinary evening burned into Donna's mind and now flowed freely onto the scorched pages of her introductory essay:

> . . . this dull null
> Navy I wear to work, and wear from work, and so
> To my bed, so to my grave, with no
> Complaints, no comment. . . .
> Oh, bars of my own body, open, open!
>
> The world goes by my cage and never sees me.
> And there come not to me, as come to these,
> The wild beasts, sparrows pecking the llamas' grain. . . .
>
> You know what I was,
> You see what I am: change me, change me!

Remarkably, Donna had achieved what Melville had accomplished in "The Line." She had used objective description in her early paragraphs to launch a philosophical portrayal of quiet suffering and the human condition. But she'd done Melville one better. By revealing her mother's painful, unvarying existence and her own exploitable vulnerabilities, Donna had created an unrivaled power and immediacy rarely achieved in letters beyond the intense domain of the troubadours, whom William of Aquitaine allegedly brought north from Spain.

I applied a rare, but well-deserved "A" to Donna's first assignment and then added several lines of positive evaluation and encouragement. But I didn't acknowledge I saw the skull beneath the skin. I'd leave that observation for another essay on another day. I was really tired then. It had been a truly eventful twenty-four hours. And the following day when Catherine arrived, I had to be rested. "Who knows," I thought, "the sun may never set again."

I placed all the papers in the course folder, walked over to the Magnavox, rummaged through the large record bin, and unearthed a most appropriate vinyl for the occasion. I seated the diamond stylus carefully at the whirring edge of the flawless LP, eased into bed, turned out the reading lamp, and listened quietly and reverentially in the soothing darkness to the undeniable essence of courage in a surprisingly undaunted major key.

The thirty-one-year-old Schubert had written the Quintet only months before the disease and the cure finally conquered his unyielding determination to survive. He was a realist. He knew he was dying; but there were no signs here of despair, bitterness, or regret. Despite the unconventional cellos, I heard no autumn, farewell, or impending doom in the *Allegro*, *Scherzo*, or *Allegretto*. Perhaps you could have challenged me on the *Andante*. Very well then, but I didn't detect misery, gloom, and hopelessness. I sensed harmony and a pure serenity of soul. As the tranquil E major triumphed over the turbulent F minor, I drifted off to Mom, Dad, Donna, her mother, Catherine, and the serviceable woman at the Washington zoo.

They had all faced the cruel carbon randomness with a calm, reassuring dignity that no just god dare scorn. Mom knew the indomitable madness was stealing her genius. Father gave everything he had to help Mom and assure me that our family wouldn't fall apart. Donna sorely missed her father and desperately hoped one of the suitors would stay. Despite the loneliness and disappointments, Donna's mother admirably nurtured her child's empathy and expressive skills. Catherine sacrificed a lover, an education, and five years of her life for her younger siblings. And now she was taking the defiant risk of coming here and declaring from the papal balcony she had survived her errand into the wilderness and dared to aspire again. And Jarrell's unpublished, importunate supplicant continually thrust her arms into the indifferent air hoping for an immediate, redemptive change.

I slept soundly through the night until Mr. Feisty began his third open rehearsal this month just below my heavily curtained Main Street window. I lay there quietly until I constructed a promising agenda for the day: library, grocery, and then the Greyhound depot. I rolled out of bed and proceeded immediately to the inexhaustible record bin. Today required an extensive program of celebratory music: first the majestic Gabrieli *Canzoni* followed by the sublime Monteverdi *Vespers*. As the Gabrieli fanfare began, I moved over to the morning window, separated the heavy burgundy drapes, and gazed northward from my grand Venetian palace toward Saint Mark's with its five enormous, cross-crowned cupolas shading the gilded nave.

But now back to reality, back to McGill and the reading

I had to get done before Catherine arrived. I hadn't cracked a book yet for the Early American Literature course. So I made an executive decision to finish the primitive Bradstreet, Taylor, and Wigglesworth poetry before leaving for the library and resuming my ongoing battle with the didactic Mr. Richardson.

Again, there was method to my madness. I'd listen to the glorious Renaissance brass as I plowed through the fiery, sulphurous poems of their strange new world. Bradstreet would be okay. Taylor would be acceptable. But the Wigglesworth verses would be highly suspect, especially given the titles of the lengthy puritanical poems I had been strongly encouraged to review for our midterm exam: "God's Controversy with New England," "The Day of Doom; or, A Poetical Description of the Last Judgment," and the "Meat Out of the Eater; or, Meditations Concerning the Necessity, End, and Usefulness of Afflictions unto God's Children, All Tending to Prepare Them for and Comfort Them under the Cross."

After two painful hours of tedious explication, I was free to continue devouring the scintillating *Pamela* in the library reading room. Bradstreet, Taylor, and Wigglesworth had achieved the impossible. They had managed to turn Richardson's novel into a riveting page-turner. I just couldn't wait now to get to the library and find out what happened after Mrs. Jewkes discovered Pamela was missing from her double-locked and barred chambers. So I showered, dressed, and rushed off to campus to get as much reading done as possible before heading to the grocery and then to the Greyhound station. I'd warned Catherine earlier that given my penurious condition, we'd be eating most of our meals above the lush cityscape in my elegant but less expensive Rainbow Room loft.

On the way to campus, I commiserated with several of my grousing Early American Lit classmates; assured Professor McMasters I'd attend his Halloween soiree the following weekend; and accepted a generous offer from a fellow graduate student of two complimentary passes to the theater department's production of a recent Jean-Paul Sartre play the next evening at eight.

I was really proud of myself. I got into the narrative, especially as the rake, Mr. B., attempted seducing the virtuous Pamela to become his mistress. But unfortunately, I hit the wall again many pages later at Pamela's epistolary entry, "Saturday morning, the third of my happy nuptials." I now realized I'd passed what I thought would be the denouement, and I still had more than one hundred and fifty anticlimactic pages to read beyond the climactic wedding bells and the honeymoon night.

I suspected the moralizing Richardson would use the last third of the book to pound home two shopworn platitudes: reformed rakes make the best husbands and virtue is always rewarded. I looked at my watch and discovered I had only an hour and a half to run by the grocery, drop off the provisions at the apartment, and rush to the terminal so I'd be there when Catherine arrived. Discretion being the better part of valor, I regrettably silenced Richardson for the time being, stashed my book and papers in my briefcase, and headed out onto Main Street through the venerated Haldeman Arch.

To ensure I purchased the freshest meats and produce for our weekend meals, I decided to splurge and shop at the boutique market on Herman Street just off the square. Several colleagues had recommended the small, family-owned store, but warned me it was a bit pricey. They joked that the local definition of "being wealthy" was strolling through the market's narrow, packed aisles with one of three seldom-used shopping carts. And they weren't joking about the charges either. When the checkout clerk handed me the painful register receipt for payment, a whimsical thought flashed through my head: I certainly hoped my brimming cart had impressed my fellow shoppers as much as the total grocery bill had just shocked my assets and liabilities. But no time to dwell on the past; I had to get the two large bags of groceries to the apartment and then rush over to greet Catherine's bus four blocks north of the square.

I walked quickly back to the apartment, and with the perishables safely stowed, I double-timed it past the busy courthouse still straining under the pressures of a late Friday afternoon surge. When I finally made the turn onto Crittenden and crested a small hill, I was amazed to see an architectural masterpiece. The McGill Greyhound station was a streamline art moderne wonder with dark blue enamel facing, white trim, long horizontal lines across the front, and graceful curving forms at either end.

I entered the small waiting room, stood in a short line for no more than five minutes, and then asked the attendant for the status of Catherine's bus. The pleasant fellow proudly proclaimed it was running on time and should arrive in no more than fifteen minutes. I sat down on one of the long wooden benches, stared vacantly into the splashy, colorful display containing the latest Li'l Abner and Blondie comics, and then began focusing on a stimulating schedule for our weekend activities.

Feeling jumpy, I checked my watch several times during

my brief planning session. But just as I expected, no bus and no Catherine. When the attendant's bold prediction inevitably expired, I stoically moved outside to the right of the double doors, where pacing passengers and dispirited greeters had congregated, naïvely anticipating a rare on-time arrival. About twenty minutes after joining the madding crowd, I actually heard Catherine's bus before I saw it. It was the unmistakable, mellow roar of a straight-eight Buick engine accelerating and shifting into second gear after having stopped at the Forrest and Crittenden intersection a hundred yards or so up the road.

And then the vehicular masterwork appeared at the top of the small rise, gradually slowed, and finally rolled to a stop lengthwise between the Dr. Pepper machine and the local paper box. The long horizontal lines of the twenty-nine-passenger Clipper classic combined with its elegant curves running along the roofline and tapering at the rear strongly echoed the streamline art moderne architecture of the depot, which now served as the Clipper's elegant temporary home. In short, an aficionado could cleverly describe the Clipper classic's sleek design as Art Deco on wheels.

The moment had finally arrived. As the heavy blue door swung open, the enthusiastic tidal wave of greeters rushed uncontrollably toward the dark, narrow opening at the front of the bus. I positioned myself strategically at the rear of the pulsating throng between the besieged Greyhound and the nearest double doors into the station. The only downside to my positioning was I couldn't see who was descending the stairs until the crowd had tossed them about, closely evaluated them, and finally discarded them out the back of the scrum as a curious child rummaging through a toy box for a favorite doll or daring plastic soldier.

After several minutes of assessment, the castaways began appearing at the undulating edge of the beast. First a stocky, goateed fellow wearing horn-rimmed glasses, a charcoal fedora, rumpled maroon suit, and black string tie. Obviously a migratory professor returning to Capistrano. Next, a dazed elderly couple locked arm-in-arm returning home from a brief annual visit with their eldest daughter, whose uncompromising husband coolly tolerated their annoying presence in his restrictive lockdown domain. Next, a twenty-year veteran of an elite ranger unit who'd boarded a bus here in '38 and scaled the cliffs at Pointe du Hoc was now returning home, not to grateful flourishes but to an indifferent, frenzied, self-absorbed din.

And then Catherine was there, walking toward me, smiling broadly and stretching her arms out to the side signaling an affectionate embrace to celebrate the end of our beginning. I pulled her in close and held her tightly. We said nothing. We let the silence and our senses express the warmth pulsing through our souls. We were tacitly acknowledging a homecoming that was a long time coming. I stepped back, held her at arm's length, and gazed into her large brown eyes. Silence. She continued smiling. I spontaneously pulled her in again, slid my hand up under her long auburn curls, and whispered, "Welcome home." She pressed her body more firmly against mine and responded, "Believe me, I've wanted this for a very long time."

We stepped back, shyly glanced down for an instant, and then moved over to the side of the bus where the driver was busily retrieving luggage from the cargo bay and lining the colorful suitcases up along the curb. Catherine checked the tags on several pieces of the latest Samsonite before finding her own small suitcase at the far end of the row. I motioned for her to hand me the overnighter, and we began strolling up Crittenden toward Forrest. I was really hoping we'd see someone I knew. She looked so beautiful that day in her flowing turquoise dress and navy blue beret sweeping down across the right side of her perfectly shaped forehead. The poet Herrick would surely have forsaken Julia's glittering vibrations to have gone a-Maying with my dazzling Catherine that day.

Since we didn't meet anyone on the way back to the apartment, I spent most of the time describing various historical, geographical, and mythical points of interest with occasional splashes of humor and significant dashes of local color. As we climbed the stairs toward the Rainbow Room, we ran into Anna, who was just completing her latest mail delivery. She gave us both the once-over and then proceeded with compulsive twice- and thrice-overs of the small suitcase and my attractive female companion. I knew she was calculating—two plus two equals five. But I remained silent and proudly projected a knowing, enigmatic smile worthy of the lady in the Louvre.

After stowing Catherine's luggage and presiding over a brief tour of the scholar's garret, I said, "How about a visit to Hudson's downstairs to celebrate your arrival with a worthy choice of sundae, shake, or three-scoop float?"

Catherine rushed the door and teased, "Sounds great to me. I'm starving."

We raced down the steps, slid into one of the wooden booths with tall, straight backs, and reached for the foot-high menus standing in the metal racks attached to the small personal jukeboxes touting the latest and greatest hits.

"What'll it be?" I asked.

"I'll have the 'treat of the day,' the hot fudge, double-scoop 'Friday sundae.' What are you having?"

"One of their seven-out-of-ten cherry shakes," I said. "Even if they don't come close to those monsters the Millers whip up in Louisville."

When our orders arrived, a magical hour of shared desserts and warm recollections began. With each successive caring spoonful exchanged, I became increasingly convinced our shared motive was inexorably evolving from one of honest gustatory curiosity to a subtle, subterranean desire to share so much more, which had been missing from both of our lives for so many years.

As we walked out onto the street, I proposed a trip around Professor McMasters's lucrative square. Since it was Friday and getting late in the day, most of the establishments had already closed, and we were reduced to admiring the creative displays in the family-owned storefronts. But fortunately, I deviated from the plan and recommended walking up toward campus to see if any of the shops along the main drag were still open for business.

We were in luck. The front door to the Off Again, On Again, Gone Again antique shop was still open. The store would normally have been closed by now, but the proprietor, Mr. Finnegan, was busy preparing boxes of glassware, jewelry, and old hand tools for an auction he was holding on the premises Saturday afternoon. We asked permission to look around. He told us to take our time because he wasn't going anywhere for at least another hour or two.

It didn't take very long to conclude Mr. Finnegan missed his real calling as a librarian. He'd arranged the shop's contents into orderly categories, subcategories, and sub-subcategories. And as Catherine and I passed the category: music, sub-category: players, and sub-subcategory: high-fidelity consoles, I was obliged to explain the providential provenance of my magnificent Magnavox.

Twenty minutes into our browsing, we drifted off into our own interests—Catherine into handcrafted jewelry, games, and first editions and I into classical LPs, old coins, and currency. After surveying the money and flipping through the eclectic record collection of a local actor who'd recently moved to Hollywood, I began moving from room to room searching for Catherine. I finally found her on the top floor in a small room at the back of the segmented building—category: amusements, sub-category: games, sub-subcategory: board games. She was sitting at a table inspecting the unique pieces of a handmade chess set. I walked over and sat down opposite her at an elegant mahogany and maple antique board with a warm, midbrown border and cream and dark brown squares. The pieces were stunning and appeared to be historically accurate. The pawns, knights, kings, and queens had all been hand painted, dry brushed, and washed to a glowing acrylic finish.

But who were these medieval forces facing off across this exquisite two-by-two wooden plain? The one set of warriors appeared to be European and the other Muslim. The European pawns and knights wore bright rounded silver helmets and dark gray armor with intricate, interlocking mail. They carried bronze-tipped spears and large white triangular shields with painted red crosses coursing from top to bottom and side to side. While the rooks were the typical medieval turrets common to many standard sets, the bishops were outfitted in gray cassocks, red tunics, and brilliant white ceremonial caps. The king was dressed in blood-red armor, carried a matching red rectangular shield, and waved an enormous black-and-silver sword above his imperial head. The majestic queen stood firmly at her husband's side wearing her imposing crown and a long white robe with gold buttons and crimson belt.

At the opposite end of the battlefield, the Egyptian pawns and Syrian knights wore tapered silver helmets, dark green armor, and thick white sashes streaming down across their chests and wrapping firmly about their waists. They carried long, black-tipped spears and large oval shields with alternating panels of bright green and polished silver. In contrast to the European pieces, the Muslim rooks were of a unique design—dark blue onion domes with bright gold tips and swirling fields of glittering stars. The bearded Muslim holy men wore bright-red-and-charcoal robes, braided silver belts, and luminous white traditional headdresses. The sultan wore crimson armor, carried a gray circular shield, and thrust his silver scimitar into the air to rally his mighty forces. His noble wife stood nearby, elegantly dressed in a long black robe and a sheer black veil concealing a confident, approving smile.

"Historical figures from the Middle Ages?" I asked.

Catherine smiled and nodded. "You see that European knight there? The colors on the horse are those of the villainous Reginald of Châtillon, Lord of el Kerak, which leads me to believe the other European knight here must be the chivalrous 'white knight,' James d'Avesnes."

I shrugged my shoulders. "Can't help you with that one."

Catherine then gained real momentum, pointing to one piece after another. "This Muslim knight must be the brave, towering el-Tawil and the other over there the dreaded leader of the Assassins, Rashid al-Din Sinan." And the names continued rolling easily off her tongue: Guy of Lusignan, Sibylla, El Melek el-Adel, Philip II Augustus, Gerard de Ridefort, Conrad of Montferrat, and Karakush. I was impressed.

"You think the board represents any particular battle or a specific period of time?" I asked.

Catherine smiled again and replied, "If I were betting, I'd say it represents the Siege of Acre on the Mediterranean between Damascus and Jerusalem."

Trying to recover from the shock of her detailed knowledge of the crusades, I countered with an arcane observation. "Did you know Acre was the first major confrontation of the Third Crusade, and the siege lasted almost two years, from August 1189 until July 1191?" I paused and then continued raising my level of play. I pointed to the European king and said confidently, "This must be Richard the Lionheart." I then turned to the sultan figure and continued, "And that should be Saladin." And after exhausting my knowledge of the pivotal conflict, I concluded, "That's a helluva grip you have on medieval history, Catherine. You do a lot of reading on your own?"

She flashed a broad smile, which immediately escalated into a cunning laugh. She hesitated for a moment, picked up one of the European knights, pointed the base in my direction, and revealed the historical identity clearly etched on the bottom of the piece. I playfully wagged my finger and began laughing at the innocent ruse she'd perpetrated at my expense. "I want you to know I won't soon forget this," I teased. And as we pushed back from the small table, I added sincerely, "And I won't forget this set here either. It's one of the finest I've ever seen."

Catherine nodded.

I asked, "Is there anything else you want to check out while we're here?"

She shook her head. "Believe it or not I think I've seen everything in here at least twice. I'm ready to go when you are."

"Fine with me," I replied. "Let's head back up to Rainbow Row and prepare a feast fit for King Richard and the mighty Saladin!"

It was a pleasant if quiet walk back through the cool evening. When we reached the apartment, I said, "Why don't you take a seat at the 'blue moon' while I get things ready?"

"The blue moon?" she asked.

I laughed. "Yeah, my dinette table in there. It's round and has a blue laminate top, so—voilà!—'the blue moon.' You can take a seat and keep me company while I pull dinner together."

"Sorry, Andrew, that's not me. I feel guilty if I'm not pitching in."

I respectfully relented and dashed over to the kitchen cupboard to fetch the Holy Grail, Gutenberg, and Septuagint rolled into one—my great-grandmother's personal cookbook from the 1870s, *Housekeeping in the Blue Grass: A New and Practical Cook Book; Containing Nearly a Thousand Recipes*, which had been edited by the "distaff congregants" of the Presbyterian Church of Bourbon County.

I then walked over to the kitchen table and proudly displayed the cherished family heirloom—a two-hundred-page volume with dark green cover, gold lettering, and gilded blades of bent bluegrass. "It's seen better days. The cloth corners are worn. You can see the board showing through from underneath. The spine ends here are missing about a quarter inch of cover. The gilded edges have darkened some, and the text has dimmed a bit." I paused and continued defensively, "But none of this wear and tear is because of neglect or abuse. It's a sign of love and respect, a sign of generations returning time and again to the age-old southern recipes in here."

As I lay the prized book down in front of Catherine, a number of handwritten memories fell out onto the table— Mom's "Hundred Dollar Cake," Grandma's "Chess Pie Delight," and Great-grandma's "Almond Rum Torte with Whipped Cream Icing." After reminiscing for several minutes about the good times associated with the recipes, I suggested an initial division of labor. "How about you bookmarking the pages we'll be using tonight while I rustle us up a couple of genuine mint juleps to celebrate our bluegrass reunion beyond the borders of the Commonwealth."

"So what's on the menu tonight, Chef?"

"Well, I thought we'd do it up right: a main course of country captain chicken with baked stuffed squash and an okra, corn, and tomato mélange."

"Sounds delicious. You have a dessert in mind?"

"Yeah, a quickie but very tasty. Oranges au caramel."

"Despite the sundae, all this talk's making me hungry. Let's get started."

"Mint juleps coming up!"

After dinner we moved from the kitchen into the "uni-room." Catherine sat down at one end of the sofa while I walked over to the Magnavox and surveyed the possibilities. I don't know why I chose to play the *Requiem*; these were some of the happiest hours I'd experienced in a long time. Perhaps it was just as simple as acknowledging the beauty and power of the piece. I next walked over to the Art Deco bookcase, where I kept an unopened bottle of Carvalhas Vintage '48, which I'd received as a graduation gift from a close college friend who'd grown up in rustic Iberia. When Manuel handed me the generous present after the graduation ceremony, I humorously but seriously swore to him I'd only sample the highly praised port on an occasion worthy of such a fine vintage.

So there was never any question in my mind about opening the valued bottle that night. Our auspicious reunion had clearly met the lofty standard I'd set when accepting Manuel's gift. I uncorked the magical wine and successfully filled two small Paris goblets without disturbing an unwanted decade of bitter sediment. We raised our glasses, acknowledged each other silently with warm smiles, and then experienced the rich coffee and caramel flavors, almost syrup-like in their Foz do Douro intensities.

I don't know whether it was the wine, the music, or the parallel progression of our mothers' lives, but we spent the rest of the evening with Leonardo roaming the landscape for answers to things we didn't clearly understand. It all began innocently enough with a polite inquiry. "Any change in your mother since we last talked?"

"No, no real changes even though she's getting the best

of care in the long-term facility. . . . By the way, how are your parents doing?"

I thought it was time to let her know about Mom. "My dad's doing just fine. He's teaching in Urbana. Wish I could say the same for Mom, though. We had to commit her to Our Lady of Hope. She broke down and never recovered. Things just kept getting worse and worse over the next ten years."

Catherine shook her head. "It's unbelievable."

"What's that?"

"We've been running along parallel tracks all this time, both of us having to adjust our lives to our mothers' worsening conditions." Catherine paused and then pointed to the Magnavox. "You couldn't have picked a more appropriate piece than the *Requiem* there."

I nodded. "I can't imagine the loss Brahms felt when his mother died unexpectedly of a stroke. I mean, to be moved so much to write such a masterwork for her. . . ."

"You see this as a conventional requiem?" she probed gently.

"Yeah. I believe it's patterned after the Latin mass for the dead. You have the somber B-flat minor second movement and the text admonishing us, 'For all flesh is as grass.'"

Catherine took a sip of her port and rubbed her finger around the rim of her glass. "May I suggest an alternative interpretation?"

I shrugged. "By all means. No pride of authorship here."

"Well, I think there are elements missing you'd expect to find in a conventional requiem."

"For example?"

"There's no prayer for the souls of the dead, no last

judgment, no separating of the sheep from the goats, and no wailing and gnashing of teeth. No, on the contrary, I see the *Requiem* as an act of consolation for the living. An assertion that all would be well again. You see, for me, it's not about the dead but the living."

"I don't see it. How do you get there?"

"His choice of text for the opening movement, 'Blessed are they that mourn; for they shall be comforted.' Brahms is urging us to take courage, to never lose hope despite the losses, despite the sorrow. I'll give you that the overall tone of the music is somber, but all seven movements end with an affirmation of rising optimism."

The wine continued flowing, and our discussion broadened widely to *Lear*, then "Bartleby," and finally to Crane's elegiac "Chaplinesque." We agreed that Shakespeare had it right:

> As flies to wanton boys, are we to the gods.
> They kill us for their sport.

That Melville hinted at a path to salvation:

> What shall I do? What ought I to do? What
> does conscience say I should do with this man,
> or rather ghost? Rid myself of him, I must; go,
> he shall. But how? You will not thrust him, the
> poor, pale, passive mortal—you will not thrust
> such a helpless creature out of your door? You
> will not dishonor yourself by such cruelty? No,
> I will not, I cannot do that. Rather would I let

him live and die here, and then mason up his remains in the wall.

But it was Crane who clearly recognized that in the midst of our suffering all we really had was each other:

> For we can still love the world, who find
> A famished kitten on the step, and know
> Recesses for it from the fury of the street. . . .
>
> We will sidestep, and to the final smirk
> Dally the doom of that inevitable thumb
> That slowly chafes its puckered index toward us. . . .
>
> The game enforces smirks; but we have seen
> The moon in lonely alleys make
> A grail of laughter of an empty ash can,
> And through all sound of gaiety and quest
> Have heard a kitten in the wilderness.

The port and the lateness of the hour ultimately took their toll. I suggested we'd better get some rest because we had another long day ahead of us. I pulled the sofa bed out for Catherine and retrieved my rolled pad and several thick blankets from the closet. I lay my gear on the floor near the bookcase a gentlemanly distance from Catherine's bed. When she returned after changing into her nightgown and rose chenille bathrobe, she firmly embraced me and thanked me for the great day.

I walked over to the luminescent switch and waited until

Catherine had climbed over the substantial ridge and rolled down into the valley before I finally doused the lights. And after reluctantly deciding my customary commando sleepwear would be highly inappropriate for the current occasion, I blindly crawled onto my firm pallet in full battle array—sweatshirt, jeans, and woolen socks.

It became very quiet. And as I lay on my back in the calming darkness, I first detected my heartbeat and then became aware of Catherine's soft, regular breathing as she fell into a deeper sleep. I then recalled a Klosé duet I loved performing with my instructor so many years ago. The short French work was discordant from the first measure onward with the woodwinds adopting divergent rhythms and then blazing separate melodic paths up and down the scale. There were strong hints of improvisational jazz throughout the piece a la Debussy.

But totally cacophonous? Almost, but not quite. And it was that aspect of the work that I found so appealing. In the last three measures, Klosé meshed everything. The irregular rhythms became synchronous and the disparate melodies richly harmonious. Discord became concord as the earlier tensions resolved. I could clearly see the similarities. Our lives mystically echoed that favorite childhood duet, and we were now joyfully playing the last three hopeful measures. We were at the end of our exploring. We'd arrived where we'd begun and eased comfortably into our beginning for the first time.

8

Bxc7 O-O   Bd6 Qf7

FROM OUR POSITION at the center of the steaming cauldron, we couldn't discern the autumnal rim or hear the sprites and spirits sing. Catherine had been a good sport and had risen well before dawn to hike the serpentine mile through Birnam Wood for a spectacular sunrise on Hecate Lake. We'd untied one of the university boats, paddled far from shore, and pointed our birch bark canoe slightly to the southeast for an unobstructed view. A thick, smoky mist of long-stemmed shiitake gently swayed above the rippled surface of backlit clouds and the first roseate light of day. We'd become ancient warriors seeking signs from holy fire. The sky-goddess appeared, slowly ascended above the jagged peaks, and cast her golden ciphers across our handmade bow. Her message was both concise and clear. We should now drive De Soto into the sea.

As the sun rose higher above the copper hardwoods, the brilliant linear reflection slowly receded across the lake and finally collapsed into a giant solar sphere of brilliant white. We then pivoted to the north, slowly rowed back toward the beach, and stowed our canoe in a small boathouse near the tree line. We began walking counterclockwise around the lake and discovered the old amphitheater for the Pantheon Shakespeare Festival held outdoors annually beginning sometime in the early

1930s. If anyone ever initiated a serious contest to identify the seven wonders of the modern world, this Tennessee thespian masterpiece would surely appear in the top tier of man-made candidates. The university architects based their design on the great masterwork of Polykleitos the Younger, the theater at Epidaurus dating to the fourth century BC.

The WPA workers sculpted the seventeen semicircular rows of seats out of the gradually sloping limestone hillside, which wrapped around a large portion of the circular orchestra paved with pink Tennessee marble. Because they had fortuitously chosen to use the existing limestone for the seats during construction, the builders miraculously replicated the heretofore-unmatched sonic quality of the Epidaurian wonder. Attendees swore you could hear the unamplified actors and musicians clearly from even the back row of the architectural tour de force.

While several Greek plays were offered over the years, *Agamemnon*, *Oedipus*, and *The Clouds*, the primary emphasis was on Shakespeare's comedies. Yet, the inaugural production and the final play twenty years later were performances of Shakespeare's major tragedy, *Macbeth*, which provided modern place names for several nearby geographical features, including Birnam Wood, Hecate Lake, and the large community garden, Banquo's Feast.

The good news: in 1950 the wealthy alumnus and Broadway producer Byron Franklin had generously donated one million dollars to the university for the sole purpose of constructing a state-of-the-art theater facility in Dawes Hall. The bad news: Mr. Franklin loved the Pantheon summer theater but hated the electrical storms and the giant mosquitoes, which often plagued the outdoor performances. His strict donor instruction was simply to abandon the bedeviled Hecate Lake site for the increased comfort of a safe indoor venue. Sad to say, the choice was easy for the school administrators—mandated generosity cruelly trumped the outdoor magic of Ariel, Puck, and Oberon. So the unwitting, well-intentioned university abandoned the wondrous site in 1951.

We slowly walked about assessing the theater's current state. While the stone orchestra and theatron had suffered little lasting damage, the wooden skene and parodoi had begun to rot from the alternating extremes of the high summer humidity and the winter's lingering snows. A number of boards had either splintered or completely disappeared from the long passageways that the chorus and some messengers had used for their exits and entrances.

The skene was in especially poor condition, not only because of the weather, but also because of the secretive Dionysian initiations that occurred in the frame structure most weekends of the year. To combat the destruction and the debauchery, the administration first posted warnings, which mostly went unheeded. So the university leaders ultimately resorted to the much more effective but inelegant solution of permanently boarding up the only entrance from the stage.

Catherine raced up the limestone stairs to the last row of the semicircle and sat down on one of the large irregular slabs. I moved into the orchestral ring several feet in front of the weathered skene, looked up toward Catherine, and recited lines from an earlier undergraduate production:

Lovers and madmen have such seething brains,
Such shaping fantasies, that apprehend
More than cool reason ever comprehends.
The lunatic, the lover and the poet
Are of imagination all compact:
One sees more devils than vast hell can hold,
That is, the madman: the lover, all as frantic,
Sees Helen's beauty in a brow of Egypt:
The poet's eye, in fine frenzy rolling,
Doth glance from heaven to earth, from earth to heaven;
And as imagination bodies forth
The forms of things unknown, the poet's pen
Turns them to shapes and gives to airy nothing
A local habitation and a name.

I lowered my head and then responded to Catherine's obligatory bravos with an exaggerated salute that would sweep the stars from the blue threshold. She laughed, ran down the wide steps, and briefly rewarded my unrehearsed cameo with a warm, playful embrace. We moved to the center of the sunlit circle and surveyed the majestic theatron a final time, glorying in its storied past while respectfully mourning what might have been.

Catherine and I left the amphitheater, continued our winding circumnavigation of the glinting lake, and came to the harrowing passage across Gorgon Ravine. The roiling hell-broth flowing from a prehistoric hole in the side of the cauldron had over time become the rushing headwaters of Acheron Creek, which had carved a gorge creating the breathtaking Hurlyburly Falls.

The long, narrow, swinging footbridge spanning the

dramatic abyss was undeniably both the creepiest and most scenic walkway this side of the Mississippi. Its handmade construction out of used cable, conventional wire fence, and old barrel staves added to the sense of adventure and eeriness. So after reading the primitively painted sign at the head of the unnerving arc, "Fair is foul, and foul is fair: Hover through the fog and filthy air," we gripped the thin handrails and moved out onto the swaying span, distractedly spending most of our time looking out over the stunning rainbow vista rather than down through the substantial spaces between the warped whiskey staves.

As we neared the far side of the ravine, we nervously began picking up the pace, which added exponentially to the swaying, which in turn stoked even higher levels of anxiety. When we finally reached the rocky ledges of terra firma, Catherine and I spontaneously shouted, embraced, and triumphantly thrust our arms in the air. We took one final look back at the narrow, rocking bridge and then proudly resumed our emotional, counterclockwise journey. First, we'd felt the sadness associated with the abandoned theatrical jewel, and then, the intense fear related to the swinging bridge; but now we were about to experience the joyous inspiration of Marvell's Garden.

This respected, decades-long exhibition had invited leading sculptors worldwide to submit "provocative works" for an "artistic, chiaroscuro integration into the compelling labyrinth of forests, caves, and cliffs surrounding mysterious Hecate Lake." Despite its remote setting, the show was always well attended with most patrons undoubtedly approaching the wilderness venue from the more conservative clockwise direction.

Catherine and I picked up a detailed guide and actually

entered the exposition through the first work of the competition, "Forest within the Basilica," consisting of four steel flying buttresses joining at the midline above the wooded path, metaphorically supporting the weight of the forest canopy and perhaps the sky and providing an inspired man-made gateway into nature's holy sanctuary. We moved on to the next discovery, "Forsaking a Life for the Soul," which featured two inverted, elongated, hammered-copper pyramids wedged into the accommodating fissure of a lichen-covered ledge.

The early German Romantic poet and philosopher, Novalis, inspired the next sculpture, "More Closely Connected." Here, a large black metal question mark appeared to be climbing out over the serrated rim of a decaying stump. We also heard quiet moans emanating from its former trunk moldering among the mosses and the fiddleheads. As we neared the enigmatic work, we could clearly read the lengthy inscription etched into the flattened, curved back: "Everything visible connects itself with the invisible, the audible with the inaudible, the sensitive with the insensitive, and probably the thinkable with the unthinkable."

After exploring twenty-one additional presentations, encompassing the stimulating, the confrontational, and the incendiary, we approached the final installment, "Forlorn Tenderness, Relentless Longing," a six-foot-high gray metal casing with three long, narrow apertures resting gently against a tall elm and partially wrapping itself about the tree at the top edge of the rounded steel. As we stood there transfixed before this poignant work, we leaned into each other, quietly accepting our beleaguered pasts and acknowledging the growing confluence of our hopeful lives.

On the way back to campus, I realized it was time to broach a sensitive subject—the activity I'd planned for one o'clock that day. Attending a college football game on a clear, crisp, blue-gray October afternoon would be a no-brainer for a high percentage of university undergraduates, but the storied gridiron was at the nexus of our pasts and our future. Anderson, the star guard, had been my closest friend and Catherine's high school flame. I slowed, turned to her, and said, "I've gotta run something by you."

"What's that?" she asked.

"Ah, the next major stop on the agenda."

"Why's that?"

"I don't want to hurt your feelings."

She looked at me quizzically and probed, "Hurt my feelings? How?"

"Dredging up memories of the past. Of what might have been."

She shrugged. "Dredging up memories? Doing what?"

"Going to the Pantheon football game this afternoon. You know . . . Ray having played football and everything."

She gazed into my eyes and said, "That's sweet, Andrew, your thinking of me like that. But no worries. The present far outweighs the past. And remember, you said as much yourself at the reunion. You told me it was time to begin thinking about myself and to get on with my life. So let's get on with my life and get out to the stadium!"

I breathed a sigh of relief, grabbed her arm playfully, and said, "Whoa! Not so fast! Let's first make a quick stop at the Rainbow Room for a little bite to eat before heading out with the crowd. Sound like a plan?"

She smiled, tapped me on the shoulder, and replied, "Since you say it's about snacking, it sounds great to me!"

We hurried back to the apartment, had some sharp cheddar on rye, and then quickly joined the boisterous masses walking the six blocks south to Panther Field. As we approached the horseshoe-shaped stadium (of course, the north end was open to accommodate the strong, bitter winds of the frigid, late-season games), the colorful conference pennants were whipping in the upper winds and the band was enthusiastically playing the Panther fight song. How could I help myself? As the adrenaline surged through my arms and across my chest, I began mumbling along, "Pounce, Panthers, pounce."

We were lucky to have gotten some of the last unreserved seats near the top of the stadium. I'd forgotten it was homecoming weekend; the place was packed. We climbed to our perch and slowly scanned the historic venue, where in their prime, the Panthers held the Illini's Galloping Ghost to minus yards rushing and two weeks later played Rockne's Horsemen to a virtual tie, losing in the last minute of play.

But the Panthers had fallen on hard times and throughout the fifties had suffered one humiliating defeat after another. The outcome of this season appeared to be tracking with all the rest. So far this year, Pantheon had barely beaten the lowly Falcons and had lost their other five games. And what were the prospects for this afternoon? I envisioned David and Goliath, Thermopylae, and the siege of Bastogne combined. The Panthers were up against their conference rivals, the Screaming Eagles, who had just climbed to number three in the country in the national polls.

The slim hope we had that afternoon was based primarily

on our enthusiastic, humorous second-year head coach, who'd astonishingly recruited several competitive defensive players, introduced an innovative, wide-open style of play, and had gotten his players to buy into the new program. The other source of optimism was derived from the intriguing statistic that the Panthers had lost the five games by a total of only twenty points. But as they used to say in vaudeville, "That ain't buying the baby a new dress"; or putting it even more succinctly, "Close, but no cigar."

It was an inauspicious beginning. We lost the coin toss, and the Eagles elected to receive. We kicked off, and their halfbacks chewed up massive chunks of yardage, first blasting off tackle and then slicing student body right. Their purple bruisers were driving our defensive players back off the line of scrimmage by at least five yards on every play. But at every sporting event, there's one defining moment that sets the tone for the rest of the game; and that action surprisingly came very early in the first quarter.

The Eagles had marched across midfield. Their quarterback called a "39 left," sending their halfback wide on a pitchout around left end. Our cornerback did his job, making an aggressive move up toward the line of scrimmage to turn the play inside. The Eagles pulling guard, who was supposed to level the defensive cornerback, missed the block, allowing our man to cream their halfback and drive him into the Panthers' bench. Believing our player was guilty of a late hit, several Eagles players took offense and started swinging at anyone standing along our sideline. As the scuffle intensified, the entire Eagles team erupted, charged across the field toward our players, and the momentous battle of Hattin was on.

Coaches, trainers, and the walking wounded all joined in the melee. Arms were flailing, jerseys ripping, and helmets flying through the air. Security personnel intent on stopping the brawl were quickly swallowed by the churning mass of young, muscular gladiators. As the fight continued I looked over at Catherine, who was on her feet. I didn't know how she would feel about such jock brutality, but when she caught me looking at her, she flashed a big grin to let me know she was thoroughly enjoying herself.

The crowd was going nuts, and their frenzied roar reached a crescendo when one of the injured Panthers broke his crutch over an opponent's head. And it was only after some ten minutes of the finest mayhem that the engulfed police somehow began to quell the uprising from within the belly of the beast. Cooler heads prevailed, and a semblance of order was finally restored.

As the combatants returned to the field, I wondered how David would respond to Goliath's aggression. During the next series of downs, it appeared the Eagles had begun again where they'd left off, racking up huge gains on every play. The nose of the ball was now on the Pantheon ten-yard line. It was first and goal. With plenty of pass protection, the Eagles quarterback rolled out to his right, then fired a perfect strike into the end zone, hitting his tight end squarely on the pads. But the second-team all-American must have taken his eye off the ball: the football bounced into the air, careened off the helmet of the Eagles' secondary receiver, and landed in our safety's hands. Interception! Touchback! Our ball on the twenty! The band struck up the Panthers fight song. The crowd exploded, and the old stadium began to rock.

And now for some bad news: our offense sputtered and

did a three and out as Catherine and I chewed our nails to the quick. But there was some good news. Our above-average punter launched a high end-over-end kick headed for the sideline, which the Eagles receiver elected not to handle. The ball took a strange bounce and rolled to a stop on the Eagles' thirty-three. After a dropped pass on first down and a seven-yard gain on second, the first quarter ended with the unexpected score of Eagles 0, Panthers 0.

As our old high school coach observed, good teams play consistently throughout the game, but great teams can raise their level of play to a higher gear when needed. Between the quarters, the Eagles coach screamed, grabbed facemasks, and pounded shoulder pads. "Look out, here comes the tidal wave," I thought. Their head coach was still gesticulating wildly as his players returned to the field. And sure enough, their fullback took the handoff and rumbled up the middle for twenty yards. The onslaught continued until our defense miraculously stiffened, and the Eagles had to settle for a disappointing seventeen-yard field goal. Eagles 3, Panthers 0.

The Eagles kicked off, and our return man caught the ball cleanly and eased in behind our flying wedge. When their defensive players smashed into our blockers, our small return man disappeared into the purple vortex. But several seconds later the cheering swelled to a roar. What a beautiful sight! Our return man had bounced free from the flying bodies, had gotten behind the Eagles' last defender, and was streaking toward pay dirt! Any flags? No. Touchdown! As the band fired up the fight song, Catherine and I began screaming at the top of our lungs, jumping up and down and hugging everyone within a five-yard radius. The extra point was good, and the scoreboard told an astonishing tale. Panthers 7, Eagles 3.

I knew all hell was about to break loose. We kicked off, and just as I had expected, the Eagles drove down the field in six long-yardage plays to our twenty, where we again stopped their momentum. It was fourth and three. The Eagles took a timeout, and their coach opted for the three points rather than risk going for it on fourth down. The kick was good, and the score was still an amazing Panthers 7, Eagles 6. We received the following kickoff, ran for one first down, and ran out the clock in the first half.

Catherine and I celebrated halftime excitedly comparing notes with our bench mates; unconsciously inhaling several hot dogs and a soda; briefly observing our top-notch "Marching Fifty"; and then beginning to dread what was inevitably about to happen in the second half. The teams returned to the field, and we received the kickoff. The Eagles were baited for bear. After forcing our halfback to fumble, they immediately drove into our red zone. But again through luck and determination, our defense stopped them. And on fourth down, the Eagles attempted a field goal at the open north end of the stadium. The wind had begun swirling in the late-afternoon shadows and pushed the kick wide right.

The first twelve minutes of the last quarter were fought in the trenches with the ball never penetrating the opponent's thirty-yard line. But then it happened. With less than three minutes to play, the Eagles' right halfback took a shuttle pass, slipped out to the sideline, and scored the go-ahead touchdown. The extra point was good, and the score with a little less than two minutes to play was now a more rational Eagles 13, Panthers 7. In a matter of seconds, the Eagles' late score had sucked all the oxygen out of the stadium, causing rabid Panthers fans to docilely and dejectedly collapse into their seats. But I watched our players as they broke the huddle to prepare to receive the final kickoff. Two good signs: the players had their heads up and they were actually running out to their positions on the field.

As expected, the Eagles' kickoff specialist didn't use a tee; he placed the ball directly on the ground and squibbed it past our up-men. Our returner fielded the ball at the twenty and was driven out of bounds at our own thirty-four. Two dropped passes later, we were still on our thirty-four with a minute five to play. We needed ten yards to get a new set of downs. Every player and fan in the stadium knew we had to throw down field.

As the Panthers broke the huddle, we all spontaneously rose to our feet, got back in the game, and screamed with what was left of our raspy voices. Our quarterback dropped back to pass but then surprisingly handed the ball off to our left halfback on a delay. And from our seats high in the rafters, we could watch the overall play unfolding. It was almost in slow motion. The running back hit the hole between the left guard and center; their falling middle linebacker raised a desperate arm to grab a vaulting ankle; and our halfback broke beyond the initial clash of brawling linemen, splitting the seam between the two deep defensive backs. And as the final seconds ticked off the clock, the race was on for the end zone.

Over the years college football has provided many memorable games: Carlisle stunning Army in 1912; tiny Centre College shocking Harvard in 1921; and Carnegie Tech blanking Notre

Dame in 1926. While everyone loves a winner, many of us admittedly cheer for underdogs and are occasionally rewarded with either mild surprises or genuine upsets. And only on extremely rare occasions do we experience upsets that exceed the "mild" or the "genuine" and rise to the level of the truly "legendary."

But in the fading sunlight and long shadows of that late-October afternoon, the 1959 Panthers joined Carlisle, Centre, and Carnegie Tech at the pinnacle of gridiron magic. The astonishing final score from the coliseum was Panthers 14, and the mighty third-ranked Eagles 13. As we filed out of the raucous old stadium that unforgettable Homecoming Day, a young local sportswriter was unknowingly typing his own legacy as he crafted a now legendary headline for his thrilling report on a college game for the ages: "God Is Alive! He Played Left End for the Panthers During the Last Minute of Play."

Despite the bulky woolen sweaters and the intense excitement, Catherine and I had both begun shivering in the cool shade on the western side of the stadium. I immediately suggested warming up in the celebratory atmosphere of the Two-Way Café. When we arrived at the iconic eatery, Catherine and I crammed into an accommodating, overflowing booth of graduate students strategically positioned only five feet from the waitresses' station.

We boldly ordered "the works": "crater-size" bowls of "volcanic" five-way chili with spaghetti, chopped onion, dark kidney beans, crisp oyster crackers, and sharp shredded cheddar. But halfway through our first frosted draft, I checked my watch and broke the news we couldn't stay much longer at the party. We had one final activity remaining on the day's demanding agenda—attending the theater department's production of Sartre's existential play, *No Exit.* Being the trooper she had always been, Catherine laughed, raised her draft, and said, "On to the theater! The play's the thing!"

So after quaffing our beers, we rushed back to the apartment for a quick shower and a change into respectable theater attire. We then hurried over to Dawes Hall for the seven o'clock performance. When the lights dimmed and the actors' voices first rang out from the back of the hall, I was convinced we were in for a stimulating evening of cutting-edge theater. As Garcin and his valet-guide descended the stairs toward the Second Empire drawing room, Catherine and I immediately pivoted toward the aisle and began assessing their enigmatic, *in medias res* dialogue:

> GARCIN [*enters, accompanied by the* VALET *and glances around*]: Hmm! So this is it?
>
> VALET: Yes, Mr. Garcin.
>
> GARCIN: And this is what it looks like?
>
> VALET: Yes.
>
> GARCIN: Second Empire furniture, I observe. Well, well. I dare say one gets used to it in time.
>
> VALET: Some do. Some don't.
>
> GARCIN: Are all the other rooms like this one? I certainly didn't expect this! You know what they tell us down there?
>
> VALET: Really, sir, how could you believe such cock-and-bull stories? Told by people who'd never set foot here.

We remained completely engaged throughout the provocative play and participated in a standing ovation for the exceptional production. As we filed out of the Franklin Theatre, several graduate classmates invited us to join them at the Two-Way to discuss Sartre's work and continue the gridiron victory celebration. But Catherine and I opted to return to the apartment for a few quiet hours alone before her departure late the following morning.

When I opened the door to the Rainbow Room, I spotted a folded paper on the carpet. "What's this? It's . . . it's a note from the landlord, Professor McMasters. Oh, damn! He's asking a favor. Wants me to drop by tomorrow morning to help him rearrange his apartment. He's trying to buy more space for his annual Halloween soiree. He's got a relatively small space, and I hear he invites a cast of thousands. . . ." I looked apologetically at Catherine. "I'm afraid I can't refuse. But we'll make it work. How about I wake you up just before I head over to his apartment and then meet you downstairs at eleven tomorrow morning? That'll give us enough time for a leisurely walk over to the Greyhound terminal. What do you say?"

"No problem, Andrew. Believe me I understand. I'll be packed and ready to roll."

"Oh, thank you! You're a good egg, kiddo." I grinned and squeezed her arm.

I moved over to the Magnavox, scanned the collection for an appropriate work to discuss Sartre, and placed the revolutionary *Große Fuge* on the turnstile. Could there be any better piece echoing Sartre than the highly introspective, mysterious, dissonant Fugue composed when the maestro was totally deaf?

I poured us a glass of vintage port and sat down on the sofa bed opposite Catherine.

She savored a sip of the thick ruby wine and declared, "It's genius!"

"Genius?"

"Yeah, condemning the three of them to the hell of an eternal love triangle that mirrored the three-way relationships they'd fashioned here on earth."

I smiled and nodded my agreement, allowing her to drive the conversation.

Catherine took another long, slow sip of port, sighed deeply, and said, "You know, I admire Sartre's wit, but I disagree with his philosophy."

"How so?" I asked.

"I'm more in Camus's camp. We live in an absurd, meaningless world. We quest certitude, but all we get back is a cruel cosmic silence of bleak indifference. I just can't make the leap from there to Sartre's 'hell is other people.' I'll concede human beings can be bastards at times, but close relationships are our only real buffer against alienation and despair. To my way of thinking, 'other people' are often the source of much of our confusion and angst; but they're also a fountainhead of comfort and meaning."

I nodded and smiled. We spontaneously raised our Paris goblets for a genuine toast "to us," and then finished off the remaining Vintage '48.

9

Bxf8 Rxf8   dxc5 Nd5

WHEN I WAS ready to leave, I quietly sat down on the side of the bed, gently ran my fingers through Catherine's hair, and realized "the center of the magic circle was one fair form that filled with love the lifeless atmosphere." She began stirring. She opened her eyes, smiled, and whispered, "Good morning."

"Good morning," I replied. "Sorry to wake you, but I have to get over to the professor's place. I'll meet you downstairs at eleven."

She sat up, softly embraced me, and promised, "No worries. I'll be packed and ready to go."

Being focused on completing the professor's master plan by eleven o'clock and ensuring Catherine boarded her return bus an hour later fortunately prevented any feelings of sadness before her departure. I first sensed the deep, enduring loneliness while watching her Greyhound pull out into heavy traffic and disappear over the slight rise on Crittenden Drive.

After wandering aimlessly about the neighborhood for more than an hour, I reluctantly returned to my apartment and discovered Catherine had left a gift at the center of the kitchen table. I was stunned. They were all there—Reginald of Châtillon, James d'Avesnes, Rashid al-Din Sinan, King Richard and Saladin preparing for the Siege of Acre. Catherine must have gone back to the Off Again, On Again that morning, while I was at Professor McMasters's.

Looking closer, I discovered a folded note at the center of the board. I opened it and read the only paragraph on the page, a thank you for "the happiest and most rewarding days" she'd experienced in years. But there was more below the paragraph—a descriptive notation of a chess match with an introductory comment: "I'm playing the Muslim figures (white); you're playing the European pieces (black):

1. Nf3 Nf6 2. c4 g6 3. Nc3 Bg7 4. d4 0-0
5. Bf4 d5 6. Qb3 dxc4 7. Qxc4 c6 8. e4 Nbd7
9. Rd1 Nb6 10. Qc5 Bg4 11. Bg5 Na4 12. Qa3 Nxc3
13. bxc3 Nxe4 14. Bxe7 Qb6 15. Bc4 Nxc3 16. Bc5 Rfe8+
17. Kf1 Be6 18. Bxb6 Bxc4+ 19. Kg1 Ne2+ 20. Kf1 Nxd4+
21. Kg1 Ne2+ 22. Kf1 Nc3+ 23. Kg1 axb6 24. Qb4 Ra4
25. Qxb6 Nxd1 26. h3 Rxa2 27. Kh2 Nxf2 28. Re1 Rxe1
29. Qd8+ Bf8 30. Nxe1 Bd5 31. Nf3 Ne4 32. Qb8 b5
33. h4 h5 34. Ne5 Kg7 35. Kg1 Bc5+ 36. Kf1 Ng3+
37. Ke1 Bb4+ 38. Kd1 Bb3+ 39. Kc1 Ne2+ 40. Kb1 Nc3+
41. Kc1 Rc2#

I sat down at the table and began moving the pieces as indicated in her notation. Was there a hidden meaning buried here? After a classical opening, Catherine makes a minor mistake at move 11, Bg5, losing momentum playing the same piece twice. I seize upon her weak move and initiate a brilliant series of sacrifices ending with an unbelievable queen sacrifice on move 17.

Catherine takes my queen, but I capture a significant number of her pieces: two bishops, a rook, and a pawn. In the endgame, I effectively coordinate my remaining pieces and force checkmate, while Catherine's queen remains powerless at the far end of the board.

What was the meaning here? What was her intent? From a purely tournament chess perspective, the obvious morals would be (1) don't waste time during the opening moving the same piece twice before effectively positioning your other pieces, and (2) significant sacrifices are likely to succeed as long as the central file is open and your opponent's king is in the middle of the board. From a historical perspective, the outcome here was the same as in 1191—after a long struggle, the Crusader Kingdom of Jerusalem (and I) had secured a rare victory over the Egyptians and Syrians (and Catherine).

But in my gut I felt she was sending a stronger albeit subtle personal message that she was willing to "surrender," not so much surrender to me as make a courageous commitment to a meaningful relationship with me. If this latter interpretation were true, would it mean a weighty decision to leave her parents, siblings, and hometown to live in McGill? If my reading were true, where would she live? Would she attend school? How would she support herself? I sat at the table for some time assessing the possibilities before finally deciding to postpone telephoning her. I would wait until we'd both had sufficient time to sort through our motives and feelings.

In the interim I knew I had to hit the books and remain completely focused until McMasters's soiree the next Saturday evening. Where to begin? Since Catherine had just left, I was unwilling to make the ultimate sacrifice of finishing the last one hundred and fifty anticlimactic pages of *Pamela*. That would be beyond the pale. So what would it be? Shakespeare, Byrd, or F. Scott Fitzgerald?

The play assigned for my early Shakespeare course was *The Comedy of Errors*. I remembered reading the work as an undergraduate. It's a warm, energetic play that welcomes us to a world of freedom where anything is possible. The farce would surely take my mind off my loneliness. And the young Shakespeare's themes would also be appropriate for the occasion. He borrowed them from the Greek, Roman, and Commedia traditions. He added feelings of human suffering, longing, and grief to the conventional farcical elements and ultimately argued optimistically that what was lost could be found again. I'd been denied a relationship with Catherine in high school, and she had lost her first love to college. Perhaps we were now in the final hopeful act of our own uplifting comedy of errors.

The assignments for my Early American Literature course were William Byrd's quirky *History of the Dividing Line* and his *Secret History*, which ironically had been added as supplementary reading for my undergraduate American history honors course several years earlier. Rereading Byrd's unconventional frontier exploits now would surely take my mind off Catherine's departure—the worldly wench who'd injured her wrist, whom Byrd's men plied with rum and then undressed; the seafarer who humbly labeled himself a hermit but who "forfeited that title by suffering a wanton female to cohabit with him"; and the extraordinary, rejuvenating bear meat, which Byrd's men had relied upon during much of their time away from home:

> I am able to say that all the married men of our
> company [they had all been compelled during
> the survey to rely largely upon this monot-
> onous food] were joyful fathers within forty
> weeks after they got home, and most of the
> single men had children sworn to them within
> the same time, our chaplain only excepted who,
> with much ado, made shift to cast out that im-
> portunate kind of devil by dint of fasting and
> prayer.

My remaining option was reading the model definition essay and assigning specific topics for the students in my experimental composition class. I sampled the first two paragraphs of F. Scott Fitzgerald's "The Crack-Up" about nervous breakdowns and immediately decided to work on the undergraduate course preparation. After reading Fitzgerald's informal and extended definition of a "crack-up," I began drafting essay assignments for my students: (1) Fitzgerald says he was a mediocre custodian of his talent. Write an expanded definition of your own talents or those of an associate. (2) Write an expanded definition of "vitality as an incommunicable force." (3) Write an expanded definition of "the salt hath lost its savour." (4) Keep a log for a week capturing the events in your life *and* your feelings about them, choose a specific entry, and then write an extended definition essay. (5) Write an expanded definition of the ability to hold opposing ideas in the mind simultaneously.

I must confess I saved this last assignment for Donna, who'd offered convincing insight into Melville and written so eloquently about her mother's "dull, null" existence. I knew she'd witnessed suffering up close and had a gift for *describing* her mother's lingering pain and isolation. But could she now, as a writer, take her skills to the next level, moving from the facts of her mother's existence to its meaning? Would she use Fitzgerald's poignant observation in the second paragraph as a philosophical catalyst to bravely describe the human condition?

> [T]he test of a first-rate intelligence is the ability to hold two opposed ideas in the mind at the same time, and still retain the ability to function. One should, for example, be able to see that things are hopeless and yet be determined to make them otherwise.

And as an exceptional writer, would she ultimately come down on the side of Camus, agreeing that nihilistic literature cannot exist because the act of writing is in itself an ironic, provocative testimony to myth trumping history and affirming our lives?

By Tuesday afternoon I'd proudly achieved all my short-term objectives: provided feedback to my composition students; assigned topics for their next essays; reviewed *The Comedy of Errors*; skimmed Byrd's *Secret History* and his *Dividing Line*; and yes, even suffered through the final pages of *Pamela*, including the narrator's "brief observations" (four pages!) about the major characters, who were meant to "inspire a laudable emulation in the minds of any worthy persons." So now a reward was definitely in order. I would stop by Hudson's for a cherry shake and telephone Catherine to thank her for her thoughtful gift.

Armed with a substantial coffer of coins, I dialed Catherine's number, and she picked up. "Hello."

"Hello, Catherine. It's Andrew. . . . How you doing?"

"Fine. And you?"

"No complaints . . . and before I forget, thanks for the antique chess set. It's a great gift."

"It was the least I could do. You showed me a great time: the football game, the play, the sculpture garden. I'll never forget the weekend."

"Me neither." I paused and then probed lightheartedly, "Ah, I have a question."

"Yeah."

"The chess notations below the paragraph you wrote. . . ."

She laughed mischievously and asked, "Did you play out the forty-one moves?"

"Yeah, I sure did. And I was wondering if you'd buried a message or two in the early moves or the endgame?"

She confessed with a laugh, "Well, if you really have to know . . . yeah." She paused and then asked, "So how'd you read the hidden message?"

It was now my turn to play coy. I opened with my safe "tournament chess" takeaways from her descriptive notations. I replied, "I believe you're saying, 'Don't waste time during the opening' and 'Significant sacrifices can succeed if the central file is open and the opposing king is in the middle of the board.'"

Assuming the farcical role of a high school instructor, Catherine responded, "I've got to give you credit for a perceptive explanation, but I'm sorry, unfortunately, your reading's incorrect. You want to try again?"

"Sure. Why not?" So I posited my second risk-free analysis, the "historical" interpretation. "You're mirroring the actual outcome of the Siege of Acre during the Third Crusade. After a long struggle, the persistent Europeans defeated the resilient Egyptians and Syrians. . . ."

Catherine laughed and coyly prompted me. "Take one more shot. Third time's a charm."

But thankfully, before I could reply, the operator interrupted requesting more money. I now had time to collect my thoughts and draft an effective response. And after depositing the coins in the payphone, I decided to increase the risk level incrementally without going all out. I'd ask a series of oblique questions rather than make unambiguous assertions. Depending on Catherine's responses to each tack, I'd ask increasingly more probing questions until I fully understood the enigma buried within her notation.

I cleared my throat and asked hesitantly, "Ah, does the message have anything to do with our friendship?"

Catherine quietly agreed, "Yes."

"Does the notation in any way imply you're returning to school?"

She again answered softly, "Yes."

I then moved my queen down to king's row. "Should I infer you're willing to make a strategic move . . . leave your parents, siblings, and hometown and live somewhere else?"

She replied, "Yes."

And now the pace quickened. I moved my bishop into position on the opposite side of the board. "Are you implying McGill?"

She gently answered, "Yes."

My knight took one of her two remaining pawns. "Applying to Pantheon?"

She whispered, "Yes."

I boldly angled my queen out from king's row. "Are you suggesting commitment to a meaningful relationship?"

She responded decisively, "Checkmate!"

"Oh, Catherine. Nothing would make me happier."

And after feeding the interloper my remaining coins, we began planning Catherine's future in McGill, temporarily avoiding the sensitive issues of where she'd live and how she'd support herself.

For the rest of the week, the wind was at my back. Nothing could faze me. Professor Wagner had bestowed one of his infamous forty-eight-hour "action assignments" on me; and honestly, it was a real enigma from the start: "If an incunable is located with a small engraving attached to the last page, who most likely was the owner in 1825?" But I didn't approach the undertaking as a pain in the ass but as an interesting scholarly challenge, which all told consumed six valuable hours discovering the simple answer, "the Bodleian."

During this memorable week, I also launched an energetic discussion of *Pamela* with my undergraduate English students, who had no idea how much I disliked the novel nor could they fully appreciate the effort expended breathing life into Richardson's static epistolary form. Like a wily veteran thespian who had thoroughly learned his lines, I paced at the front of the class, praised Richardson's disciplinary contribution to the rise of the novel, while subconsciously admiring the opening chapters of *Joseph Andrews*, which I had begun reading the day before. I couldn't wait to explain how Fielding had begun writing his second parody of Richardson's *Pamela*; stumbled upon the seductive Lady Booby and the uncontrollable Parson Adams; and fortuitously crafted a humorous, picaresque novel worthy of Cervantes.

It was uncanny. As the weekend approached, my good fortunes multiplied. First, on Friday night I joined a fellow English instructor for a performance of Tati's Academy Award–winning film, *Mon Oncle*, about a man who wanders about the city eloquently humanizing his impersonal, complex world with simple acts of beauty and grace. This Chaplinesque Parisian opens a window in his modest loft and hears a bird sing, but only for an instant. His childlike curiosity demands he open and shut the window until he fully understands when and why the bird sings. Aha! As the window pivots, it reflects a beam of light into the nest, tricking the bird into thinking the morning has broken. Monsieur Hulot playfully positions his window at the perfect point of reflection, prompting the lark to sing gently throughout the night.

Next, there was the football game on Saturday afternoon. Pantheon had left the friendly confines of Panther Field to play its powerful cross-state rival. I opened a can of chicken noodle, cranked up the small Philco, and suffered the first uninspired half alone in the Rainbow Room. The score after two quarters was Wildcats 13, Panthers 0. The third quarter was much the same, a stalemate played between the twenty-yard lines. But toward the end of the third quarter, the Panthers began showing signs of life. For the first time that afternoon, the offense drove the ball deep into Wildcat territory but was stymied five yards short of pay dirt. Pantheon settled for a routine field goal, making the score at the end of the third quarter Wildcats 13, Panthers 3.

As the fourth quarter began, there were growing signs divine intervention may be at play again that week. On the ensuing kickoff, the Wildcats fumbled and the Panthers recovered and marched in for a score: Wildcats 13, Panthers 10. Throughout the fourth quarter, both defenses played valiantly; and with a minute forty-five to play, we gained possession for a final attempt to drive the ball down the field. As the Panthers rolled inexorably toward the Wildcats goal, the radio screamed. I paced and then pounded out a drumbeat on the kitchen table. I was now convinced God had indeed shown up again to block for the Panthers during the last minute of play. And on the final snap of the game, our halfback drove up the middle and miraculously broke the plane of the goal. The final shocking score from eastern Tennessee: the lowly Panthers 17 and the highly regarded but stunned Wildcats 13. After savoring the rowdy postgame interviews, I hurried down to the Two-Way to join students and alumni for another unexpected victory celebration.

And the momentous weekend wasn't nearly over. I had several beers with colleagues at the Two-Way, diplomatically excused myself, and hurried back to the apartment to dress for the highly anticipated McMasters Halloween soiree. When I arrived fashionably late at a little past eight, many of the new English Department faculty members had already made an appearance. I deposited my trench coat on the pile of outerwear at the center of the professor's bed, then ladled out a large mug of warm, bubbling Witches Brew and began making the introductory rounds.

The attendees were a strong, eclectic group of young but established artists and scholars who had been hired to teach creative writing and literary scholarship. William Swain had studied at Wesleyan and Stanford, had written several incisive articles for the *American Scholar*, and was currently assigned undergraduate courses in Milton, Chaucer, and Shakespeare. Walter Talley had attended Vanderbilt for both his undergraduate and graduate degrees and was what I would call a hybrid. He had already gained recognition both as a twentieth-century literary scholar and as a compelling novelist whose first two massive works had climbed the charts into the top ten. During the fall semester, the highly regarded Professor Talley was teaching graduate creative writing courses in the novel and short story forms.

Thomas Gould earned his undergraduate degree from Tulane, traveled west for his doctoral work at UCLA, and completed his dissertation on the treatment of reality in Thackeray, Dickens, and Trollope. Professor Gould had been hired to teach undergraduate and graduate nineteenth-century courses and to establish a solid Victorian Studies division within the English Department. Donald Sanders, by contrast, had studied premed at Notre Dame, fell in love with words along the way, and opted for a Ph.D. in English from Columbia University. The associate professor was another hybrid, teaching medieval English literature by day and writing poetry at night. Before arriving at Pantheon, he had published two acclaimed volumes of verse, *La Belle Époque* and *Lamentable*

Predilections. Willis Ridley had attended Northwestern as an undergraduate and the University of Chicago for his doctorate. His primary interests were nineteenth-century European psychoanalysis and literature, which inspired his soon-to-be-published dissertation, *Freudian Influences on Literary Biography and Scholarship*.

The remainder of attendees I met during my initial rounds was just as talented, energetic, optimistic, and accomplished as the professors Swain, Talley, Gould, Sanders, and Ridley. After ensuring I had introduced myself to everyone in attendance, I returned to the buffet table for another mug of the highly popular Witches Brew, which Professor McMasters swore he concocted every year in his bathtub to dramatically enhance both the potion's viscosity and its otherworldly flavor.

About an hour into our All Hallows festivities, there was a loud knock at the front entrance. I opened the door, and a young couple strolled in. They passed by me without saying a word or making eye contact and sauntered over to Professor McMasters, who was busy circulating a tray teeming with an assortment of toasted seafood canapés. After handing off the hors d'oeuvres and stowing the couple's jackets in the bedroom, Professor McMasters began making the formal introductions to those of us who had never met the late arrivals.

As the threesome approached my latest position guarding the heavily depleted punch bowl, the engaging young fellow shifted his English Oval to his left hand, smiled broadly, and extended his right arm toward me. Professor McMasters quickly stepped forward to introduce us, fondly identifying the guest as the avant-garde playwright Jeffrey Kline, who had temporarily joined the faculty as an adjunct professor teaching dramaturgy and overseeing graduate theater practicums.

I immediately sensed Jeffrey was a counterintuitive blend of warm, engaging personality and over-the-top, pretentious flair. In my own head, I resolved Jeffrey's glaring dichotomy by separating his inner charm from his glaring sartorial panache. I assumed his flamboyant fashion statement was intended to advertise his cutting-edge dramas while simultaneously downplaying his rural, bourgeois background with its all-too-conventional social ethic.

Jeffrey was undeniably handsome: a tall, muscular, tanned body; long, dark brown curls; large brown eyes; a straight, thin nose; and a square, clean-shaven chin. But here again I could detect an obvious tension. His matinee idol, OK Corral features were severely at odds with his flashy, overly refined, coral, yellow, and cinnamon outerwear. The young dramatist explained that after attending Michigan and the Yale School of Drama, he landed an invaluable backstage position at the Ritz on Broadway, which opened the door to important theatrical connections and to experienced feedback from confidants enthusiastically reading rough drafts of his early manuscripts.

After allowing this brief exchange of biographical and collegial pleasantries, Professor McMasters gracefully pivoted toward the playwright's gorgeous companion and proudly announced, "May I introduce the exceptional poetess, Bianca." That's right; the professor didn't mention a last name for La Belle Dame sans Merci. Bianca was following the customary tradition of the great romantic lyricists, but with a twist. While she was using only a single name as Shelley, Keats, Wordsworth, or Byron, Bianca chose to use her given rather than her family name. And as I had discerned with Jeffrey, there was a tension, a duality between her soft, striking femininity and a fiery undercurrent of passionate volatility.

While she had now reached her early to mid-thirties, Bianca still retained the stunning appearance of a highly marketable fashion model. She was at least five feet ten inches tall with glossy raven curls flowing down over her bare shoulders. She had all the required facial features—high cheekbones, a small straight nose, full sensuous lips, and almond-shaped, crystal clear blue eyes. She extended her hand, arched her left brow, smiled warmly, and gazed directly into my eyes. After several seconds of magnetic, glowing silence, I smiled, distractedly turned toward Professor McMasters, and acknowledged my familiarity with Bianca's first collection of poems, *Serra de Sintra*.

From earlier press accounts and book reviews, I had learned her father was Portuguese and her mother was German. The parents still lived in the north of Portugal on a seventy-acre quinta at the confluence of the Douro and Pinhão rivers, the acknowledged epicenter of the port winemaking world. Bianca's father inherited their storied vineyard from his father in the 1920s and had continued producing critically acclaimed wines rivaling those of the nearby Quinta de Vargellas and Quinta do Vesúvio.

Bianca's mother, for her part, had a stellar operatic career with the Staatsoper Unter den Linden in Berlin, collaborating with the conducting giants of her day, Furtwängler, Klemperer, and Bruno Walter. She was the understudy for the soprano, Sigrid Johanson, in the premiere of Alban Berg's *Wozzeck* in

December 1925 and assumed the key role of Marie when Ms. Johanson left the cast the next spring. It was after one of the April performances that she met her future husband backstage. He had traveled to Germany pursuing a highly lucrative business venture and wanted to experience the finest operatic productions in Western Europe.

After a year of demanding transcontinental train rides between Berlin and the Douro, Bianca's mother retired from the stage, married the dashing entrepreneur, and moved permanently to the palatial estate. The following year, Bianca was born in the ivied manor house and then spent most of her childhood gamboling among the idyllic hillsides overlooking the ruined castles and haunted monasteries of the fertile Douro Valley.

When she had completed her secondary education at the German school, Bianca left rural Pinhão to study literature and languages at the University of Coimbra, where she, as her mother had before her, fell in love with a foreigner and followed him back to his home country. After traveling to the States with the visiting professor, she shared an off-campus apartment with him for several riotous years near the tragic estate once owned by Charles and Anne Lindbergh. During her stay in Hopewell, Bianca studied creative writing at Princeton, began thinking seriously about poetry as a full-time profession, and penned the first of her elegiac love poems, undoubtedly fueled by her tumultuous affair and lifetime familiarity with the distinctive Portuguese tradition of fado.

Several hours into our Halloween soiree, everyone had gravitated to the sofa and chairs in the comfortable book-lined study and formed an admiring circle around the lovable professor emeritus. Over the course of the next half hour the conversation inexplicably evolved from alcohol-induced frivolity into a lively academic discussion of a postwar philosophical movement sweeping Europe and permeating its literature, theater, sculpture, and painting.

I suspect few of us participating in that fireside conversation understood we were actually in the process of creating our own dynamic movement and a vehicle to disseminate both its tenets and its creative works. But to be fair to our attendees, many scientific, economic, and societal advances serendipitously evolve out of man's quest to either improve his living conditions or more clearly understand the vast unknown.

Did Bjarni Herjólfsson plan to discover North America in 986? Absolutely not. According to the *Saga of the Greenlanders*, the Norwegian was simply trying to visit his father, who had recently immigrated to Greenland. Three days after leaving port, Bjarni Herjólfsson's ship was buffeted by severe storms, blown off course, and fortuitously pointed in the direction of undiscovered lands. While he and his crew chose not to go ashore during this voyage, they did report back about this new temperate region southwest of Greenland. A decade later, Leif Ericson heard the story, bought Bjarni Herjólfsson's ship, assembled a crew of thirty-five, and soon established a Viking community at L'Anse aux Meadows, Newfoundland. It was the first recorded European attempt at settlement on the North American mainland half a millennium before Columbus sailed from Spain.

And why did the Messrs. Burbage, Henslowe, Shakespeare, Jonson, et al., build their seven wooden O's? Clearly to provide the public a needed service and generate a hefty return on their investments. And the fortunate by-product of their lucrative ventures? A life force informing the western mind: *Lear, Hamlet, Othello, Tamburlaine, Faustus, Epicoene, Malfi,* and *Volpone*.

Ironically, it was our animated host, the retired economics professor, who first identified the opportunities and led the inspired charge to devise plans of implementation. "What's the most dynamic philosophical construct under discussion in Western Europe today? Has a similar dialogue ensued in the United States? If we were to launch an exploration of provocative ideas, shouldn't we strive for a sustainable critical mass, say, for example, among creators and discoverers readily available on a vibrant college campus? How would we express our ideas? Through poetry? Novels? Plays? Essays? How would we share our latest thinking first among ourselves for feedback and refinement? Monthly or quarterly meetings, perhaps here? And how would we then disseminate our latest works beyond our university circle?"

After running up "interrogatory hill," Professor McMasters paused to catch his breath; and during this brief interval, the room spontaneously erupted into an audible buzz of excited, undisciplined sidebar conversations. Several minutes passed, and then our rejuvenated host waved his arms to silence our speculation. He cleared his throat and began racing downhill, quickly answering his previous questions in precise order: "Everything I've read recently in the journals points to a burgeoning existential movement throughout the arts. If there's anything going on in the States, it's still under the radar.

"So paraphrasing Colonel Parker at Lexington, if we mean to have an American movement, then let it begin here with many of us nurturing its development. You're all scholars, poets, novelists, or dramatists. You would create; and we could meet here monthly or quarterly to discuss your latest thinking. And the vehicle for wider distribution? How about publishing a modest literary journal to showcase our own existential works? I'm open to suggestions, but doesn't *The Messenger* have a certain ring to it?"

The professor smiled, settled back into his overstuffed chair, and awaited the group's response to his unrehearsed remarks. We sat there momentarily in breathtaking silence, assimilating what we had just witnessed—a peerless grandmaster advancing a forceful strategy, posing his third question while simultaneously crafting the answer to a still undisclosed, incisive question number five. We then slowly began nodding our acceptance of his sweeping proposal, rose to our feet, and vigorously applauded the professor's game plan. After unanimously agreeing to hold our first formal meeting the third weekend of November and targeting the following April for publication of the inaugural issue of *The Messenger*, we moved over en masse to the buffet table, filled our mugs a final time, and proposed a hearty toast to our success.

Throughout the evening's festivities, I had primarily adopted the Verver-Brand strategy—quietly and unobtrusively observing the guests' interactions from a safe distance. With Bianca's arrival, the party dynamics changed radically from a fully integrated, interactive single group of collegial professionals to three distinct rival groups with intensely conflicting agendas. There were the male attendees immediately gravitating to Bianca; the older women surrounding a fiercely jealous Jeffrey;

and the younger wives of the wayward men coalescing around a plausible conviction that it would only be a matter of time before this appealing addition to the faculty would spell trouble for someone in this crowded upstairs room. And to no one's surprise, the unholy alliances prevailed until the disparate groups finally migrated to the study and encircled their charming, inventive host.

Since Professor McMasters had appointed me special assistant du jour, I stayed to help the guests reclaim their coats, strike the set, and most importantly, undertake the lion's share of the considerable postparty cleanup. And of course, who would be some of the last invitees to leave? You guessed it: the playwright and the poet.

Jeffrey stepped forward, shook my hand, and moved away to thank the professor for his gracious invitation. And then what I had successfully avoided all evening was now about to happen. As if on cue, Bianca walked up, smiled, gazed directly into my eyes, slid her long fingers up under the lapels of my sport jacket, and whispered, "Where have you been all evening, red beard? We didn't get a chance to speak. I understand you are taking graduate courses and teaching. I'd like to hear more about what you are doing. Perhaps we could meet next week in the faculty lounge."

Fragmentary, conflicted thoughts raced through my mind: Catherine's genuine commitment; Bianca's obvious flirtations; an apprehensive lover; perilous departmental politics; a strong physical attraction; instinctive reluctance; a logical dead end; while on the other hand, no truly viable alternative; a relatively safe public venue; minimal consequences; so what the hell, once more unto the breach, dear friends, once more. I stared into Bianca's transparent blue eyes, smiled broadly, and confidently agreed to meet her the next week in the faculty lounge. Bianca tugged lightly at my lapels, nodded her approval of our professional tryst, and triumphantly turned away toward the door. As the exceptional couple disappeared down the long, dark hallway, I immediately began rationalizing my decision, significantly downplaying the risks, admittedly reveling in her beguiling beauty, all the while knowing I was now playing with Icarian fire.

With everything I had on my plate, the week passed quickly, and I was now standing at the front of the faculty lounge surveying the near-empty room. I took a deep breath to compose myself; and then, with my heart pounding out of my chest, I moved to a back table and stood opposite Bianca. She was so absorbed in her writing that she didn't sense I was standing there. I cleared my throat and whispered, "Bianca."

No response.

A little louder now. "Bianca . . ."

Startled, she jumped and looked up. "Oh, Andrew. I'm sorry. I . . . I didn't know you were standing there." She paused and added dreamily, "I was in another world."

I nodded and agreed good-naturedly, "Yeah, I could tell you were really lost in your work."

Bianca stood up, extended her hand, and smiled coolly. "Glad you could join me. Here, take a seat."

Trying desperately to break the ice, I responded, "Before that, how about I brew us a coffee?" And then to close the sale,

I declared, "Faculty here say I make a mean espresso. I could conjure one up for you if you'd like."

As she sat back down, she replied, "Well, in that case, Andrew, show me what you got."

"How do you take it?" I asked. I wondered if she could hear my heart beat.

"Straight up. No sugar or cream," she said.

Still trying to warm things up, I said, "Now you're talking. Why people ruin espressos with all that junk sure beats me." I then turned and shouted back over my shoulder, "Two triples coming up before you can put pencil back to paper!"

As the top-of-the-line commercial machine ground, whirred, pumped, and poured, I reflected, "You know, this is nothing like what I had pictured all week waiting for today to happen. Her demeanor is far different, in fact, the opposite of her behavior during the soiree. Maybe it's the environment, the atmosphere. After all, this is the faculty lounge where eyes peer and tongues wag. Or perhaps it's her way of saying, 'I'm sorry, Andrew, but after a week of careful consideration, I find you don't rise to my lofty standards.' And then again, maybe she had already sensed I was nibbling at the bait; and instead of launching a full-on frontal assault using her beauty and sensuality, she would set the hook now with a rearguard action, employing her intellect and creativity." I shook my head, grabbed the cups, and headed back to the table determined to crack the code.

After handing her the demitasse, I felt I had just been thrown into an international barista competition. Bianca carefully inspected my handiwork and then began offering her Old World assessment of my New World technique. "Still too hot to drink.

That means you heated the cup. Good. . . . A golden brown layer of crema on top. Not bad. . . . And now the final test—the taste." She took several sips, swirled the viscous liquid around in her mouth, and announced her final judgment: "Rich? Yes. Bitter, but not too bitter? Yes. And just the right thickness? Yes." She nodded and then declared her verdict. "Not bad, Andrew, not bad at all."

Bianca paused and then segued from the refreshments to what felt to me like an informal job interview. "So tell me now about some of your other talents. I understand you're taking graduate courses and teaching."

I didn't know where she was headed, so I just nodded and went with the flow. "The graduate courses, ah, Shakespeare: The Early Plays, American Literature to 1800, and An Introduction to Graduate Studies."

"Interesting. So what's involved in the Intro to Grad Studies course?"

"Primarily exploring research tools."

"Like . . . ?"

"Oh, like specialized reference materials, various research methods, bibliographies and the like."

Bianca continued probing. "And what courses are you teaching?"

"Oh, a sophomore-level course on the rise of the novel. You know, eighteenth-century England beginning with Defoe, Richardson, Fielding, and Sterne."

"Others?"

Totally flummoxed, I shifted in my seat and replied, "Ah, an experimental advanced writing course."

Bianca tapped her pencil on her folder and asked, "Experimental? How's that?"

Trying to quickly finish the gauntlet, I rattled off a skeletal outline of Dr. Wagner's signature course. "I only saw the students once, for the first class of the semester. After that, everything has been handled by internal mail. That's how the students get their assignments, how I get their essays, and how they get my feedback."

To be honest, I really wasn't enjoying the gentle grilling, even if I was being interrogated by one of the most beautiful, seductive women in the world. My instincts said it was time to counter, time to shake things up, politely but firmly drive a bishop into her king's row. "Speaking of writing, Bianca, if I might ask, what were you working on so intently when I walked up? Already drafting a sonnet for the inaugural *Messenger*?"

Signaling she was willing to relinquish the lead for now, Bianca shook her head and said, "No, no sonnets yet. I was just going where the voices lead me."

I gazed into her eyes, smiled nervously, and probed, "And where were the voices leading you just now?"

Becoming a bit more engaged, she answered, "To my second love, fado."

I looked away, embarrassed, but responded truthfully, believing that to do otherwise would just be digging a deeper hole. "Fado? To be honest, about all I know about fado is that it's a Portuguese genre involving sad songs. But I'd really like to learn more about it."

Warming to the subject, Bianca leaned in and said, "As the literal translation of *fado* implies, it's about doom. Fortune.

Destiny. . . . It's from the same Latin root as the English word 'fate.' Bubbled up out of the docks and barrios in the early 1800s, not surprisingly, a lot of the lyrics describe living hard lives at sea or in the ghettos."

Relieved that I was in the ballpark, I leaned in and said self-deprecatingly, "Well, at least you can give me partial credit for mentioning the sad songs."

She nodded and smiled. "That's right—songs filled with feelings of resignation and what we call *saudade*.

"*Saudade?*"

"Yes, you would translate that as 'longing.'"

Sensing an opening to at least partially salvage my image, I said, "Fado sounds a lot like our American blues—melancholy oozing up out of the juke joints in the Mississippi delta, poor blacks singing about their lives on hellish plantations, resigned to a fate of hardship and suffering. . . ." I paused and then confessed, "You know, Bianca, people think I'm crazy; but I don't focus on the sadness in the narratives. I take an alternate view. I find the courage in the narrator's willingness to soldier on. To endure."

Bianca reached across the table, grabbed my forearms firmly, and exclaimed, "Yes, Andrew! Yes, that's it!" She paused and then continued reflectively, "That's . . . that's exactly how I feel, what I'm trying to convey when composing these 'sad' songs. You see, I don't want people leaving my concerts with their heads hanging low. I want them walking out into the streets with their heads held high, ready to, as you say, 'soldier on.'"

We gazed into each other's eyes, nodding, smiling, but saying nothing. Allowing the silence to flash hopeful messages about our future.

10

f4 Rd8   N2c3 Ndb4

EVERY DEVOTED STUDENT of Plutarch knows
Pheidippides ran only twenty-two miles to reach the Athenian assembly and announce the Greek victory at Marathon.
And every serious marathoner knows he or she must run an
additional four and two-tenths excruciating miles because the
British royal family demanded outstanding views of the finish
line during the 1908 Summer Olympics. So like the legendary Greek before us, my classmates and I had completed the
formidable course requirements up to and through the final
research paper with more than a week to spare. But playing
the role of Edward VII on behalf of Alexandra, our beloved J.
Alfred extended the standard course beyond the finish line and
assigned one additional "action assignment" for each of us just
before final exams were scheduled to commence in our other
graduate courses. And these last "action assignments" were not
trivial. They ranged from determining the date the Bishop of
London delivered a specific sermon during the reign of Queen
Elizabeth I with the Treasurer and the Keeper of the Privy Seal
in attendance to identifying three idiosyncrasies of the English
painter John Varley, beyond the habit of tossing his wife across
the table to several of his students.

My assignment was another classic. J. Alfred first quoted a passage from Virginia Woolf's novel *Orlando*:

> The Court was at Greenwich, and the new King seized the opportunity that his coronation gave him to curry favour with the citizens. He directed that the river, which was frozen to a depth of twenty feet and more for six or seven miles on either side, should be swept, decorated and given all the semblance of a park or pleasure ground, with arbours, mazes, alleys, drinking booths, etc. at his expense.

The professor next indicated the quotation was an accurate description of an Elizabethan "frost fair," which Londoners would hold during harsh winters when the Thames had frozen solid. My surreal task was to identify at least five documented winters spanning the sixteenth and seventeenth centuries during which the citizenry actually held these "frost fairs."

This was going to be like running ten extra miles rather than the excruciating four and two-tenths. Where in the hell do I start? I could spend a lifetime thumbing through the various histories of England searching for specific references to annual weather phenomena. My mind had already numbed; and physically I felt I was pushing my pencil across the page while taking notes in my final classes. First, I thought almanacs might be the magic bullet; but then I remembered they were predicting weather not actually recording it. Next, I considered the possibility of volumes of recorded weather. I did find three books, *British Floods and Droughts*, *Climate in Everyday Life*, and *Weather*; but none was helpful in completing my mission from hell.

As I teetered on the edge of panic, I tilted back on two legs of my library chair and stared above the impressive stacks of the graduate reference room to collect my thoughts. And then the likely answer miraculously appeared, right there on the wall above the twenty massive volumes of the OED—a reproduction of Turner's 1827 oil on canvas, *Mortlake Terrace*, depicting commercial and fashionable boat traffic on a bend of the Thames near the Royal Botanical Gardens at Kew. Since English sailors had depended on the river for their livelihoods over the past millennium, perhaps there would be historical accounts of river conditions for the two centuries currently under review. Hope springs eternal; so off to the card catalog in search of the theoretical holy grail, comprehensive maritime records of the Thames extending back to the early 1600s.

I couldn't believe it. There they were—five immaculate, comprehensive volumes of historical river data covering the last thousand years. Over the next several hours I researched the sixteenth and seventeenth centuries and even discovered several brief contemporaneous accounts of a frozen Thames:

> 1537—King Henry VIII, with his queen (Jane Seymour . . . who was to die late in the year after giving birth to the future Edward VI) rode on the ice-bound river from London to Greenwich.

> 1608—Ice formed on the Thames in London,
> sufficient to bear all sorts of sports, perambula-
> tions and even cooking. The frost lasted overall
> for some two months.

I was gaining momentum. Why not trace the references back to the first recorded "frost fairs" on the Thames? Would it be the fifteenth century? No. There was an extended account for 1310:

> London Bridge arches were damaged by ice
> during the severe winter. The Thames was fro-
> zen solid. There was a frost-fair on the Thames
> in London; 'sport' was also held on the riv-
> er. People walked across the channel, danced
> around a fire built on the ice and chased a small
> hare on the frozen waterway.

Would it be the fourteenth century with the 1310 account? No. Thirteenth century? No again? I actually found the first recorded reference for the year 1150, ironically the same year chess was purportedly introduced into England:

> The frost lasted from December to March,
> and the frozen river was crossed on foot and
> on horseback. The Thames at London Bridge
> supported loaded wagons.

And as I drafted my response to J. Alfred's "action assignment," I envisioned not just running, but sprinting to the finish line with a flourish: "From 1150 through the seventeenth century, there were twenty-three winters in which the Thames was recorded to have frozen over at London and 'frost fairs' were held: 1150, 1205, 1270, 1282, 1310, 1408, 1410, 1435, 1506, 1514, 1537, 1565, 1595, 1608, 1621, 1635, 1649, 1655, 1663, 1666, 1677, 1684, and 1695."

After completing my own course work, I still had to finish grading the last of the papers for the advanced composition class. The students' final assignment was to read Fiedler's model essay emphasizing the moral obligation of serious fiction and then write an essay of argument and persuasion based on one of Fiedler's observations. The provocative piece contained many important assertions, one of which in particular I thought might inspire Donna's last essay: "In the end, the negativist is no nihilist . . . but chooses to render the absurdity he perceives, chooses to know it and to make it known." Based on her first essay of quiet suffering and the human condition and her second supporting Camus's and Fitzgerald's affirmative belief that nihilistic poetry and fiction can't exist, I believed she would pick up on the Fiedler thought and expand her previous arguments.

But no. Instead, she chose a passage from Fiedler's initial paragraph as the basis for her final work:

> Most of my best literary friends, at any rate, considered it strategically advisable to speak of novels and poems purely (the adverb is theirs) in terms of diction, structure, and point of view— remaining safely inside the realm of the format.

Donna opened with a broadside against the New Criticism movement established at Vanderbilt in the early 1920s and espoused by such respected scholars, poets, and writers as Warren, Brooks, Ransom, Tate, Riding, and Moore. She disagreed with their notion that each literary work should stand on its own and be analyzed in a vacuum, with no regard either for its cultural and historical milieu or the author's likely intentions. Donna believed rejecting these highly effective interpretive tools severely limited the reader's ability to fully appreciate the power, scope, and meaning of the overall work.

After clearly stating her opposition to the New Criticism, she circled back to Camus, but not in the context I'd anticipated. Donna declared she ardently supported the philosopher's belief that myth ultimately triumphed over history. She then asserted poets continue writing the all-important myth of America and that current scholars could not effectively interpret the individual works without fully understanding the influences and linkages between the major poets spanning the last one hundred years.

Donna next described the negative impact the period leading up to the Civil War and the war itself had on the country's confidence and national spirit. Before, during, and after the American Revolution, the citizenry respected their clergy, politicians, and entrepreneurs who continuously reinforced the dynamic concepts of providence, manifest destiny, and the strong likelihood of stunning success. But not long after Appomattox, it became clear the country's optimism was quickly waning and the previous leaders could no longer convince their constituencies the future would be so much better than the past.

The nation required a "societal handoff" to a new generation of leaders, speaking a new language and employing an entirely new medium. Long before anyone fully understood the problem, Emerson had prophetically announced who should replace the theologians, politicians, and businessmen:

> I look in vain for the poet whom I describe. We do not, with sufficient plainness, or sufficient profoundness, address ourselves to life, nor dare we chant our own times and social circumstance. If we filled the day with bravery, we should not shrink from celebrating it. Time and nature yield us many gifts, but not yet the timely man, the new religion, the reconciler, whom all things await.

And as Emerson had prophesied, out of the destruction, bleak prospects, and despair of the war, a discouraged people finally heard the "barbaric yawps" of a new voice announcing a new mythic vision for America:

> The past and present wilt—I have fill'd them, emptied them,
> And proceed to fill my next fold of the future. . . .

> I too am not a bit tamed—I too am untranslatable;
> I sound my barbaric yawp over the roofs of the world. . . .

> I bequeath myself to the dirt, to grow from the grass I love;
> If you want me again, look for me under your boot-soles.

After describing Whitman's critical role as "the timely man, the new religion, the reconciler," Donna moved on to Hart Crane, who acknowledged the "Meistersinger's" contribution and continued the mythic vision of America in *The Bridge*:

> But who has held the heights more sure than thou,
> O Walt!—Ascensions of thee hover in me now
> As thou at junctions elegiac, there of speed
> With vast eternity, dost wield the rebound seed. . . .
> Our Meistersinger, thou set breath in steel;
> And it was thou who on the boldest heel
> Stood up and flung the span on even wing
> Of that great Bridge, our Myth, whereof I sing!

Dad always said he taught to learn. I never knew exactly what he meant until Donna pushed me to the limits of my familiarity with American poetry, referring to William Carlos Williams as the next link in the mythic chain. My knowledge of Williams's poetry was limited to his 1923 volume, *Spring and All*, which contained the highly anthologized "Red Wheelbarrow" and "By the road to the contagious hospital." Donna argued that at the beginning of *Paterson*, Williams fuses the city and the narrator into an epic protagonist, who become the animating force for his world. As city, he is the provider of energy and goods; and as man, he is a mythmaker that bestows life on his imaginatively created dreams:

> Paterson lies in the valley under the Passaic Falls
> its spent waters forming the outline of his back. He

lies on his right side, head near the thunder
of the waters filling his dreams! Eternally asleep,
his dreams walk about the city where he persists
incognito. Butterflies settle on his stone ear.
Immortal he neither moves nor rouses and is seldom
seen, though he breathes and the subtleties of his
machinations
drawing their substance from the noise of the pouring
river
animate a thousand automations. . . .

Williams firmly believed the bold exploration of the local, of specific things, would result in the discovery of a new, mythic world blossoming all about him:

Say it, no ideas but in things—
nothing but the blank faces of the houses
and cylindrical trees
bent, forked by preconception and accident—
split, furrowed, creased, mottled, stained—
secret—into the body of the light!

Donna then suggested Charles Olson was the logical heir to American mythmaking. Williams had mentored Olson, and they had both lectured at the innovative Black Mountain College near Asheville. As for my knowledge of Olson, the poet had only come up once or twice in casual conversation back East in undergraduate school. I had never read his *Maximus Poems*, which Donna indicated was the specific work attached to the mythic arc. Where Whitman used the country, Crane the Brooklyn Bridge, Williams the Passaic River and Paterson, Olson chose the craggy seaport town of Gloucester as the springboard for his epic myth of America. Gloucester was Olson's *polis*, a Greek word for an ideal city-state, and Olson declared *polis* was his eyes to witness the specific, the local, and the concrete:

> I have this sense,
> that I am one
> with my skin
> Plus this – plus this:
> that forever the geography
> which leans in
> on me I compel
> backwards I compel Gloucester
> to yield, to
> change.
> Polis
> Is this

With probative acts of seeing *and* knowing, the poetry takes over; the epic takes control. The poet can no longer remain anchored to "the roofs, the old ones, the gentle steep ones on whose ridge-poles the gulls sit."

If Maximus were silenced, who then would pick up the mythic mantel? Donna believed it would be a young Californian from Half Moon Bay, a Wallace Tyndale, who had only published two slim volumes but both had received high praise. She argued the mythic elements were all there in his early work—there in the diction, tone, theme, imagery, and the allusions to the earlier mythmakers from Whitman through Olson:

> Sunrise.
> Claret wing dips,
> Sweeps, soars
> O'er glinting arc.
> Vibrant, taut,
> I lift to receptive, flowing warmth;
> I drive piling among loving sinew
> Beyond Far Rockaway
> To gifted Gloucester
> And the unicorn.
> Measures pulse,
> Swirl, fuse.
> Prologue and Myth are one.

Donna concluded her assignment arguing reality had now fused with the symbolic. While Tyndale's predecessors had all conjured the myth near the Atlantic coast, this Californian had stretched the mythic arc well beyond the continental divide to the far Pacific.

There was no question here about the grade. Donna had excelled throughout the semester. She had earned her A. My only problem was I had no way to distinguish her superior evaluation from the top scores of many others, who had also performed quite well during the experimental course. In fact, in a normal year, the other "A students" would have been highly praised for their results. But they were in a situation similar to Shakespeare's creative peers, who crafted exceptional dramas that were then quickly forgotten and unfortunately still receive little notice or staging today. After applying the A to Donna's paper, I turned the cover page over and wrote a sincere message thanking her for the provocative, illuminating essays and encouraging her to continue taking courses to further refine her skills.

I packed up my belongings strewn all about the library carrel and headed over to the English Department to place the students' last feedback in their mailboxes and record their final grades in the official registry. It had finally stopped snowing. The dark gray blanket had drifted off to the east, and the late-afternoon sun had broken through the remaining thin layer of clouds, providing little warmth, just long, charcoal shadows and several fading slants of January light. The stinging wind had swung around to the north and had begun depositing deep drifts of powdered snow against the limestone buildings and the ivied walls surrounding much of the arctic quadrangle. I tightened the long laces on my indomitable Chuck Taylor's, pulled the wide woolen collar of my navy pea coat up firmly around my neck, lowered my watch cap, and blazed a momentary trail along a swirling path to a distant Redman Hall.

After finishing my administrative tasks in the nearly empty office, I headed down to the faculty lounge to brew some Oolong and open my healthy stack of aging departmental mail. As I sat at one of the heavy wooden tables overlooking the glistening silver winterscape, Professors Talley and Sanders dropped in for their last "leaded" coffee of the day. Since I was severely behind in reviewing my correspondence, they informed me Professor McMasters had announced a *Messenger* update meeting at his apartment for the coming Thursday evening. Contributors were to report their progress on potential submissions for the inaugural issue in April. While Talley indicated he was working on the third draft of two short stories, Sanders said he had completed two sonnets, "Sacred and Demonic Flames" and "The Fruits of Aphrodite," and was currently working on a third still unnamed lyric. I had missed the inaugural November meeting with a racking migraine, but confirmed I would definitely join them at McMasters's for the second gathering. I then excused myself and returned to opening the daunting stack of mail. I wanted to get back to the apartment as soon as possible and begin cleaning. Company was coming to stay for a while day after next.

I had the magical streets to myself as I zigzagged through the challenging mogul field, which the struggling plows and conscientious proprietors had sculpted earlier in the day. The tall, curved streetlights cast pale yellow cones downward onto the swirling drifts, animating faint, elliptical galaxies billions of light-years away. It was a special time. The snow was fresh and clean, and it mirrored the flashing holiday lights still streaming from the festive shops and the snowbound bungalows lining McGill's heavily tinseled streets.

This rare winter storm reminded me of the good times I'd had as an undergraduate out East. During the Christmas season, several of my roommates and I would drive up old Route 7 through Cornwall Bridge, New Canaan, and Great Barrington to everyone's ideal image of Christmas in New England—idyllic, charming Stockbridge. We'd always park on the opposite side of snowy Main Street, watch the low sun fade behind the Sleeping

Giant, and wait for the brick and wooden buildings to waken with the warm amber glow of interior lights.

There were large decorated evergreens at both ends of the block, one at the entrance to the quaint two-story brick library and the other in front of the historic Red Lion Inn. There was also a bright, garlanded tree standing in a large picture window on the second floor of the Stockbridge Shops. The lady who owned the bakery with the heavenly raisin bread had told me earlier Rockwell had rented the space above the shops for his apartment and studio and had created some of his most admired *Saturday Evening Post* covers there: *Breaking Home Ties*, *Girl at Mirror*, and *The Discovery*.

After surveying this joyful, celebratory scene from the far side of the street, we would step over the steep mounds, dodge the children's playful snowballs, and join the bustling last-minute shoppers moving frantically among the galleries, boutiques, and antique shops. Because of our financial straits, our Berkshire shopping itinerary was never long; but it always included a nostalgic stop at the Country Store for Squirrels, fireballs, and my all-time favorite, Mary Janes.

As I'd expected, my frozen journey home became much easier when I crossed Forrest Avenue and walked the last lonely block to my apartment. I was really convinced Professor McMasters never slept. He was always tackling a second and third task simultaneously. And true to form, sometime during that afternoon, he must have hired a battalion of conscientious teenagers to clear all the sidewalks around the square. Espousing the high correlation between customer satisfaction, loyalty, and revenue generation, the economic dynamo was always advising,

"You take good care of your customers, and they'll take good care of you."

When I reached the outside entrance, I kicked the remaining snow from my rigid All-Stars and trudged up the dim stairway with every intention of remedying more than two weeks of custodial neglect. But after emptying the cupboard of its last can of sardines and finishing the quickly fermenting orange juice, I realized my heart was not really into housekeeping that evening. I rationalized I still had an entire day to complete the mission before Catherine arrived. So I sat down on the sofa and began reminiscing with some sense of satisfaction about this all-important first semester of graduate studies.

Since I'd performed well as an undergraduate, I thought I'd do well in my doctoral classes. But despite the past successes, I still heard small voices questioning whether the outcome would be the same as before. And to provide full disclosure, the one course that gave me real pause was J. Alfred's introductory course. He had a reputation. He was demanding. And most importantly, he was my mentor. Somehow I dodged all the bullets and established a relationship with him based primarily on a mutual respect for scholarship.

Beyond the graduate studies, I also had concerns about the advanced composition and novel courses I was teaching for the first time. While I understood the source of my anxiety, my apprehension didn't dissipate until at least a third of the way through the semester. Once I'd graded several exercises, something clicked, and the tension spontaneously began disappearing. The rise of the novel course, however, was the more problematic of the two classes. I believed the anxiety lingered because, as I indicated earlier, I had to doggedly fight my way through Richardson and unleash some of the greatest performances of *léger de main* produced in a university classroom. But by semester's end I could happily report none of my students ever suspected my actual distaste for the author's rigidity, morality, and epistolary works.

I don't want to leave the wrong impression here. I thoroughly enjoyed teaching these superior undergraduates. And there were some truly magical moments. Besides the discussion of Melville's "Chapter LX: The Line" and Donna's essays in the experimental course, arguably the most intellectually stimulating and pleasurable moments involved the class discussions of Sterne's avant-garde, eighteenth-century masterpiece, *Tristram Shandy*. I don't believe there would be anyone in the course who'd strongly disagree with my personal assessment. We all felt *Tristram* appeared as fresh today as when Sterne penned the work over an eight-year period beginning in 1759. It was a theatrical tour de force, a pioneering anti-novel, which few understood at the time.

Everything was new in *Tristram*, especially the typography, the formatting, and the tortured plot. There are short, one-sentence chapters; misnumbered chapters; black, blank, or marbled pages; squiggles and dashes; index fingers pointing to passages; an abundance of italics and Gothic letters; and entire pages of Latin text. The dedication "To the Right Honorable John, Lord Viscount Spencer" appears at the beginning of volume 5, more than two hundred and fifty pages into the work.

And at the end of the sixth volume, after drawing schematics depicting the multitude of digressions appearing throughout the first three hundred and fifty plus pages of the book, the narrator promises a volume 7, which he indicates will be like "a line drawn as straight as I could draw it, by a writing master's ruler . . . turning neither to the right hand or to the left." Of course, Sterne has set us up for the joke—volume 7, containing almost fifty pages and forty-three chapters, is one total digression having nothing whatsoever to do with the rest of the work.

One of the students suggested if we didn't know how Sterne had drafted the book, we could have easily come to the conclusion he first wrote a straightforward novel, threw the pages into the air, and then reassembled them in a totally random order. Her remark gave me an idea for a bit of lighthearted scholarship, since all my students were in the throes of midterm exams. How about an in-class storyboarding exercise to straighten out the plot? Using a play-on-words to provide a hint, I asked the students to explain the "thrust" of the novel. One of the playful fellows in the back of the room responded immediately that Tristram is attempting to understand the peculiarities in his nature and eventually identifies two key moments primarily responsible for his eccentricities: (1) on the verge of being conceived, his mother interrupts his henpecked father to determine whether he has forgotten to wind the clock, and (2) while Tristram is relieving himself out an open window as a young lad, the sash slams down on his genitals.

After an animated half hour of analyses, we'd identified the fictional chronology of key events ranging from 1644 to 1767 and then listed where those sequential events occurred in the book. We concluded that to tell the story in strict chronological order, we'd have to restructure the nine volumes as 2, 6, 8, 9, 1, 3–5, and then full circle back to volume 2 with the digressive volume 7 standing alone.

I smiled nostalgically, looked about the room, and then spotted another neglected pile of mail that I'd allowed to accumulate for several weeks. I had scanned the envelopes daily and stacked them neatly on the small, damaged end table, successfully hiding the annoying, indigenous cigarette burn. During those weeks of neglect, I had taken the time to open only one letter, the one from Catherine, which had arrived three days ago during the mad rush to the finish line. Since I was really feeling the pressures of finals week, I must confess I only skimmed the four pages primarily to ensure everything was still on track for her Saturday afternoon arrival. After I had confirmed Catherine would be on the weekend Greyhound, I set the letter aside, rationalizing I would fully savor her words soon after finishing my tests and professorial responsibilities.

So I now leaned back into the sofa and began reading the news, most of which related to Catherine's academic plans. After indicating she had received an acceptance letter from the admissions office, she explained she would definitely be living on campus in university housing. This was an immutable regulation. All incoming female undergraduates regardless of age had to live either in a dormitory or a sorority until completion of their sophomore year.

She said she'd decided to undertake a premed curriculum and was happy to be arriving early so that "the wily veteran" could assist the "struggling freshman" with the registration process and course selection. One course, however, had already been set. Since she'd successfully completed high school honors classes in anatomy, biology, and chemistry, Catherine had appealed to the Anatomy Department requesting admission to the upper-level embryology-comparative anatomy course, "Morphogenesis of the Vertebrates," and had been granted a waiver to enroll in the demanding advanced class.

Catherine also indicated she'd been awarded a partial, needs-based scholarship but would have to work part-time to bridge the shortfall. Since she'd be studying medicine, her first choice for employer would be the McGill General Hospital, which she described as a highly respected teaching facility. She concluded her letter by again thanking me for helping her to sort through the issues, bring closure to the past few difficult years, and synthesize the compelling life lessons concealed within the decisive match, the "Pearl of Zandvoort."

11

Nd6 Qf8   Nxb7 Nd4

IT NEVER MADE sense to me, a death sentence so soon after birth. Why the compression? Why the non sequitur? Some kind of cosmic joke? But this wasn't the time for an existential conversation. Catherine had just dropped by the office after her job interview to eagerly announce she'd been hired as a nurse's aide in the pediatric cancer ward at McGill General. I gave her a big hug, congratulated her on her good fortune, and invited her down to the faculty lounge for a laudatory Darjeeling.

As we sipped our tea, I shook my head and said, "You've sure made a lot of headway since you got here late Saturday afternoon."

"Yeah, I got right on it. Let's see, I've settled in the dormitory, registered for classes, purchased my books, and finalized my financial aid package," she said with a smile.

"Impressive! But as I said before, the only concern I have is your workload. I mean, being a freshman, getting used to everything and working part-time. And the courses aren't trivial. Besides the sophomore-level anatomy course you petitioned to take, there's advanced German, inorganic chemistry, ah . . . ah . . ."

Catherine chimed in, "Calculus . . . and . . . and advanced English composition."

"Yeah, and that composition course puts the icing on the cake. Of all the instructors, you ended up with my graduate school mentor, J. Alfred Wagner. He's notorious for tormenting undergraduates at least once every academic year."

"I know it'll be challenging, Andrew, but I want to get the premed requirements out of the way as soon as I can. And you know I'm not afraid of hard work."

"I know you're not. I know." I paused and made a pivot away from the sensitive academic workload subject. "Speaking of hard work, when do you start at the hospital?"

"Next Monday morning. I'll work full-time all next week before school starts. Make a little extra money. But when classes begin, I'll be working part-time." She paused and then switched gears. "That's enough about me. How about you? What have you been up to while I was away? . . . Oh yeah, I remember. You were going to a Halloween soiree. How'd that work out?"

"I can't lie. It was pretty good."

"Pretty good? Like what?"

"Professor McMasters's homemade Witches Brew. The buffet. The toasted seafood canapés."

"Just the food was 'pretty good'? What about the people? Any interesting folks show up?"

I nodded. "As you'd expect, a number of scholars. But there was also a novelist, a poet, and . . . and a dramatist. They'll be artists in residence and be teaching a course or two."

Catherine probed gently, "Anything else?"

I paused, replaying the soiree in my head and exclaimed, "Ah, I almost forgot the most exciting thing of all. *The Messenger*."

"*The Messenger?*"

"A literary journal. It's Professor McMasters's idea. The creative artists in the department will contribute original existential works, mirror the movement that began in Europe after the war. I'm going to be one of the editors."

"Oh, Andrew, that sounds fantastic. How exciting for you."

"Yeah, a bunch of us contributors and editors got together for an update meeting just the day before yesterday."

"How'd it go?"

"Great! I could tell that everyone's serious about getting the journal up and running. Professor Talley filled us in on the short stories he'll contribute. Sanders described his poems. Gould said he was polishing off an exploratory essay on European existentialism, and Ridley says he has a promising essay, 'The Impact of Physical and Mental Trauma on Beckett's Worldview.' I know the names don't mean anything to you now, but you'll meet all the players soon, and I'm sure you'll find them fascinating. And I'm sure others on staff will want to contribute to the project too. You know, poetry, short stories, a play or two and the like."

Catherine sat up and exclaimed, "I'd love to get involved, working with such a creative group! It'd be so stimulating."

I smiled and pushed back gently, "Now, Catherine, remember, it's your freshman year. You're already working part-time. . . ."

"I know, I know." Catherine paused and looked at her watch. "Wow, it's getting late. I better be heading back to the dorm and get some reading done. I want to hit the ground running a week from Monday."

"I know you're working full-time this coming week and I'll be tied up with course prep, so how about I pick you up at your dorm late Saturday afternoon. We can walk back to the Rainbow Room and prepare an exquisite dinner for two. What do you say?"

She smiled broadly. "I say count me in!"

The following morning I walked over to Redman Hall for a scheduled meeting with J. Alfred Wagner. It was so much different now. I knew what to expect. I had been in the arena with the man and escaped with my life. While there was less tension and more collegiality in the room this time, everything else remained the same—the cigar stub, the clutter, the crew cut, the blue oxford shirt, the rolled-up sleeves, and the navy bowtie with the small magnolia blossoms.

The brief agenda was to firm up my spring curriculum and discuss the two undergraduate courses I would be teaching. Since I had taken Early American Literature and Shakespeare's Early Plays in the fall, it was very easy to settle on two of my three graduate courses, American Literature, 1800—1900, and Shakespeare's Major Plays. The third selection required a bit more time; but after weighing the pros and cons of several tempting choices, we agreed on Contemporary Theater from Shaw to the Present.

As for the undergraduate courses, we decided I would be teaching one section of English composition and a 200-level experimental workshop, Topics in American Literature and Culture. Doctor Wagner and I just had to fill in the blanks. What would be a scintillating subject that the English majors and I could really enjoy? The magnificent bastard had done it again! He had conjured up a topic that would synthesize my classroom responsibilities, my love of trains, and my extracurricular activities on *The Messenger*.

For whatever godforsaken reason, J. Alfred had been reading Nels Anderson's pioneering 1923 field-based study, *The Hobo: The Sociology of the Homeless Man*. He was on a roll. Why not base the seminar on Anderson's work, perhaps something like The Literature and Myth of the American Hobo? We brainstormed and identified at least three additional texts: Woody Guthrie's *Bound for Glory*, Ben Reitman's *Sister of the Road: The Autobiography of Boxcar Bertha*, and Jack Black's *You Can't Win*.

My creative juices were flowing now. I suggested setting the stage with an introductory examination of the wanderer through the ages from Odysseus to the Canterbury pilgrims, to Humphrey Clinker, Moll Flanders, Tom Jones, Oliver Twist, and Huckleberry Finn. As the professor rose from his chair, he added, "And don't forget Chaplin." I rose, nodded in agreement, shook his hand, and quickly left the office with so much more energy than when I had entered the room. My next stop would be the library to retrieve copies of the aforementioned texts, which would serve as the framework for the experimental seminar. This was going to be fun; I had never heard of any of the authors other than Woody Guthrie, let alone having read any of the assigned works.

The prospects of teaching another probing, innovative course had also highly motivated me to delve into some of the other challenges lurking in my own graduate school classes. I checked the syllabus for the American literature course and determined the midterm paper would be due soon after we had completed our discussions of Melville and Poe. I immediately began mulling over several potential topics for the midterm requirement.

But it was a serendipitous visit to the Unicorn Bookstore that inspired my future choice of subjects. I had actually gone to the quaint establishment seeking copies of Olson's and Tyndale's poetry, which Donna had referenced in her argument and persuasion essay at the end of the first semester. When I located Olson's poems, I noticed another of his books lying facedown on the dusty shelf. Everything was coming full circle. Olson's title was *Call Me Ishmael*, the opening line in Melville's *Moby-Dick*.

I opened the Melville study and read Olson's prologue, which cited Owen Chase's narrative of the whaleship *Essex* "struck head-on twice by a bull whale, a spermaceti about 85 feet long, and with her bows stove in, filled and sank." I continued skimming the next few pages and stumbled on the following intriguing observations:

> Among the Egyptians Horus was the god of writing and the god of the moon, one figure for both, a WHITE MONKEY. . . . [Melville] had a pull to the origin of things, the first day, the first man, the unknown sea. . . . He sought prime. He had the coldness we have, but he warmed himself by first fires after Flood. It gave him the power to find the lost past of America, the unfound present, and make a myth, Moby Dick, for a people of Ishmaels. The thing got away from him. It does, from us. We make AHAB, the WHITE WHALE, and lose them.

I next climbed the curved stairs to the second floor and quickly found a copy of Chase's narrative. I flipped the book over and read the descriptive notes on the back cover. The publisher described Chase's *Shipwreck* as the first in a series of American seafaring works including Poe's *Narrative of Arthur Gordon Pym of Nantucket* and Melville's *Moby-Dick*. Voilà! Game, set, match! The mythmaker Olson had opened my eyes to a midterm topic.

I had read *Pym* and *Moby-Dick* as an undergraduate. The word *white* in the Olson passage now added new, significant connectivity and meaning to the two works. Melville must have read *Pym* before launching his whale. I now remembered the ending of Poe's novel—Pym and Peters had escaped an ambush near the South Pole, stolen a small boat, and begun drifting south in the milky white waters. A fine white powder then began to fall around them, and a mysterious white animal floated by their small canoe.

Next, they encountered a large white curtain with indistinct images flitting about behind it, as gigantic, white birds began flying out from behind the inexplicable veil. Pym and Peters were finally caught up in a strong current, which steered them inexorably toward a violent chasm. At the last instant, a huge shrouded figure with skin the perfect whiteness of snow rose in their path, perhaps in a vain attempt to save them from plunging over the steep cliffs to a certain doom.

I placed the Chase volume under my arm and headed back downstairs to locate a copy of *Moby-Dick*. I remembered my undergraduate professor describing "The Whiteness of the Whale" as a key chapter to understanding Melville's major theme. There it was now, chapter sixty-two. I raced through paragraph after paragraph; and finally, lightning struck:

But not yet have we solved the incantation of this whiteness, and learned why it appeals with such power to the soul; and more strange and far more portentous—why, as we have seen, it is at once the most meaning symbol of spiritual things, nay, the very veil of the Christian's Deity; and yet should be as it is, the intensifying agent in things the most appalling to mankind. Is it that by its indefiniteness it shadows forth the heartless voids and immensities of the universe, and thus stabs us from behind with the thought of annihilation, when beholding the white depths of the Milky Way? Or is it, that as in essence whiteness is not so much a color as the visible absence of color, and at the same time the concrete of all colors; is it for these reasons that there is such a dumb blankness, full of meaning? . . . And of all these things the Albino Whale was the symbol. Wonder ye then at the fiery hunt?

As I read the passage, I could hear the echoes from *Pym*: "whiteness," "soul," "veil," "milky," "white." But it was so much more than the diction. It was the profound common meaning buried within the paragraphs and summed in a single word, "ambiguity." Melville and Poe were depicting existential ambiguity. Camus would have felt very comfortable with the thinking: "indefiniteness," "heartless voids," "immensities of the universe," "annihilation," "white depths of the Milky Way," "dumb blankness full of meaning." Pym and Ahab both died attempting to pierce the veil. Ahab's symbolic quest for existential certitude was the true reason for the "fiery hunt":

> Hark ye yet again—the little lower layer. All visible objects, man, are but as pasteboard masks. But in each event—in the living act, the undoubted deed—there, some unknown but still reasoning thing puts forth the moldings of its features from behind the unreasoning mask. If man will strike, strike through the mask!

I returned *Moby-Dick* to the shelf and headed for the cash register at the front of the store with a spring in my step. After happily paying for my purchases, I exited onto Main Street with Chase's *Shipwreck*, Olson's *Call Me Ishmael*, and a midterm paper well under control.

It had snowed again from late Friday night into Saturday morning, rejuvenating the fading, packed layer deposited by the rare blizzard the previous week. Books had been off limits all day as I cleaned house and ventured into the frozen wonderland seeking quality ingredients for Catherine's promised meal. Despite the icy walks and skidding taxis, I managed to arrive in the dorm lobby precisely at five o'clock. I called up to her room to let her know I was waiting.

When the elevator doors opened minutes later, my mind flashed back to Catherine descending the Greyhound steps and slowly gliding toward me. The flowing dark green autumnal dress had been replaced by winter slacks and a rich hunter green gabardine coat, belted, with turn-back cuffs, and generously trimmed in thick shearling. But what did remain from that earlier visit was the striking, romantic navy blue beret sweeping down across the right side of her attractive forehead. She smiled, brushed lightly against my cheek, and gently pulled me toward the door.

On the way over to the apartment, we walked arm-in-arm beneath the radiant streetlights speaking quietly about what we had accomplished over the past few days. As we passed through a modest residential neighborhood near campus, our serious discussion abruptly ended when we stopped to help a small boy and girl, perhaps a colleague's children, finish the jolly snowman they had begun on their front lawn. It was a magical moment for us. Hope, rare laughter, and the innocent memories of a shared childhood fused in the frosted twilight further strengthening the growing bonds between us.

The laughter and the reminiscences continued as we sautéed the veal, whipped the potatoes, and prepared the Caesar salad Cardini style. When the sumptuous feast was artfully arranged on the laminated "blue moon," we sat down, raised our manhattans in the shimmering candlelight, and toasted a promising future in McGill. Even stowing the leftovers and washing the dishes failed to alter the upbeat mood. And after restoring the kitchen to better than its original state, we picked up the flickering tapers and moved quietly into the living room.

I searched the record bin for an appropriate selection and positioned Mendelssohn's *Calm Sea* on the turntable. I placed my candle on the Art Deco bookcase next to the medieval board and sat down near Catherine to share the sublime, mythic opening, which musically expressed how I felt when we were together. As we listened to the lengthy overture, our eyes were drawn to the glimmering Siege of Acre, where the candlelight animated Richard, Reginald, and Saladin.

It was the ideal moment to personally thank Catherine for the special gift and the priceless message she had hidden within her ingenious note. I never mentioned the word *commitment*, which was the acknowledged thrust of her brief thank you. I was determined to give her the space she needed to resolve any doubts she had about our relationship before acting on her pledge. She had suffered enough and sacrificed so much for everyone else in her family. The timing would be on her terms.

But as the evening progressed, the earlier banter became softer recollections and finally a mystical stillness. As the silence deepened and the music filled our senses, we found ourselves gazing into each other's eyes and realizing the time was now. We curled into each other, gently kissed, and softly began exploring the dreams that for so long had been denied to both of us.

Catherine and I didn't see much of each other the following week. She was working full-time at the hospital, and I was busy preparing lectures for the two classes I was teaching. And to top it all off, we had to cancel the weekend because I had contracted the worst kind of flu. On the second day of classes, Catherine stopped by my private office in the afternoon to check on my condition. After entering, she closed the door behind her, slipped her arms around the back of my neck, and told me how much she had missed me. Despite my protestations about likely contagion, she smiled, leaned in, and passionately kissed me.

After several moments of silent embraces, I cleared a stack of books off my visitor's chair. "Here, take a seat. So, tell me, how've the first two days gone?"

She laughed. "Okay so far. I've only had two classes, but I'm already fluent in German."

"Really?"

She nodded and began speaking, "Der junge Mann, der 'Englisch spricht, ist gerade zum Chef gerufen worden.'"

"I'm impressed!"

She laughed aloud.

"What's so funny?" I asked.

"Those are the only words I know. My German professor wanted us to memorize the sentence because it illustrates many of the finer points of German grammar."

"Seriously, what does it mean?"

Catherine responded lightheartedly, "The young man, who speaks English, has just been called into the boss's office."

I laughed and replied, "Well, I don't care what it means. It still sounds impressive." I paused and then asked, "You said you'd had two classes. What was the other?"

"The Morphogenesis of the Vertebrates."

"The comparative anatomy/embryology course?"

"Yeah. It's even better than I thought it would be."

"How so?"

"We've been looking at cross sections of seventy-two-hour chick embryos, and it forces you to think three-dimensionally so you can visualize the blastocyst, the blastopore, the ectoderm . . ." Sensing my eyes were beginning to glaze over trying to comprehend words sounding more foreign than the German she'd reeled off earlier, Catherine quickly changed the subject.

"You got time to walk over to the Anatomy Department in Carmichael Hall? It's where I'll be doing my laboratory work. I'd like to show you around."

I shook my head teasingly and replied, "I don't know, Catherine, I've still got a lot of prep work to finish." I paused and smiled. "But your wish is my command. So let's go!"

As we entered the gross dissection lab, I fully understood why I intuitively thought Catherine would make an excellent doctor or surgeon. For the past few months, I had witnessed a steadiness and unflappability that would serve her well in a crisis environment. Here we were walking through a large room with at least a dozen long rectangular tables overflowing with severed arms and legs. They had the color and appearance of orange paraffin, which we normally associate with the waxy lips and noses of young Halloween goblins. Thankfully, the stumps were capped with a thick layer of surgical gauze. Catherine didn't flinch.

Like a docent in a museum Catherine calmly pointed out the key exhibits in each gallery. "Here we have our arms and legs. Here we have our torsos. Over here we have our heads in jars. And over there, running along the outer walls, we have a cadaver, which has been cross-sectioned into one-inch-thick slices from head to toe." She then guided me over to the wall for a closer inspection. "You see these three cross sections here?"

I nodded warily. "Yeah. . . ."

"They're slices through the stomach. You see the white chunks and round green things there?"

I gulped and replied, "Yeah."

"It's undigested turkey and peas—the main course this fellow had requested before they executed him."

I didn't respond. I just shook my head in awe.

She next led me down some metal stairs to a dimly lit basement, which reeked of formaldehyde. When she flipped on the switch, we were standing near a large circular vat. As we moved closer to the tank, I could see a number of bodies floating about in the acrid fluid.

She pointed. "You see the gaff over there on the wall?"

"Yeah."

"You see the gurney over there against the cabinets?"

I nodded, not sure I wanted to hear this.

"Those are my new tools."

"Tools?"

"Yeah. I've taken on a second job to earn a little more money."

"I'll probably regret asking . . . but doing what?"

"Fishing the cadavers out of the vat here, loading them on the cart, and taking them upstairs for graduate-level dissections."

I just shook my head. When we are confronted with the truly grotesque, our minds have the uncanny ability to formulate strange associations. All I could think about was Stevenson's short story, "The Body Snatcher," in which Fettes and Macfarlane attend medical school and are responsible for paying shady men for cadavers they use in gross dissection classes.

As we climbed back up out of the underworld, I said, "It's beyond me. I don't know how you do it. Honestly, it ain't my cup of tea, but more power to you." I smiled wryly, and Catherine took my hand, a glint in her eyes. We then walked out onto the front steps of Carmichael Hall, briefly kissed, and made plans to see each other over the weekend before going our separate ways for the evening.

The next morning I attended my first two classes, Contemporary Theater and Shakespeare's Major Plays. Professor Harbin assigned Shaw's *Candida* for the following week. I had seen the play in hometown repertory, when I was fairly young; but frankly all I remembered about the long work was a wife, a husband, and a young poet, who had learned to live without happiness. Thankfully, Professor Maxwell had begun his Shakespeare course with the highly underrated history play, *Richard II*, which featured some of the most elegant language of the Elizabethan Age:

> How sour sweet music is,
> When time is broke and no proportion kept!
> So is it in the music of men's lives. . . .
> For God's sake, let us sit upon the ground
> And tell sad stories of the death of kings. . . .

But it was my experimental workshop in the afternoon, my "hobo class," that supplied the memories we continually expect but rarely experience. I entered the filled room, walked to the lectern, and quickly opened my notebook. I was almost ten minutes late. I had run into Jeffrey Kline on my way over to Redman Hall. He was excited about a one-act play he would be submitting for the inaugural issue of *The Messenger*. The absurdist plot would be something of a blend between Ionesco's *Chairs* and Simpson's *Resounding Tinkle*. I listened patiently, resisting every impulse to glance at my watch before finally extricating myself and running the rest of the way to class.

I now hurriedly located my opening remarks and began speaking: "Through much of our century, the hobo's been the foremost symbol of American freedom. Using Anderson's *The Hobo: The Sociology of the Homeless Man*, Guthrie's *Bound for Glory*, Reitman's *Sister of the Road*, and Black's *You Can't Win* as guideposts, we'll explore the myth of this celebrated, iconic figure of the open road. We'll place this twentieth-century itinerant in context by examining wanderers throughout the ages, from Odysseus to the Canterbury pilgrims, to Tom Jones, Huck Finn, and Charlie Chaplin."

I paused briefly and for the first time lifted my head to scan the room; and there she was sitting on the far aisle in the second row. Our eyes locked. I stifled a broad smile, quickly looked down at my notes, and continued reading. "We'll examine why the hobo has been romanticized as a symbol of freedom, why the vagabond is fading from our collective consciousness, and what this disappearance implies about our current culture." My delivery now was so much different than it was just moments before. My voice rang out. I hoped my students would feel the anticipation, excitement, and optimism I sensed, knowing Donna had signed on for another semester.

When class was over, I paid Professor McMasters a visit to drop off my rent check and find out how he was progressing with *The Messenger* layout. As he opened the door, he exclaimed, "Hey, Andrew! Come on in. Willis is here dropping off his manuscript."

Ridley rose from his chair and extended his hand. "Good to see you, Andrew."

I shook his hand firmly. "Good to see you too, Willis."

The professor jumped in, "Would you like to join us in a cup of breakfast tea, Andrew?"

"No, thank you, sir, I'll pass. I can't stay long. I was just dropping off my check and seeing how you're making out with *The Messenger*."

"So far so good. Everything's still on track for an April launch! Counting Willis's essay here, I've already gotten four manuscripts for review." A blast of noise greeted us from the kitchen. "Excuse me, boys. The kettle's whistling. I'll be back shortly with the tea, Willis."

As the professor rushed off to the kitchen, I resumed our conversation. "So you've finished your paper, Willis? Congratulations. What's the title again? Something like, 'The Impact of Physical and Mental Trauma on Beckett's Worldview,' wasn't it?"

"Yeah, that's right."

"Sounds fascinating. I love Beckett. Tell me how you made the argument."

Sensing I was sincerely interested, Ridley enthusiastically launched into an overview: "Since few in the States would be familiar with Beckett, I begin with the obligatory biographical material, you know: Good Friday, 1906; Cooldrinaugh in Foxrock; Oscar Wilde's school; Dublin University; *Wisden Cricketers' Almanack*; Trinity College; École Normale Supérieure; helping Joyce research *Finnegans Wake*; publishing a defense of Joyce with William Carlos Williams; observing Lucia's disturbing mood swings; making it clear he came to see the master and not the daughter; and finally being booted from the Robiac circle by Joyce, the outraged father. I then finish the introductory paragraphs highlighting Beckett's early works of poetry, short stories, and full-length prose.

"After the opening, I move on to Beckett's first plays to introduce the existential emphasizing 'patience,' 'waiting,' 'ordeal,' and charged phrases such as 'cosmic indifference,' 'void of meaning,' 'tragic absurdity,' and 'the incontrovertible fact of dying.' I then quote the early comic novel, *Murphy*, to illustrate Beckett's point of view." He looked down at his essay and began reading:

> Some hours later Cooper took the packet of Murphy's ashes from his pocket, where earlier in the evening he had put it for greater security, and threw it angrily at a man who had given him great offence. It bounced, burst, off the wall on to the floor. . . . By closing time, the body, mind and soul of Murphy were freely distributed over the floor of the saloon; and before another day had been swept away with sand, the beer, the cigarette butts, the glass, the matches, the spits, and the vomit.

"Man, that's good stuff!" I interjected.

Reveling in my enthusiasm, Ridley smiled and said, "Yeah, really packs a punch!"

The professor returned and said, "Excuse me. I don't want to interrupt but here's your tea, Willis."

"Thank you, sir. If you don't mind, would you please put my

cup on the end table over there." He laughed and added jokingly, "As you can see, I'm really on a roll."

Professor McMasters responded in kind. "Yeah, I can see, and far be it from me to get in the way of that express barreling down the rails!"

After we shared a good laugh, the professor sat down in one of his overstuffed chairs, and I set the ball back up on the tee for Ridley. "So following that great quote from *Murphy*, where did you go next?"

"I argue that Beckett's life experiences greatly influenced his major plays. First there's the theme of 'waiting.' I explain Beckett had been part of the French underground fighting the Germans during their occupation of France. When Beckett's resistance group was betrayed, he fled south and lived there for years hidden with friends in a small village hotel. What were they doing? Waiting for the war to end, and nobody knew when that would be. So Beckett and his friends passed the time trying to find topics for conversation; and when they ran out of one topic, they had to find another. And that is the pattern of the conversations in *Waiting for Godot*."

"Wow! So that's why the dialogue is all over the place. I've seen the play twice and had no idea why the conversations were so disjointed, jumping from one thing to the next. . . . Sorry, Willis, go on. This is really fascinating."

"Well, I next identify a potential source for the themes of randomness and chance pervading Beckett's works. While walking home from a Parisian restaurant with friends, Beckett was stabbed by a known pimp. One of Beckett's lungs was pierced, and the knife barely missed his heart. His old friend, Joyce, came to the rescue, securing a private hospital room and a qualified doctor to treat him. Fortunately, Beckett fully recovered from the attack, but it left permanent psychological scarring.

"Beckett later visited the attacker in prison and asked why he had been stabbed. The assailant, ironically named Prudent, answered, 'I don't know why, sir. I'm sorry.' Beckett later described the irrational denouement: 'The desperado got off with two months, not bad for a fifth conviction. I am still without my clothes, taken away from me at the time as pièces de conviction and never produced. I have now to prove they ever belonged to me.'"

Professor McMasters jumped in. "Pretty grim view, huh, Willis?"

"Not entirely, sir. Toward the conclusion of the essay, I explain Beckett's vision was not entirely bleak. While his existential antiheroes were often miserable, morbid, and morose, they could display hopeful signs of cheerful pessimism, just as Beckett had done while walking through a London park. It was a beautiful summer morning, sunny, the grass green, the birds singing, blossoms blooming everywhere. Beckett observed how beautiful everything was. His companion said, 'Yes, Sam, on a day like this it is good to be alive.' Beckett rejoined, 'Well, I wouldn't go as far as that.'"

I looked over at Professor McMasters and declared, "Willis's essay sounds pretty solid to me. What do you think, sir?"

He got up, walked over to Ridley, slapped him on the back, and replied, "I think Willis is ready for print!"

After reassuring the professor I would be dropping by regularly to help with the editing, I eased out of our impromptu meeting and began walking the short distance from Professor McMasters's place back to my apartment. But as I sauntered along, I glanced over toward the courthouse square and got a real jolt. I discovered the town fathers had apparently approved a worthy expenditure—additional floodlighting to fully illuminate the impressive dome and, unfortunately, the large cod weathervane that continually pointed toward Rainbow Row declaring I was a "fish," a chess dilettante, a failure.

When I opened the apartment door and flipped on the lights, I discovered Anna had been unusually busy that day. Seven pieces of mail were scattered about on the floor near the door. I gathered up the envelopes, tossed my books in the corner, and sat down to scan the letters. There were only two pieces of correspondence. The rest was either advertising or, even worse, bills.

The first of the two notes was actually a message from Catherine conveying a brief description of her initial encounter with J. Alfred Wagner and her first writing assignment. She said she felt very comfortable with her first project because she would have "home-field advantage." Through some unbelievable luck of the draw, J. Alfred had tasked her with analyzing the purpose, structure, diction, and tone of Faulkner's 1955 essay on the Kentucky Derby, "Kentucky: May: Saturday." "Reminds me of those old field trips we went on back in high school," she wrote, and I recalled our school visits to Lincoln's tiny cabin, Stephen Foster's "Old Kentucky Home," and the thoroughbred museum beneath the twin spires at the historic Downs. I smiled and honestly wondered why the gods were so supportive of her when they'd never lifted a finger to help me navigate J. Alfred's minefields.

I now turned to the other note, which had actually traveled through the postal service. I didn't recognize the elegant flowing script on the envelope; and there was no return address. How intriguing. I tore open the letter and immediately determined the correspondent. My heart began racing; it was Bianca. She said she wanted to meet to discuss her planned submissions to *The Messenger* and to explore a potential opportunity for the summer months after the semester had ended. The meeting place would be the student union, the time, two o'clock. She concluded her note with an enigmatic message in Portuguese, which I didn't understand:

> *A sua vida (. . .)*
> *Isso não é o meu amor; é apenas a sua vida.*
>
> *Amo-a como ao poente ou ao luar, com o desejo de que o momento*
> *fique, mas sem que seja meu nele mais que a sensação de tê-lo.*

12

Nxd8 Bb5   Nxe6 Bd3

I ARRIVED AT the student union ten minutes before our two o'clock meeting. I walked the length of the block-long building and waited for Bianca in the reading room. Although she was fifteen minutes late, I didn't mind. I got to soak up the beauty and elegance of the room, especially the eight stained-glass Sir Gawain masterpieces. Upon her arrival, we found a quiet space away from the madding crowd and sat down in a pair of blue upholstered chairs.

Bianca broke the ice by commenting on the stained-glass windows, which then allowed me to settle my nerves by relating a brief summary of *Sir Gawain and the Green Knight*. But rest assured, I steered as far away as I could from Lady Bertilak's repeated temptations of our well-intentioned hero. After getting Sir Gawain on his way back to Camelot, I turned to the business at hand, asking the gorgeous temptress to read several of the sonnets she proposed for the inaugural *Messenger*. We talked for hours and about much more than just business.

Not long after that charged meeting in the student union, I became convinced of two things: Bianca's latest poetry far exceeded the threshold for inclusion in *The Messenger*, and I would never exchange a McGill summer with Catherine for a whirlwind trip to Europe with engaging colleagues. Bianca's latest poems were so much more deeply personal than those of her previous volume, *Serra de Sintra*. Her earlier works reminded me of a Wordsworth composing lengthy pieces in reflective tranquility near Racedown or Tintern Abbey, fusing the physical and emotional to "clearly see into the light of things." But Bianca had now become the urgent Keats of "I Cry Your Mercy" and "When I Have Fears." She had moved beyond the extended, recollected landscapes near Coimbra to intense, personal sonnets of unrequited emotions, immediacy, and soulful isolation. I would have guessed she composed the poems more than a year ago, before the onset of her serious relationship with Jeffrey; but she hinted she had only begun writing them last year toward the beginning of November. When Bianca had finished reading several of the sonnets aloud, I enthusiastically congratulated her and promised to become a strong advocate for their inclusion in volume 1, number 1.

And then she surprised me again, this time with a generous offer of an all-expense-paid trip to Europe. Before Catherine's arrival on campus, I would have immediately accepted Bianca's invitation to fly to Portugal with her and her chosen retinue of Kline, Talley, and Sanders. Bianca's wealthy, entrepreneurial father had suggested she invite several guests at his expense to visit the Douro region near Pinhão to celebrate the sesquicentennial anniversary of the founding of the family's port wine business. And to top it all off, after the Douro festivities, the comprehensive itinerary would continue with engaging stopovers in several additional regions of the historic country. It would be an evolving and involved experience.

Bianca had just concluded her poetry reading when she detailed this unique offer. She gazed into my eyes and waited expectantly for my response. Under the circumstances, I just couldn't bring myself to say "no" right there on the spot. At that point I felt politic deferral trumped blunt refusal. And my ad hoc strategy appeared to work. When I asked if I could have some additional time to firm up my summer plans before responding definitively, she nodded, appearing relieved that at least I hadn't rejected her proposal outright.

Because of my heavy workload, the weeks passed quickly from winter into early spring, when the midterm exams and papers were due. I had guessed correctly that a highlight of the semester would be Donna's work in the "hobo class." As with her essays in the previous experimental composition course, Donna's midterm hobo paper surprised, delighted, and educated me. I began reading the first few paragraphs and remembered her earlier quote from William Carlos Williams, "Say it, no ideas but in things—." Her strategy would be to lay down a solid, fact-based foundation and then use these "things" to launch her "ideas" about absurdity, indifference, and a quest for certitude.

She first referenced Nels Anderson's sociological research, asking his questions and then supplying his scientific answers. Questions: "Why do men leave home? Why are there tramps and hobos? What are the conditions and motives that make migratory workers, vagrants, and homeless men?" Answers: "From the records and observations of a great many men the reasons they leave home seem to fall under several heads: (a) seasonal work and unemployment, (b) industrial inadequacy, (c) defects of personality, (d) crises in the life of the person, (e) racial or national discrimination, and (f) wanderlust." Donna pointed out that reasons (a) through (e) primarily related to causes well beyond the control of the tramp (i.e., they are potentially existential) and that it was only the last point (f) that the vagrant had any real hope of controlling at all.

Throughout her discussion of Anderson's innovative research, Donna skillfully incorporated real-life stories from Woody Guthrie's autobiography, *Bound for Glory*, to support and enliven the scientific findings about riding the rails, living in camps, and picking commercial fruit. But Donna left most of the enlivening to passages from Jack Black's 1926 influential autobiography, *You Can't Win*, and Dr. Ben Reitman's 1937 tour de force, *Sister of the Road: The Autobiography of Boxcar Bertha*. Donna quoted liberally to depict the hobo's real world, from Black's freight hopping, burglaries, drug abuse, arrests, and jailbreaks to Boxcar Bertha's free love communal farms, whorehouses, hobo jungles, and her questionable circle of associates—bohemians, extremists, pimps, and tramps.

At this point, Donna moved from "things" to "ideas." She provided the necessary literary backdrop, briefly describing the "wanderer contributions" of Homer, Chaucer, Defoe, Fielding, Dickens, Twain, and Hart Crane. She then circled back to Shakespeare to launch an extended discussion of a major theme—how the playwright had used dialogue between kings and jesters to depict reality and the human condition.

And as I would have expected after reviewing Donna's essays last semester, she then made a brilliant, near half-millennium leap from Shakespeare to Beckett. She argued that as Shakespeare's wise fools had taught their kings about alienation, indifference, and despair, Beckett's tramps today teach us about absurdity and angst in a meaningless world.

Since few readers would have been familiar with *Waiting for Godot*, Donna provided a brief synopsis and then turned to the existential themes in Beckett's play—nothingness, absurdity, and death. Inspired by the starkness and nihilism of the years following World War II and the birth of the atomic age, existentialists saw the earth as orbiting a minor star in a remote location within the Milky Way, a galaxy containing billions of stars, in a universe of billions of galaxies. Small, helpless, insecure man had by chance (or as a cosmic joke) been dropped onto this tiny, insignificant planet surrounded by a vast universe of void and nothingness.

She then concluded her assignment by emphasizing Beckett's message to all of us delivered through his tramps in *Waiting for Godot*—confront the nothingness, absurdity, and death with courage:

> Let us not waste our time in idle discourse! Let us do something, while we have the chance! It is not every day that we are needed. . . . To all mankind they were addressed, those cries for help still ringing in our ears! But at this place, at this moment of time, all mankind is us, whether we like it or not. Let us make the most of it, before it is too late!

It was clear from the assignment there had been no diminution in either Donna's enthusiasm or performance from one semester to the next. As I was applying another well-deserved "A" to another of her highly refined essays, I had an idea that I believed could further motivate the highly talented undergraduate. I would recommend including Donna's insightful essay in the inaugural issue of *The Messenger*.

During the two weeks following midterms, Professor McMasters's apartment became a vortex of literary activity and, for the most part, my home away from home. After determining which of the submissions would make the final cut, the professor and I worked feverishly on the definitive formatting and editing to meet the printer's strict deadline. Because of my classroom and lecturing responsibilities, the process was touch and go all the way; but we succeeded in delivering the valuable package to the Beauregard Press at four forty-five on Friday afternoon, just fifteen minutes before the company's rigid closing time. The professor and I were admittedly conflicted. While on the one hand we were relieved to have met the challenging schedule, on the other hand, we knew we would never feel entirely at ease until we had had a chance to review the finished product poised for an aggressive national and intercontinental distribution.

So the long-anticipated publication date finally arrived. Professor McMasters had reserved the richly paneled Wittenberg Room in the student union to celebrate the launch of the first North American journal solely dedicated to the publication of existential poetry, fiction, drama, and essays. Among the invitees were the inaugural contributors and their families, members of the English and Theater Departments, senior university personnel, advertisers including research companies and university presses, and the print and broadcast media.

The stately banquet room was filled with large round tables and a dais, which had been erected opposite the massive doors at the far end of the cavernous room. This narrow platform held a central lectern and a dozen seats of honor, lined up from one end of the stage to the other. There was also a small semicircular space between the dais and the first row of tables reserved for the Pantheon Players, who serenaded us with Praetorian Tafelmusik throughout the celebratory feast.

After everyone had enjoyed a surprisingly tasty meal catered by the university's hospitality majors, the professor emeritus stepped to the microphone and introduced himself lightheartedly as the "McMasters of ceremonies." The joke worked; everyone groaned. The spry old fellow then walked over to a sturdy easel and flipped back a thick gray cloth, which had been concealing an enlarged facsimile of the table of contents for the inaugural issue. As he announced each of the works, the professor pointed in the direction of the author, who then rose to an admiring, heartfelt round of applause:

CONTENTS

INTRODUCTION

ESSAYS

When the last of the contributors had finished reading brief excerpts from their works, I stepped down off the dais, squeezed between the crowded, congratulatory tables, and found Catherine standing alone at the back of the room. She embraced me and whispered how proud she was of my work on *The Messenger*. As the admiring guests began milling about the packed room, I sensed they were on the verge of witnessing the same striking phenomenon I had observed six months before at the McMasters's Halloween soiree.

Many of the mesmerized male guests, advertisers, and media personnel had already begun slowly gravitating toward the captivating poetess, first isolating Jeffrey and then tightening a libidinous circle around their smiling, alluring prey. I tried desperately not to stare, but I, too, was drawn to her powerful animal spirit. As the lurid dance continued, Catherine glanced over at her spellbound lover and began tugging lightly at his arm signaling it was well past time to leave. Oddly enough, once we had exited the building, Catherine never passed judgment on the suggestive conduct of anyone, including me. But despite her reticence, I knew damn well the banquet that day would be the last time Catherine and Bianca would ever be in the same room together.

The longer I live the more strongly I believe Ahab had it right. There is some unknown reasoning thing lurking behind the unreasoning mask. While the spring semester had admittedly had its challenges, Catherine and I truly enjoyed our minimal time together. In fact, almost everything about our relationship was positive and symbiotic. Everything was going so well, that is, until several weeks after celebrating the launch of *The Messenger*. Catherine stopped by the office to drop a bombshell.

"I don't know how to break this, but I won't be staying with you at the apartment over the summer."

I didn't respond immediately. I was in a state of shock. All the planned summer activities—the canoeing, the picnics, the hiking, the concerts, the museums, and yes, even the gentle lovemaking—flashed before my eyes and vaporized in an instant. I took a deep breath and calmly asked, "Where you heading?"

She glanced down dejectedly and answered, "Back home."

"Back home? Why? You just made a clean break. Why risk everything going home?"

"Father needs me. He wrote this week he's having so much back pain he's got to have surgery. Without an operation he can't continue traveling for his job. So he wants me to come home and help him out until he can get back up on his feet."

"Catherine, not being an asshole or anything, but haven't you sacrificed enough for the family? Can't one of your brothers or sisters look after him now? Most of them are old enough to shoulder the responsibility."

"Father doesn't think so. He believes I'll help speed his

recovery. He promises he'll do everything in his power to get well so I can be back on campus for the fall semester. Honestly, Andrew, I really think I need to go." She paused and gazed into my eyes expecting a response.

So with the grimmest of gallows humor, I smiled and responded, "Well, in that case, I guess the mountains will have to come to Mohammed. How would I ever make it through the summer without seeing you at least once?"

She smiled, slipped her arms up around my neck, and whispered, "Thank you for understanding and not making this any more painful than it already is."

Throughout the remainder of the semester, I increasingly frequented the faculty lounge for strong black coffee to combat the constant workload fatigue. At least twice a week, I would run into Talley and Sanders, who knew I hadn't committed to the European trip. Since we got along socially and professionally, I tolerated their good-natured prodding because I believed they sincerely wanted to see me board the outbound plane.

Following Bianca's proposal earlier in the semester, I had seen her only that one time at *The Messenger* banquet, which never lent itself to speaking about her offer. But just before the last day of final exams, the stars aligned and the triumvirate surrounded me in the faculty lounge and politely demanded an answer. In hindsight, I don't know whether it was their effective cajoling, my disappointment in knowing I would be alone most of the summer, or my unfulfilled desire to visit the Old World, but I smiled and formally accepted Bianca's generous proposal. It was now an official party of five—Talley, Sanders, Kline, Bianca, and the potential fifth wheel, me. And I knew I would have to find just the right time down the road to explain to Catherine how I would be spending part of my summer "alone."

Knowing Catherine would have to vacate her dorm on the Saturday after finals, we planned on her staying at my place overnight before boarding the Greyhound Sunday morning. Following the routine I had adopted for all her other visits, I cleaned the apartment and then went shopping for the unique ingredients to prepare another exceptional albeit expensive meal.

Compared to that special winter night when we toasted our future, listened to Mendelssohn, and made love for the first time, the atmosphere that spring evening should have been at least as joyous, if not more so. We were in the same apartment. The meals were comparable. And we had more than survived a hectic semester; we had prevailed over it. But realizing Catherine was leaving the next day and we would most likely not see each other for several months cast a pall over what should have been a festive occasion. So throughout our subdued candlelit evening, there were many long moments of probing, reflective silence. Speech had become superfluous. We gazed longingly into each other's eyes and clearly understood what the other was feeling. We would try to remain strong, look beyond the months of separation and lose ourselves for a final time in gentle lovemaking.

We held each other throughout the sleepless night, as if vainly trying to prevent something precious from slipping away. When I heard the distant chimes and saw the early summer light, I kissed Catherine softly on the forehead, told her to stay in bed a while, and rolled out instinctively in the direction of the kitchen. Since Catherine had an early bus to catch, I wanted to ensure a proper Sunday send-off with stacks of buckwheat pancakes, thick slices of lean bacon, and genuine Vermont maple syrup. As expected, the rich, nostalgic aromas became irresistible, and in no time, Catherine had risen, slipped quietly into the kitchen, hugged me, and begun eagerly sampling the first batch of golden dollars right off the griddle.

Just before sitting down to breakfast, I walked over to the console and chose a meaningful symphony for our last few hours together, Mahler's Fifth in C-sharp Minor. There was no need playing the first two movements. Catherine and I had already spent much of our lives in a haunting minor key attempting to reach beyond the "high point," only to lose momentum and fall back into the familiar shadows.

So we began with the third movement, the lengthy *scherzo*, which was the keystone on which the Fifth pivoted from despair into radiant exuberance. The music reflected the changes in Mahler's life. He had been seriously ill, recuperated enough to return to his composing, and had just met Alma, one of the most magnetic personalities in all of Europe. As the couple grew closer and secretly engaged, Mahler composed the tender, searing *Adagietto* for strings and harp, which we now knew Mahler conceived as a "love letter" to his beautiful, brilliant Alma.

Soon the couple married and learned Alma was expecting their first child. Again, the music reflected positively what had been happening in Mahler's life. He composed an unambiguously optimistic rondo finale with fifteen minutes of melodic fireworks. For the climax, Mahler returned to the transcendent chorale, which had been overwhelmed in the frenzied second movement but had now returned triumphant in the fifth. And the progressive tonality from the first movement's funereal C-sharp minor to the finale's brilliant D major reflected Mahler's emotional and spiritual progression over the course of less than a year. So in a way, playing Mahler's Fifth had become my love letter to Catherine with a highly positive message that we, too, could overcome the disheartening obstacles we faced that day.

The dreaded time to leave for the Greyhound terminal had finally arrived, and we strolled silently, arm-in-arm along the now familiar route. As we neared the station, we discovered Catherine's bus had already pulled into one of the spaces at the front of the building. We hurried into the terminal, purchased her ticket, and then waited outside for the boarding announcement.

As the departure time approached, anxious outbound passengers began forming a short line near the front of the bus. Catherine and I chose to stand off to the side, where we could watch the boarding process and time it so she would be the last passenger up the stairs. When the driver appeared at the door and began punching tickets, Catherine and I embraced and shared one last passionate kiss. She told me how much she loved me, promised to write, and then turned to board the bus. As she reached the top step, she paused, turned, smiled bravely, and then disappeared into the darkness beyond the narrow door.

I waited until Catherine's bus pulled out into the Sunday traffic, and then I returned to the apartment, slumped back into the sofa, and listened to the Sarabande from Bach's Cello Suite Number 5. It is simultaneously simple and complex. It contains no chords and only seventy notes, yet it mysteriously allows us to plumb the soul. I never believed the contemplative secret lay in the soft melodic beauty, but in the vast distance between the notes. So much space-time for so much thought. A slant of summer light now pierced the shadows and settled squarely on the Siege of Acre. And for the first time, I heard the chorus sing: *Months alone. . . . Bianca. . . .Commitment.*

13

Bd5 Qf5   Nxd4+ Qxd5

OUR PAN AM super 7 made the crossing in a little less than eight hours. As we approached the rugged coastline of the Iberian Peninsula, the rising sun cast a pink hue over the stratus clouds and burnished the palace dome pushing up through a low, billowy layer hugging the umber shore. The pilot steered our Boston Clipper eastward up the Tagus River, banked northward over Saint George Castle, and then gently descended toward the midtown runway. The view was spectacular as we glided low over the old city—majestic cathedrals, imposing castles, towering monuments, lush emerald parks, and brilliant whitewashed houses with classic terracotta roofs.

Bianca, Talley, Sanders, and I collected our luggage, passed through customs, and then hailed a taxi over to the Santa Apolónia Terminal for the three-hour express up the Atlantic coast to Porto. I had telephoned Catherine a week before we left to ask about her father and to announce I had decided to take a brief trip to Europe with several of my colleagues. I explained the rationale I had honed for weeks: all expenses were paid; the excursion would enrich my graduate studies; and most of all, it would ease the deep loneliness I felt not having her on campus with me over the summer.

After asking several routine questions about the itinerary,

the flight plans, and the accommodations, she focused on the "several Pantheon colleagues." I first offered Talley, Sanders, and Kline, putting off the unpleasant for as long as possible. Catherine waited patiently, seeming to know I was withholding something. I hesitated and then awkwardly revealed Bianca would be traveling to Europe with us. The long silence at the other end of the line prompted me to launch a preemptive strike. I told Catherine I could only imagine what she must be thinking given Bianca's questionable behavior at the *Messenger* celebration but then emphasized Bianca's lover would be a permanent member of the traveling group. We declared an unspoken truce and nervously changed the subject to our planned course work for the upcoming semester. And after several minutes of conversation devoted primarily to our academics, I finally had to declare I had just deposited my last coin in the payphone. Catherine wished me safe travels and then whispered, "I love you. . . . I trust you."

I believe it was the day after I had spoken with Catherine we got the exciting news that Jeffrey's first full-length play, *What Others Only Tell You*, would open off-Broadway at the Sheep's Head in early September. So understandably, while Manhattan rehearsals were in for Jeffrey, a trip to Europe with friends was definitely out. When Talley, Sanders, Bianca, and I joined the deserving playwright at the Two-Way for several celebratory beers, he was quite apologetic about canceling on us; but we smiled and jokingly responded we understood that "the show must go on."

While I should have been exhausted after the long overnight flight to Lisbon, I was actually exhilarated and in my glory riding three different trains to reach our final destination. We pulled into Porto a little past noon, transferred onto a local train for a short ride out to Peso da Régua, and then caught the narrow-gauge steam train for the final journey to Bianca's estate near the small village of Pinhão.

The view out the window was stunning: miles of winding, deep blue river flanked first by olive groves and then by ancient vineyards rising in steep, narrow terraces with supporting rock walls handcrafted over the past four hundred years. Enologists agree that this rugged landscape dictates the special character of the wines. The Douro soil is primarily bits of sharp-edged schist, which the Tinta Roriz and Tinta Cão roots must penetrate, sometimes up to forty feet, to reach life-sustaining water. And the locals swear it is this century-old struggle for survival that creates the wine's unique, powerful, full-bodied intensity.

When the steam locomotive finally slowed to a stop in Pinhão, we collected our belongings and piled out onto the platform of one of the most beautiful railway stations in all of Europe. It's exterior walls were painted a gleaming white and decorated with twenty-four large blue azulejo panels depicting the many scenes associated with the region's wine production, including the vineyards, the rabelo boats, the river, the harvest, and two landscapes—the Cachão da Valeira and the iron bridge of Ferradosa—which have sadly disappeared.

As we entered the cozy, one-room building, Bianca smiled, dropped her bags, and began walking quickly with arms outstretched toward a tall, aging fellow wearing a charcoal touring cap and taupe jacket. The poetess and the old man embraced warmly and then walked arm-in-arm over to where we were standing. She tapped the old man on the forearm repeatedly and said to us, "I want you to meet our driver and footman for going on forty years, José Guilherme. José was like a second father to me while I was growing up on the estate."

We all smiled and said in unison, "Nice to meet you, sir." I then added, "You certainly do have a beautiful country here."

Bianca tapped José lightly on the forearm again and whispered to us as if he were out of earshot, "His English isn't very good." She then turned to the old man and pointed to each of us one at a time and said, "Pappie, this is Walt, this is Don, and this is Andrew."

The old man bowed and said, "*Boa tarde. Prazer em conhecê-lo.*"

After Bianca finished the introductions, José slipped on his leather driving gloves, motioned for us to follow him out the front door, and led us over to a 1938 Mercedes Benz Cabriolet B convertible parked at the side of the station. The vintage automobile had a glossy black finish, a burgundy leather interior, and a large whitewall spare mounted on the left side of the vehicle between the front fender and the driver-side door. While José stowed as much of the luggage as he could in the small trunk, we excitedly piled into the car and held the remainder of the bags on our laps.

The winding, narrow road to the estate was both scenic and dangerous, hugging the steep hillside and mimicking the twisting contours of the Douro River below. As we neared the family estate, we crossed over the Pinhão tributary near its confluence with the wider Douro flowing westward toward the sea. When José had cleared the last span of the riveted steel bridge across the Pinhão, Bianca asked her old friend to stop the Mercedes for a moment. "*Parar o carro*, Pappie."

After he had pulled off to the side of the road, she turned around to us and said, "Look back over your shoulders there toward the river. See that bridge spanning the stream out here in the middle of nowhere?"

We all nodded and Sanders answered for us, "Yeah, but what about it?"

"Well, it dates from the nineteenth century; and believe it or not, it was designed by Gustave Eiffel."

"Eiffel. Unbelievable," I mumbled and then thought, "Well, that sight alone was sure worth the price we paid for admission."

After several additional minutes of single lanes and harrowing hairpin turns, we reached the flowering front entrance, turned in between two eight-foot-high granite columns, and proceeded up a long driveway lined with tall eucalyptus forming a dense, fragrant canopy over the wide gravel road. When we reached the two-story fieldstone farmhouse, José blasted the horn several times announcing our "on-time" arrival less than two hours late. Responding to the driver's signaling, a middle-aged couple walked out onto the concrete landing, waved, and then descended the stairs toward the circular drive at the front of the house.

The tall, graying gentleman opened the passenger-side door, and Bianca stepped out, embraced him, and spoke softly in Portuguese. "Papa, Papa, *Eu senti tanto sua falta*." She next moved over to the elegant lady standing off to the side, hugged her firmly, and exchanged greetings this time in German, her mother's native tongue, "Mama. *Ich habe dich vermisst*." Bianca then excitedly turned toward the three of us and introduced us to her parents in English. "Well, here are the three guests I wrote to you about. This is Professor Talley, the novelist." Tally gave a brief nod of his head. "This is Doctor Sanders, the poet. Remember, I sent you a collection of his beautiful sonnets, *La Belle Époque*." Sanders smiled and gave a small bow. "And now, last but not least, this is Andrew, our adjunct professor of English and resident scholar." I nodded and said a formal, "How do you do?"

Mr. and Mrs. de Silva nodded, and Bianca's father responded in perfect Queen's English, "Welcome to our home. It's so nice you could join us for the celebration."

When the pleasantries had run their course, Bianca's father first signaled José to collect our bags and then warmly requested we follow him and his wife up the front steps into the manor house, which he emphasized had been in his family since the beginning of the nineteenth century. I would describe the quinta's style as "casual elegance," a charming blend of the modern and rustic, including many traditional Portuguese features as thick stone walls, high ceilings with wooden beams, natural stone door- and windowsills, and undulating antique ceramic tile floors.

The first story of the large, south-facing farmhouse consisted of a wide hallway leading to a spacious living room with a beautiful fieldstone fireplace in the northwest corner, a formal dining room with ancestral portraits and priceless silverware, a relaxed country kitchen, and a sitting room with an old Italian tapestry covering one wall, the only room in the house where the shutters were always closed to ensure the masterpiece didn't fade in the strong southern light.

The second floor contained six bedrooms of varying size and

decor, three facing north and three south. Bianca's family had named four of the rooms after the grape varieties cultivated on the estate: Tinta Roriz, Tinta Barroca, Tinta Cão, and Touriga Francesa. The other two bedrooms had special names and were used primarily for momentous family occasions. The one in the northeast corner of the house was called Nascence, which had been used for generations as a birthing room and was only occupied otherwise when the number of family members and guests exceeded the capacity of the four customary chambers. The other room symbolically located in the sunny southwest corner was named Morte and had been used over the centuries as a quiet, meditative place to comfort family members regretfully spending their last few days in the Douro paradise before embarking on their last journey into the mysterious unknown.

For the few days before the winery's sesquicentennial celebration, Bianca served as tour guide for her "special friends from North America." Since we were in recovery mode after our long overseas trip, Bianca chartered a traditional Portuguese rabelo for a private cruise up the Douro toward the small village of Tua. With our poetess companion translating for us, the river pilot explained the history of the small ship: "Our narrow boat here is single-masted and flat-bottomed. During the nineteenth and early twentieth centuries, our barks transported casks of port wine downstream from Pinhão to be stored in the extensive cellars of Vila Nova de Gaia, just across the river from Porto. Our gold-and-black boat here is about seventy feet long, has a large square sail, and is guided by a very long steering oar, which gives it the name *barco rabelo*, meaning 'boat with a tail.'" He then nodded, turned, and moved toward the dock. After slipping the thick ropes off the pilings, the pilot jumped up onto a high platform, grasped the loom, maneuvered the striped oar, and quickly pushed us away from the moorings and out toward the center of the gently flowing Douro.

When we arrived at the town wharf in Tua, Bianca generously paid the river pilot a round-trip fare even though she had already planned our return trip via the Douro Valley Railroad. She then motioned for us to follow her up the rising, stone-walled path to the two-story, whitewashed Tua railway station, featuring a four-foot-wide border of blue Portuguese tile encompassing the building at its base; two large, stone-lined windows on either side of a thick wooden door; and a tiled, ornamental canopy extending out over the narrow inbound and outbound platforms.

After entering the charming terminal, Bianca approached an old, bearded fellow behind the counter, spoke to him in Portuguese, and then rejoined our group holding tickets for what we thought would be the short ride back to Pinhão. But Bianca surprised us and led us out onto the opposite platform.

"Whoa! Where we headed?" Sanders asked.

She smiled coyly and replied, "North. Up the Tua Valley."

"*Where to* up the Tua Valley?" Talley probed.

"One of my favorite places on earth: Mirandela."

"Mirandela?" I asked.

"A picturesque medieval city. And the ride up the valley is spectacular."

Fifteen minutes later we boarded a small steam train with three antique passenger cars and were on our way. Since there were few people riding our train that day, one of the two conductors, who was relatively fluent in English, sat down across the aisle from us and described the onerous three-year challenge in the 1880s to complete the thirty-three-mile narrow-gauge line from Tua to Mirandela: "The construction teams used dynamite every day as they continuously faced solid blocks of granite and extremely wide canyons."

To emphasize the daunting tasks the nineteenth-century engineers faced, our skilled Tua Line expert added, "We are going to be crossing over four long bridges and traveling through three long tunnels before reaching Santa Luzia at the quarter mark of our trip up the valley."

Sanders leaned over toward Talley and said jokingly, "I hope nobody here's afraid of heights or the dark."

Talley laughed and shot back, "If they are, I guess we'll just have to hold their hands to help them get through it."

After describing these remarkable engineering triumphs and the workers' unheralded sacrifices, our enthusiastic conductor switched gears and spent the rest of the scenic tour up the valley pointing out magnificent landscape features, including thunderous waterfalls and a spectacular sweeping array of wild magenta peony, heart-flowered silver serapias, and pale blue Portuguese squill.

When we reached Mirandela, we climbed out onto the platform, found the designated walkway across the tracks, and strolled along a narrowing path behind a row of two-story houses until our trail dead-ended into a jumbled outcropping of bedrock. Bianca signaled for us to follow her along a garden pathway and onto the porch of the last house on the block. She then rapped hard on the screen door until the owner appeared and enthusiastically greeted our traveling companion. "*Olá, minha querida!*"

"*Olá, Francisco! Estou realmente com fome!*" Bianca replied.

The short, portly fellow opened the door and responded with a sweeping gesture meant for all of us, "*Bem-vindo! Bem-vindo!*"

He then guided us through the back rooms to the front of the house, where we found four tables set for customers. It appeared Bianca's old friend had established a small restaurant in his private residence and prepared all the public meals in his own kitchen. I immediately grasped the successful concept—customers enjoying friendly, authentic "down-home cooking" in an officially sanctioned commercial restaurant.

Because there were no formal menus and only a tiny blackboard hanging on the wall with unintelligible Portuguese scribbling, we relied solely on Bianca to order our meals. For hors d'oeuvres, we savored a small wheel of Serra da Estrela cheese, *broa* (cornbread), ripe olives, and the highly addictive little salt-cod cakes, *bolinhos de bacalhau*. Next came the thick, flavorful kale soup, *caldo verde*, and then the pièce de résistance, Mirandela's most famous cuisine, fried *alheira*, a type of sausage made of pork, cockerel, chicken, game, and bread and spiced with garlic and a little malagueta chili pepper.

And the red wine the owner had recommended? It was some of the best I had ever tasted—velvety, vibrant, resonant, and the exceptional product of a regional quinta rising high above the Douro opposite Pinhão. As we finished the hearty home-cooked meal, our genial host stopped by to suggest a refreshing São Tomé espresso and a sugary *torta de Viana* from a local *pastelaria*. How could we refuse? So with a couple bracing espressos and painfully rich sponge cakes under our loosened belts, we lumbered back to the Mirandela Station, caught the return train to Tua, and finally boarded the last westbound express toward home.

When my dad would say, "There's no rest for the wicked," Mom would immediately interrupt to softly amend Dad's maxim, substituting the less judgmental word "weary" for "wicked." So far on this trip, I would have to side with Mom; there was so much more weariness than wickedness by a long shot. After returning from Mirandela, Talley, Sanders, Bianca, and I sat outside on the timbered veranda under a flowering canopy until almost two in the morning sipping port and pressing every bit of meaning we could out of Pessoa's eighth English sonnet:

> How many masks wear we, and undermasks,
> Upon our countenance of soul, and when,
> If for self-sport the soul itself unmasks,
> Knows it the last mask off and the face plain? . . .
> And, when a thought would unmask our soul's masking,
> Itself goes not unmasked to the unmasking.

I must admit I wasn't exactly thrilled when I heard José pounding on my bedroom door to launch another long day of pre-festival activities. After showering and joining the family for breakfast, I soon learned why there was so much enthusiasm in José's wake-up call. He was going to be our guide that day, and we were going to visit the place of his birth where he would share a secret known only to a few close friends outside his village of Vila Nova de Foz Côa.

As we drove along the back roads southeast from the estate, José pointed out with great fanfare the same historical structures and natural features that his father had proudly revealed to him decades earlier as they transported apples, plums, and figs to market. Wordsworth would have been at home here "choosing incidents and situations from common life." The countryside was dotted with almond and olive groves, small vineyards, farms, medieval dovecotes, and fortresses dating to the reign of Dom Dinis, the farmer king.

After about a half hour, our country lane intersected with another rural road running north-south. The traffic sign pointed to the left for Vila Nova de Foz Côa; but unexpectedly, José turned to the right and headed out into more rugged terrain and away from his treasured hometown. We drove south for less than ten minutes before pulling off the gravel road and parking in an open space overlooking a scenic river valley mostly covered with steeply terraced vineyards and almond groves. José jumped out of the car and opened the trunk. Bianca continued translating for the animated old fellow. "José is telling us to grab a canteen there. He says the summer heat can make us sick real fast." After we grabbed a canteen from the trunk, Bianca smiled and added, "And José also wants us to swear to absolute secrecy. Will you all swear?"

Talley, Sanders, and I looked at each other quizzically, nodded, and answered good-naturedly in unison, "Sure, sure. No problem. We swear."

José smiled broadly and responded, "*Sim! Sim!*" He then turned and motioned for us to follow him into the canyon.

As we began scrambling down the four-hundred-foot escarpment, Talley laughed aloud and shouted back at Bianca, "Hey, we didn't sign up for this! What have you gotten us into?"

"Yeah," I chimed in, "if I had known we were going to be climbing mountains, I'd have worn my hiking boots."

Sanders let out a wail. "Son of a bitch! My canteen's leaking. Looks like I pissed myself."

And despite our protestations as we scrambled down the hill, every one of us "indoorsmen" began laughing heartily because, if truth be told, we were all enjoying our adventure in the great Portuguese outdoors. When we reached the banks of the winding Côa River not far from its confluence with the Douro, we stopped and gazed out over the gently flowing waters graced with diamonds. José allowed us to rest there and enjoy the striking scenery for several minutes before shattering our reverie with another of his commands, "*Inversão de marcha!*"

Talley, Sanders, and I quickly looked over toward our translator for guidance and shrugged.

Bianca said, "He wants you to turn around now and look back up the hill."

José then quickly barked out another order, and Bianca continued translating, "José wants you to begin walking slowly back up the slope to the right toward the red, black, and gray outcroppings that are sticking out there. He says there's a surprise waiting for you a quarter way up."

When we got within six feet of the sheer vertical surfaces, we discovered engravings, an intricate combination of fine line incisions, points hammered into stone, and abrasive scratching to provide greater dimension to the etchings. What José had just unveiled was a prehistoric open-air art gallery with mysterious signs, abstractions, but mainly representations of goats, oxen, horses, fish, and deer. And on one of the larger schist surfaces, we found a fascinating lone human figure approaching several ancient horses and wild cattle. The petroglyphs ranged in size from six inches to six feet, incorporated existing rock fractures into the bold line drawings, and often formed a remarkable series of panels and compositions.

In one instance, the prehistoric artist even tried creating animation, portraying a mare being mounted by a large stallion whose three heads depicted the downward motion of his thick neck. I had to agree with José: these remarkable etchings, which he had known and kept secret since childhood, were indeed very old, thousands of years old. In fact, they were strikingly similar to photographs I had seen of the first Paleolithic parietal paintings found at the Altamira cave site in the nineteenth century.

After several hours exploring the riverbanks for further examples of the precious rock art, we readily confessed to José that the extreme heat and craggy terrain had taken its toll on his soft academic cohorts. Our guide graciously accepted our unconditional surrender to the rigors of the afternoon's archaeological pursuits and immediately suggested we pile back into the Mercedes and drive a few miles north to his homestead for a late lunch and some worthwhile local refreshments. The prospects of food, drink, and dense shade motivated all of us to invest significantly more effort in the ascent back up the steep hill to the car.

When we turned into the long driveway leading up to the farmhouse, José began honking the horn repeatedly; and by the time we had reached the historic quinta, two casually dressed men had exited the house and were standing on the front steps waving enthusiastically. José stopped the car, jumped out, gave the men bear hugs, and then motioned for us to join them. José did the introductions via Bianca's translation. "This is my younger brother, Pedro, and my youngest brother, Simão. They've both lived here and worked the farm all their lives." He paused and added lightheartedly, "I was the only lucky one who managed to escape the hard labor here, but believe me, that was only after our mother passed on. God rest her soul."

While shaking hands all around, Talley, Sanders, and I mumbled simultaneously, "Nice to meet you. . . . Good afternoon. . . . Good to see you. . . ."

Pedro then began rattling off something to Bianca in Portuguese, which produced the usual shrug from all of her traveling partners. She turned and continued translating: "Pedro says he wants us to join him in the dining room for some light afternoon fare, most of which he says has been produced right here on the farm—*sopa de chícharros verdes*—green mackerel and bacon soup; hearty *paio*—hard pork loin sausage; and spicy *chouriço*—another classic Portuguese meat." Bianca paused and Pedro said a few more sentences, then nudged her to translate. "There'll also be Portuguese rolls, ewe's milk cheese with sliced oranges for dessert, and to finish things off in Portuguese style, of course, generous glasses of vintage port from the late thirties."

Talley nodded and spoke for the three of us. "Sounds delicious." He added, "We're starving after marching all over the valley this morning!"

As we gathered around the rustic dinner table, Simão pointed to Bianca and then to me and motioned for us to take seats next to each other. He then looked over at Bianca and said something in Portuguese. Bianca shook her head and laughed aloud.

"What did he say?" Sanders asked.

Bianca continued laughing and answered, "Simão thought Andrew and I were, ah, lovers."

Talley and Sanders joined in the laughing, and then the teasing really began. Talley wagged his finger and said, "Oh! Oh! Jeffrey better not hear about this!"

Sanders piped up. "Yeah, Andrew, Jeffrey will box your ears—make mincemeat out of you!"

I was grateful when the ribbing stopped. I felt self-conscious that my face would somehow reveal something. That's when everyone sat down and began enjoying a relaxed feast. The more the wine flowed, the more the recollections between the brothers and between Bianca and José came pouring out. Bianca's translations became fewer and farther between, but Talley, Sanders, and I didn't mind. We enjoyed watching their warm interaction. While we didn't understand the drift of their conversations, we sensed the love and the memories our hosts shared during that memorable afternoon in the country.

In José's defense it wasn't his lack of driving skills that almost got us killed twice on the way back to Pinhão. It was Friday evening, and excited migrants were racing home from France preparing to party at the customary summer weddings in their hometowns. After the first excruciating near miss, I crouched down in the backseat between Talley and Sanders, closed my eyes, and coolly pretended to be taking a short nap as José negotiated one blind curve after another on the narrow dirt roads.

When we miraculously arrived back at the estate unharmed, we soon learned of slight modifications to our sleeping arrangements. Since several family members from Lisbon and Porto would be staying overnight after the following day's festivities, Talley and Sanders would now share the spacious Tinta Barroca room and I would be moving down the hall to the rarely occupied Nascence chamber at the northeast end of the second floor.

Given that the next day was the big anniversary for the quinta, we were determined to meet our goal of getting to bed earlier than we did the night before; but we missed the target by almost an hour, finally retiring close to three o'clock. When I switched on the light and entered the Nascence room for the first time, I discovered my accommodations had been upgraded considerably. While the Touriga Francesa was anything but spartan, my new room was quite large with a dark mahogany four-poster bed, oversized armoire with double doors and simple carvings, a turquoise upholstered armchair, a heavy mahogany writing desk with matching chair, and an antique smokers stand with spiraled legs in the Indo-Portuguese style. The top and sides of the bed were covered in a pale blue, gossamer-like material with delicate cherubs embroidered into the handmade fabric. It was far too big for one man, but Bianca must have insisted.

The walls of the room were a pale yellow and decorated on one side with a single eighteenth-century portrait of a mysterious, raven-haired beauty dressed in cobalt blue, and on the other with a rococo gilded mirror featuring carved wooden acanthus leaves and the original mercury glass, which had darkened considerably over the years. Opposite the hallway entrance there was a charming latticed window with a superb view encompassing the courtyard and the terraced vineyards below. And to the left of the alluring portrait, I discovered a locked door between the Nascence and the Tinta Cão rooms, which most likely had been installed to facilitate passage between the birthing room and the waiting room filled with concerned family members anxiously awaiting the arrival of a new child. The odd thing about the door was it could only be opened from the Tinta Cão room. There was no handle on my side of the door.

Since we thankfully didn't have an early out on Saturday morning, I planned on sleeping in for an extra hour or so, but the elevated conversations of the servants began a little after seven a.m. and never stopped. I fought the chatter for a half hour, but even burying my head under the thick goose-down pillow didn't filter the noise. I finally gave up, rolled out of bed, dressed smartly for the occasion, and headed down to the stone-lined country kitchen where caterers were already busily preparing the midday buffet.

After some fresh Portuguese rolls, homemade marmalade, and a couple espressos, I headed out to the courtyard where I found Talley, Sanders, and Bianca greeting early arrivals from Lisbon and Porto, including economic representatives from the Salazar government and the twelve members of the distinguished Porto Vocal Arts Collegium specializing in the Portuguese baroque masters—Lobo, Cardoso, and Filipe de Magalhães.

Guests continued to arrive throughout the morning, and Saturday afternoon the festivities at last began. Following the congratulatory speeches and the declaration of the quinta as a national heritage site, after the outstanding Portuguese polyphony, the sumptuous buffet, and the superior Douro region wines, family members and guests alike proclaimed the formal celebration an undeniable success. While I thought we might feel uncomfortable and out of place being unfamiliar with local customs and not speaking the language, Talley, Sanders, and I agreed everyone attending made us feel at home and made the effort to communicate with us, albeit occasionally with several humorous instances of linguistic malpractice. For example, everyone at our table got a good laugh at my expense, when I experimented with my newly acquired Portuguese, asking an aging relative if she would sleep with me when I meant to ask if she would be staying overnight at the quinta.

When the last of the celebrants had left Pinhão for home, Bianca's family and guests retired to the veranda to share their recollections of the day's events and enjoy several Parisian goblets of vintage port. Over time, I suspect age and the fortified wine took their toll; and one by one, the older folks excused themselves for the evening, finally leaving Talley, Sanders, Bianca, and me sitting alone reminiscing in the warm summer air. And the more the wine flowed, the more organic and discursive our conversation became, discussing everything from Vonnegut's Malachi Constant to Burroughs's William Lee and finally Beckett's Krapp, whom Bianca pensively quoted: "The new light above my table is a great improvement. With all this darkness around me I feel less alone."

After reminding everyone we had promised Bianca's parents we would join them for morning mass before leaving for Sintra, I made a motion we adjourn for the evening. Bianca concurred; but Talley and Sanders said they wanted to continue their conversation and would follow along shortly. Bianca and I walked inside and down the corridor together, then waved awkwardly when it came time to part. Although I was getting more used to her beauty and her casual sensuality, she still had a way of making me wholly aware of how uncoordinated I could be.

When I entered my special bedroom, I walked over to the window, cranked open the casement to allow the fresh country air to permeate the room, and surveyed the expansive estate cascading down to the undulating stars reflecting off the Douro. As I was about to turn back to face the room, I noticed two indistinct figures emerge from the shadows, pause for a charged moment, and then warmly embrace in the summer's sacred benedictory moonlight. I confess I reluctantly turned away, crawled into bed, and lay in the silver ambience processing what I had just learned. The bottom line for me was I really didn't care. But I hoped for their sake that only trusted friends, relatives, and faculty would ever know of the honest, growing love the two men shared.

A key then turned in the night, and the door between the Nascence and the Tinta Cão gradually swung open into my room. I sat up and peered into the adjoining space. Candlelight merged with moonlight and then "all that's best of dark and bright met in her aspect and her eyes." As Bianca slowly glided toward me, she put her hand up to her lips signaling this was not the time for words.

She moved over to the side of the birthing bed, slipped her long fingers up under the thin straps of her flowing gown, and slipped the satin chemise downward over her sensuous breasts. She climbed up over the edge of the tall mattress, pulled up close against my chest, and kissed me passionately. There was no Catherine now, no Jeffrey, only an intense, instinctive desire to embrace her and the rhythmic, dreamlike unreality of that metamorphic night.

It was not the hallway voices but the distant bells and the strong light that woke me early Sunday morning. When I turned over to face Bianca, she was no longer there; and the door between our rooms was once again locked. Had everything regressed to the norm? I showered, packed my bags, and hurried down to the traditional kitchen, where the cook was attentively stirring a large pot of cereal hanging from a swing crane positioned directly over the fire.

I was the first of our group to arrive; but soon afterward, Talley and Sanders sauntered into the room arm-in-arm, gave me a big hug, and politely signaled to the cook they desperately needed coffee. What about this open display of affection? Had they seen me standing at the window observing their courtyard embrace? Or had we now been traveling together long enough to remove their masks and confide in me? Did Bianca know of their relationship? Was I the last to know?

I sat down across the table from the relaxed lovers, bantered with them about who was more proficient in Portuguese, and savored my breakfast *galão*, which consisted of drip espresso cut with a lot of warm milk. As Talley and Sanders revisited my earlier linguistic faux pas, they stopped midsentence and began smiling at someone entering the room behind me. I swung around on the bench to see with whom they were gesturing. It was Bianca. My pulse quickened. I was dying to know how she would respond after visiting the Nascence during the night.

It didn't take long to understand her feelings this morning. Bianca approached, dropped her arms down across my chest from behind, embraced me firmly, kissed me warmly on the cheek, and said, "Good morning, my love." What was clear in hindsight now should have been obvious to all of us at the time; a natural aligning, a pairing up had begun not long after we had touched down in Lisbon. The process came full circle when Talley smiled at Bianca and extended his arm around Sanders to emphasize there was more than one pair of lovers at our table.

After a pleasant breakfast with family members who had spent the night, we collected our belongings and headed out to the courtyard. Bianca's father had made a generous offer to take two cars to mass. While José would drive the antique Mercedes, Mr. and Mrs. de Silva would use their other classic car, a burgundy, prewar Talbot 75 Saloon. And then when mass had ended, José would drive us on over to Sintra near Lisbon, where we would be spending our last few days abroad. Since the old Roman city of Viseu was nearby and on our way to the capital, we decided to attend mass in Viseu's Romanesque-Gothic cathedral dating from the twelfth century.

As we neared the city's cobbled plaza, the imposing structure came into view. The three-story façade was flanked by two very large towers and resembled a sixteenth-century altarpiece decorated with niches containing statues of the four evangelists, the Virgin Mary, and Saint Teotónio. The interior was just as spectacular with a three-aisled nave, a transept, and several highly decorated chapels representing architectural styles spanning the ages. Pedro de Escobar's a cappella motet, *But There Cried Out a Woman*, reverberated among the massive columns and sweeping arches shaking the soul to its core. We followed along with the English translation in the mass program:

A woman of Canaan cried to the Lord Jesus, saying:
Lord Jesus Christ, son of David, help me;
my daughter is grievously troubled by a devil.
And he answering, said: I was not sent but to the
sheep, that are lost of the house of Israel.
But she came and adored him, saying: Lord, help me.
Then Jesus answering said to her: O woman, great is
thy faith: be it done to thee as thou wilt.

And there could not have been a more appropriate homily delivered that morning than the one based on the first book of John, which Bianca paraphrased later on our ride over to Sintra: "He that loveth abides in the light, and there is none occasion of stumbling in him."

When the mass had ended, we stood out in the expansive plaza for a few minutes listening to the cathedral bells and vainly attempting to postpone the inevitable—the painful separation of an adventurous, talented daughter from her traditional, loving parents. Bianca's father finally made the first move, embraced his daughter, and spoke softly in Portuguese. As tears welled up in her eyes, Bianca managed a brave smile and then turned toward her mother, who was standing off to the side. Talley, Sanders, and I walked over to Bianca's father, thanked him for his hospitality, and told him we would like to return the favor if he ever visited Bianca in the States. We then piled into the Mercedes and continued waving until the stoic couple disappeared behind a line of Portuguese oaks as we rounded the first curve leaving Viseu.

We thought we had begun a four-hour, nonstop trip to

Sintra, but José surprised us and stopped off in the medieval walled city of Óbidos for a late lunch and a few minutes of sightseeing. After a sumptuous meal of baked goat and potatoes at one of Bianca's favorite restaurants, The Illustrious House of Ramires, we climbed up onto the ramparts near the castle and enjoyed views of windmills, vineyards, and narrow cobblestone streets lined with whitewashed houses sporting either old gold or royal blue accents and window boxes ablaze with geranium, lantana, and morning glory. When we climbed down from the walls, José suggested we walk over to the main street, find a *ginja* bar, and sample the city's famed *ginjinha*, a sweet brandy liqueur made locally with a fruit similar to wild cherries.

Driving from Óbidos to Sintra was like traveling from one fairyland to the next. After passing Sintra's fifteenth-century national palace and the charming blue-tiled bistro, the Café de Paris, José turned onto the Rua Consiglieri Pedroso and dropped us off at our boutique sixteen-room hotel, the oldest on the Iberian Peninsula, which we would call home for the rest of our European stay.

As we entered the lobby, Bianca revealed the two rooms she had reserved in the romantic venue were surprise gifts for "Talley the novelist, Sanders the poet, and her young literary scholar." She then explained the significance of the historic place. In July 1809, Lord Byron had stayed in one of the second-floor chambers and written part of "Child Harold's Pilgrimage":

> Poor, paltry slaves! yet born midst noblest scenes—
> Why, Nature, waste thy wonders on such men?

Lo! Cintra's glorious Eden intervenes
In variegated maze of mount and glen.
Ah me! what hand can pencil guide, or pen,
To follow half on which the eye dilates
Through views more dazzling unto mortal ken
Than those whereof such things the bard relates,
Who to the awe-struck world unlocked Elysi-
um's gates?

Later, over a unique dinner of baked fish encased in salt, a Café de Paris house specialty, Bianca bolstered her case for Sintra's importance by reading quotes from Byron's correspondence to his mother and a friend describing the very places we were now seeing:

> I must just observe, that the village of Cintra in Estremadura is the most beautiful, perhaps, in the world. . . . It is in every respect, the most delightful in Europe; it contains beauties of every description, natural and artificial. Palaces and gardens rising in the midst of rocks, cataracts and precipices; convents on stupendous heights—a distant view of the sea and the Tagus. . . . It unites in itself all the wildness of the western highlands with the verdure of the south of France.

After several glasses of Graham's Vintage '35, we stepped out of the restaurant into the cool summer evening and walked along the narrow, winding cobblestoned paths gazing into the lighted shops, marveling at the tall, conical chimneys of the national palace, and staring up at the floodlit ramparts of the Moorish castle, which had stood above the old town as a sentinel for more than a thousand years. Almost instinctively and without any conversation, we gravitated back to our hotel, exchanged brief pleasantries, and then retired to our rooms for what we all silently desired, passionate lovemaking in a storybook setting lasting deep into the night.

On our final day before flying home, we flagged a taxi and drove over to Cascais, a fashionable seacoast village not far from Lisbon, which had become the summer playground for European royalty. After a long, relaxed lunch at O Pescador's overlooking the scenic harbor, we walked arm-in-arm up the rugged, wind-blown coastline toward untamed Guincho Beach, where we stood on the sweeping cliffs above the dunes and umbrella pines and watched the Atlantic breakers crashing into the fractured boulders at highest tide. And after several hours of walking the quiet streets of tiny fishing villages dotting the rocky shoreline, we returned to a restaurant we'd discovered early on teetering for decades at the very brink of the cliffs. We ordered a round of farewell drinks and then watched the sun drop behind a low bank of clouds creating radiant bursts of roseate and pastel light.

It was a brutal early out the next morning. We had to pack our bags and leave for the airport an hour before dawn. But thankfully we were rewarded with a relaxed check-in, flawless boarding, and a smooth take-off right on time. Nevertheless, since the strong headwinds would result in at least a twelve-hour crossing back to the States, we all asked for blankets, closed our shades, and settled back into our reclined seats to catch up on our sleep.

Although I desired sleep, I knew that would be an unattainable goal for me. I had so much to think about, so little time to make the hard decisions and then to do what I thought was best for everyone. Bianca had told me the night before that she would be staying over in New York for a few days to see Jeffrey and "set everything right." Perhaps I should bite the bullet and follow through on my promise to visit Catherine before Bianca returned to campus. What would I say? Would I tell her about the European tryst? If I did, how would she react? Would she forgive? Would she reconcile?

But did I want reconciliation and the stability that that would bring? Or did I really want to risk everything and embrace Bianca's impetuosity? Did I love Catherine or was it an honest empathy for what she'd endured? Did I love Bianca or was it a blind attraction to her creativity and raw, vibrant sexuality? In a practical sense, how would the faculty react to an open affair between Bianca and me? Would Catherine want to continue our relationship if I were graduated in a few years and left McGill to teach somewhere else in the country?

Bianca had followed Jeffrey to McGill; and since he would surely not be returning to Pantheon, what would her plans be? Would she want to move on to another, more exciting venue? If so, would I be willing to drop everything I was doing at the university and follow her to her next source of inspiration? I knew one thing for sure: time was not an ally for resolving the situation. I would have to act before the fall semester began.

14

Nc2 Bxc3   Qxa2

I KNEW THE conclusion before I had ever read the story. While I was away, Anna had been very busy stuffing reams of paper under my door. As I collected the flyers, bills, and correspondence from the floor, I noticed I had received two telegrams both dated within the last few days. Both were from Dad. I inadvertently opened the second telegram first: "Son, I'm sorry to say Mom has died." Tears sprung to my eyes. "Contact me as soon as possible. We need to discuss the funeral." Stunned, though admittedly not surprised, I ripped open the first telegram, which had been delivered several days earlier. With bleary eyes I read Dad's message: Mom was gravely ill and he hoped I could get back home to see her before she passed on.

I reflexively dropped my bags by the sofa, searched around the apartment for any loose change, and then headed down to Hudson's to make the call.

"Hello . . . Dad?"

"Is that you, son?"

"Yeah. Sorry I didn't get back to you sooner. I just got the telegrams. I was out of town with friends and just got back. . . . What happened?"

"The old man's friend: pneumonia. After all your mother has been through, thank God, she didn't suffer."

"What are the plans?"

"The wake is scheduled for Monday evening at Mittlebeeler's, you know, the mortuary up the road from our old home. Your mother's idea. Every time we passed the place she would praise how they had handled the Turner child. And then when we would get back to the house, she would point to a dress hanging behind the door and say, 'Take this and me to Mittlebeeler's. No place else, you hear?'"

I smiled. "That sure sounds like Mom. So when you plan on arriving, Dad?"

"Sonya and I will be driving down from Urbana on Sunday. I don't suspect she'll want to attend the wake or funeral, you know, since your mother's relatives will all be there. . . ."

"Yeah, I understand. So where you staying?" I asked.

"I was thinking of making reservations for us at the old hotel where we used to go after your mother's concerts."

Tears welled up with the memories. "That's great. Mom would have been pleased with that."

"Yeah, I think so too. . . . So, when can you get here, son?"

"I'll hop the early bus on Sunday morning and meet you at the hotel for dinner."

"Sounds like a plan."

"I look forward to seeing you, Dad."

"Same here, son."

"Oh, Dad . . ."

"What, son?"

"Don't worry about Sonya and me. I've meant to tell you for a long time I thought you did the right thing. Thought you tried and did your best. You deserved to have a life, be able to move on."

"That means a lot, son. Thanks."

"See you Sunday, Dad."

"Yeah, see you Sunday, son."

After checking in and stowing my suitcase in the room, I headed down to the grand lobby a few minutes before six to reminisce and remember the good times with Mom. In fact, as I scanned the enormous space, I realized, despite the changes in me, nothing had changed there since the class reunion, or for that matter, since we celebrated Mom's triumphs on many Sunday afternoons. Everything was in its place—the long rectangular skylight, the soaring ceilings, the marble columns, the pioneer murals, the velvet chairs, and the massive registration desk running the length of the room. As I was looking up at the gilded antique chandeliers, I heard Dad call my name. I turned and saw him walking toward me arm-in-arm with an attractive blue-eyed, auburn-haired younger woman roughly Bianca's age.

Dad gave me a big bear hug before making the introductions. "Son, I'd like you to meet Sonya," he said, smiling briefly. "Hello," I said. "It's great to finally meet you." I made a valiant but awkward attempt to embrace her—awkward because Dad had saved a surprise for me, which he wanted to keep until we met face to face. Sonya appeared to be at least seven months pregnant. So I was potentially going to have a new stepmother and stepbrother or stepsister, and ironically our family was going to net out at a plus one overall.

But I also had a surprise for him. I told Sonya and Dad to

follow me and then led them down the hallway to the richly paneled billiard room where Capone enjoyed playing poker with friends. I motioned for Dad to sit in Al's old spot in the alcove, helped Sonya with her chair, and then took a seat across the table from the two of them. Dad surveyed the special room and gave me a puzzled look, as if wanting to know how I had managed to secure the inner sanctum for dinner. I only smiled, and to this day have never discussed the exorbitant twenty bucks I forked over to the maître d' to reserve the space for our reunion.

With Sonya joining us for dinner, it was impossible to reminisce about the Sundays we had spent there with Mom, but I think Dad and I passed several coded messages, especially when he ordered his usual Sunday baked ham and I my roast beef with gravy. Instead of discussing our family's past, we chatted about Dad's latest incomprehensible paper on subatomic particles and Sonya's fascinating work in progress, *An Introduction to Musical Theory*, which she described as flowing from the basics of musical study and steadily adding theory as the student progressed through the lessons of form, structure, texture, rhythm, harmony, and melody.

From our discussion of Sonya's upcoming publication we moved on to a general conversation of musical works, which eventually led to Haydn's glorious but often neglected Forty-fourth in E Minor known as the *Trauer* or *Mourning Symphony*. Sonya and I agreed Haydn had known toward the end of his life he had composed something very special some thirty-eight years before, since, out of all his many works, he asked that the gentle *Trauer adagio* be played at his memorial service.

So our spontaneous, probing discussion of Haydn's symphony

ironically brought us full circle to the specific arrangements for Mom's imminent wake and funeral. Dad said we should be ready to leave the hotel the following evening at six, since the viewing started at seven. He also confirmed as expected that Sonya wouldn't be attending either the wake or the church service the following morning.

Dad then looked over at Sonya but spoke to me: "We've had a long day with all of the travel. I'm afraid we need to head back to the room and get some rest." He patted her hand kindly, then looked back at me. "Sorry to cut it short, son. We'll talk more in the morning."

After wishing my dining partners a good night, I returned to my room and telephoned Catherine. When she answered, I could tell she was excited.

"Oh, Andrew, it's so good to hear your voice! How was your trip?"

"I . . . I think we'd better put that off until later when we have some quiet time together."

"Where are you? Back on campus?"

"Ah, no. I'm here. Here in Louisville."

"In Louisville? Why's that?"

"Mom died, Catherine. . . . I'm in town for the wake and funeral. She died just before I returned home from Lisbon."

She paused and then responded quietly, "I'm really sorry, Andrew. You . . . you say you're in Louisville. Whereabouts?"

"At the hotel where we had the reunion."

"You want me to come over? I can be there in no time."

"No, no. Better you stay there with your father. Take care of him."

"Well, when is the wake?"

"Tomorrow evening beginning at seven o'clock."

"Well, you can count on my being there."

"Thanks, Catherine. I'll see you then tomorrow night."

"I love you. . . ."

"Ah . . . I love you too, Catherine. Good night."

When Dad and I entered the funeral home the following evening, I was relieved on two counts: Mom's family treated Dad respectfully and they had wisely opted for a closed casket. Dad said Mom's last year of confinement and chronic disease had taken their toll, and I wanted to remember her the way she was on those special Sunday afternoons after the concerts.

Mom's relatives had also fortuitously chosen a highly meaningful photograph to place on a small wooden stand at the head of the casket. It was a publicity photo taken the week before Mom's final concert. She must have been playing the Sibelius. You could read the intensity in her face. And she was wearing the black brocade cheongsam with flame-red dragons and piping that she had worn for that final concert. After pointing out the photograph to Dad, he smiled and whispered he had recommended the picture to the family. And that was not all. He said he had also suggested Mom be buried in that special dress she always had hanging behind the door. Besides following Mom's wishes to be buried in that special dress, perhaps he was also thinking spiritually or metaphorically that God would now cure Mom and allow her to complete the Sibelius concerto in D.

As I turned away from the flower-draped coffin, old friends, family members, orchestral colleagues, and a spry but arthritic centenarian, Mom's old maestro, began entering the room. I took a deep breath and steeled myself for the well-intentioned onslaught of the customary condolences. "It was for the best." "I know just how you feel." "She is no longer suffering." But there was one positive outcome from the evening. The funeral director handed me an Associated Press wire story from the local newspaper about Mom's passing. The story avoided her public breakdown and focused only on her major achievements, especially having been one of only three female concertmasters in an American orchestra during the 1940s.

Catherine arrived a little past eight o'clock, kissed me lightly on the cheek, and apologized for her tardiness. "I'm sorry I didn't get here sooner. The part-time nurse I use when I'm going out was delayed getting home from her regular shift at the hospital." Her face was pinched in anguish.

I put my fingers to my lips and shook my head indicating no apology was necessary. I then scanned the room and located Dad, who was speaking with two of Mom's old orchestral colleagues from the string section. I slid my arm gently around Catherine's waist, guided her over to where Dad was standing, and waited briefly until the conversation had ended. I tapped my father on the arm and said, "Dad, excuse me, I'd like to introduce Catherine. We attended high school together—were lab partners—and now we're both enrolled at Pantheon. She's staying here in Louisville this summer taking care of her father, who had back surgery."

"Nice to meet you, Catherine."

"Same here, sir. But I'm sorry it's under these circumstances."

We continued speaking for several minutes, mostly about Catherine's course of studies, until Mom's aging conductor interrupted to say farewell and repeat his sincere condolences.

I then walked Catherine out to her car, discreetly embraced her, thanked her for making the effort to be there that evening, and asked her to be back at ten in the morning to join us in the limousine for the drive over to the church.

I spent another long two hours at the wake and was relieved when the last guest bid farewell and allowed my father and me a much-needed reprieve. He and I trudged back to his car and had a silent ride over to the hotel.

When Dad and I pulled into the mortuary parking lot the next morning, three young men had already arrived and were standing behind a bright red Chevrolet Impala convertible smoking cigarettes. As we carefully maneuvered into the space next to the iconic symbol of the flamboyance and flair of the late '50s, I discovered my old buddies, Knox, Anderson, and Grimes, had learned of Mom's passing and had now come to pay their respects.

I jumped out of Dad's car, swung around to the back of the Chevy, embraced each of them. "Ray! Knoxie! Grimesy! Great to see you guys!" I paused and then added, "Hey, thanks for showing up. It means a lot."

They responded simultaneously, "No problem. Best we could do."

I turned and reintroduced my cohorts to Dad, whom they had met several times during our high school years after football games. I then steered the conversation toward the usual opening topic for males, occupations. "Dad here is now teaching physics at the University of Illinois in Urbana."

Dad looked over at Grimes and eased in. "So what are you

men up to these days? It's been a long time since we celebrated that regional championship."

"I'm still working as a physical therapist at the VA, Dr. Taylor."

Dad turned to his left and asked, "What about you, Knoxie?"

"My father and I have just begun a twenty-story high-rise on the riverfront near the Coast Guard station."

Dad then completed the circuit. "And you, Ray?"

"My father and I just got some good news. We've been awarded two motel franchises, one to be built in the East End of the county near Cherokee Park and the other one across the river in Indiana near the old boat works."

Dad nodded and said, "Well, it sounds like you fellas are all happy and getting along well with your lives."

Speaking for the triumvirate, Ray responded, "Yeah. We sure can't complain, can we?"

I jumped in. "Say, after the church and graveside services, why don't you guys join us at Armando's for some rolled oysters, white bean soup, and plenty of beer. Mom would have wanted us to celebrate her life informally this way."

Knox, Anderson, and Grimes responded enthusiastically, "You better believe it! Count us in!"

As the crowd continued gathering on the back lawn next to the parking lot, the funeral director appeared, asked our family members to convene in the visitation room, and instructed the remaining mourners to drive their cars around the block and form a line behind the hearse and the two limousines. After the young priest led our family in prayer, the funeral director motioned for the eight pallbearers to approach the front of the room. Father positioned himself at the head of the bronze-colored casket, I at the foot, and the remaining six pallbearers from Mom's side of the family—her brother and some cousins I never really knew—lining up along the sides.

When the director gave the signal, we gripped the fixed handles and simultaneously lifted the coffin from the platform. Sometimes when we are under severe stress, our minds intervene to protect us from the reality of the situation. As I began thinking it was my loving mom's remains we were carrying out to the hearse, my subconscious interrupted and focused me on the disconnect between Mom's thin frame and the bulky weight we were now carrying over to the side door.

Appropriately, Mom's memorial service at the cathedral was more music than words. A string ensemble comprised of members of her old orchestra opened the celebration with Sibelius's five-movement *Intimate Voices* in D minor. Mom had played the haunting piece several times. It was one of her favorite quartets, beautifully intimate, yet heroically symphonic in development.

Next, the priest delivered a brief sermon based on the gospel according to Saint John:

> And as Jesus passed by, he saw a man, who was blind from his birth. And his disciples asked him, saying, Master, who did sin, this man, or his parents, that he was born blind? Jesus answered, neither hath this man sinned, nor his parents, but that the works of God should be made manifest in him.

It was a unique text for a funeral sermon. The priest said Mom had never been blind, far from it; but as the man in the gospel, she had been terribly afflicted. He quoted the disciples questioning Jesus, "Who sinned that he was born blind?" The priest then suggested we might be tempted to ask similar questions when we see things going wrong: "What did I do to deserve this?"

In answer, the priest quoted Jesus' response to his disciples revealing why human beings were afflicted: "It was not that this man sinned, or his parents, but that the works of God might be displayed in him." The priest argued the works of God had been displayed in Mom. He reminded us we should remember her accomplishments. He continued, "Was there sadness in her life? Yes. Tragedy? Perhaps. But I believe it was neither the sadness nor the misfortune that defined her life. No, it was how she endured her affliction—with grace, intelligence, and dignity. And *that* is the message God has chosen to deliver through Grace."

The string players now returned to conclude the services. They had chosen Sibelius's final piece for quartet, the *Andante Festivo*, a poignant single-movement, five-minute work of heartrending beauty. It is one of only a few musical compositions that accurately capture the human condition—all its hope, its love, its complexity, its loss and pain. As I listened to their flawless interpretation, I remembered a story Mom had told me about the piece, when I was no more than ten years old. After a rehearsal with the players, Sibelius looked at them and proclaimed, "Play it with more humanity!"

After helping carry Mom's casket out to the hearse, Dad and I joined her elderly mother, brother, stepsister, and Catherine in the lead limousine for the procession out to the cemetery. The ride was very quiet, but not because tensions remained between Mom's family and Dad. No, all of that had been forgiven with Mom's passing. Everyone simply chose to stare out the side windows and remember their wife, mother, child, or sister in their own special way. Catherine slipped her hand over onto mine and gently squeezed; I slowly turned toward her and gave a faint smile to acknowledge her support and reassurances that everything would be all right. Several minutes later, Dad spotted the Corinthian-style cemetery entrance with its signature limestone tower and quietly murmured to himself, "Well, Grace, you're almost home."

The nineteenth-century town fathers had demonstrated great foresight in purchasing the old Johnston farm and hiring the highly respected Hartford engineer, Edmund Lee, to design a garden-style cemetery. The crests of the rolling hills would become the primary burial grounds; the basins would be transformed into exotic ponds filled with Egyptian lotus plants; the gently sloping terraces would become the arboretum composed of willows, magnolias, hemlock, spruce, and pine; and the level grounds would be planted in gardens of rhododendron, laurel, and azalea.

The motorcycle policemen who had escorted us through a city of memories slowed and stopped near Mom's summit grave site, which had been prepared with a large green canvas awning and dark brown folding chairs. Dad and I exited our limousine and joined the other pallbearers waiting beside the hearse for our next set of instructions.

As I scanned the nearby section of burial plots, I realized the orchestra's board of directors had secured Mom a prized location among the city's past luminaries. To Mom's left, within a stylish exedra stood larger-than-life portrait statues in Athenian marble depicting the nineteenth-century Baroness Von Zedtwitz and her sister, the Marquise des Monstiers Merinville. And to Mom's right, a large black granite cross honored a successful local entrepreneur, George Keats, who made his fortune in shipping, flour, and real estate and corresponded regularly with his frail younger brother in England, the immortal poet, John.

After we had positioned Mom's casket over the grave, the priest conducted a brief committal service. He first led us in the Lord's Prayer, cast symbolic earth on the casket, and then prayed:

> In sure and certain hope of the resurrection into eternal life, through our Lord Jesus Christ, we commend to almighty God our sister, and we commit her body to the ground, earth to earth, ashes to ashes, dust to dust.

As the priest ended the prayer, he signaled the cemetery workers to release the brakes on the lowering device, and Mom's coffin slowly descended into the vault. Mom's brother stepped forward and shoveled the first dirt onto the casket, eerily producing memorable thuds of hopelessness. And then we all stood up, passed the well-groomed opening, and dropped long-stem roses into her grave.

When we arrived at Armando's twenty minutes later, I told Dad, Catherine, and Mom's family to go on inside and I would be there in a few minutes. I didn't explain why I wanted to stand outside in the hot sun; but I was waiting for Anderson. I knew he had seen Catherine and me together at the funeral, so I wanted to speak with him privately to explain the history of my relationship with his high school sweetheart.

It wasn't long before the sleek red Chevy Impala convertible rounded the corner and parked in the overflow lot across the street. As the threesome neared the front entrance, I asked Knox and Grimes to head on into the restaurant and promised them that Anderson and I would join the group shortly. I then turned to my old friend and said, "I'm sure you saw Catherine and me together today. I wanted to explain. It was only after she moved to McGill that we struck up a relationship. There'd been nothing before that. You have my word on it."

Anderson smiled and put his arm around my shoulder. "No need to explain, Andy. Our relationship ended after high school. We've both moved on. So don't worry about it. Okay?"

"Okay, then. I'm all set. I didn't want anything to come between us, Ray."

"It never has, Andy, and it never will. . . . So let's get in out of this heat and hoist a cold one to your mom's memory. What do you say?"

"I say, 'Bottoms up!'"

And as if to prove his point, when we joined the rest of the celebrants in Armando's private dining room, Anderson arranged the seating so that Catherine sat between him and me for the rest of the afternoon exchanging only the most innocent banter of longtime friends.

Several hours into the festive commemoration, Catherine pointed to her watch and said, "I've got to get going. My father's visiting nurse can only stay until seven o'clock. Since the hotel's on my way home, would you like me to drop you off?"

I nodded. "That'd be great. I've been running on fumes the last couple of hours."

As we drove over to the hotel, I said, "I'd like to visit Mom's grave tomorrow before heading back to McGill and, if you can arrange it, I'd like for you to go along."

She paused and replied, "I think I can get my sister to come over to the house and stay with Dad for a few hours. But I should be heading back by early afternoon. I don't really feel comfortable leaving . . ."

I put my finger up to her lips and said, "Shhh. I understand."

After pulling into the hotel driveway, Catherine came around to my side of the car. She embraced me, gave me a long kiss, and said, "I'm really sorry about your mom."

I nodded and replied, "Thanks, Catherine, and thanks for being there for me the last couple of days. It meant a lot." I paused and then firmed up our plans for the following morning. "I'll pick you up at your place tomorrow around ten o'clock."

She smiled and responded, "Don't worry. I'll be ready to go."

I didn't sleep well that night, but this time I couldn't blame it on the hallway noise. Everything was swirling—Mom's unexpected death; Catherine's expected reaction to my revelations; Bianca's uncertain promises; and this maelstrom's potential impact on my academic performance and professional career. I was admittedly now playing outside my comfort zone, where mistakes could multiply and their consequences compound exponentially.

I didn't want to become the chess grandmaster, Bronstein, in the "Immortal Losing Game." The pressure got to him in the first game of his match with Śliwa. He made mistakes and spent the rest of the day trying to extricate himself using elegant traps, which ultimately failed. While gaining notoriety for his valiant efforts to finesse a victory, the bottom line was Bronstein lost the game. So I understood what self-induced pressure could do, and I was determined to avoid it. I would consciously try to relax, play it straight up, tell the truth, and let the cards fall where they may.

I finally gave up on getting to sleep. So I rolled out of bed, showered, and read for a while before picking the keys up from Dad. Since I had a couple hours more to burn before meeting Catherine, I turned left onto Market and headed west toward the past. It was summer. The children were out of school, and they were already lining up outside the amusement park screaming excitedly and laughing. The longer they waited, the more the teasing, the hair pulling, and the spirited games of tag animated the long, thin queue with a slithering motion rivaling any python in search of prey. I pulled into the parking lot and walked over to the chain-link fence near the memorable twin spires. It was reassuring peering through the fence and observing the rides again in the quiet morning light before the park opened and began fashioning lifelong memories for another generation.

The iconic landmarks were still there: the penny arcade, the roller rink, the Whip, the Rocket, the Comet, and the Rock-O-Planes. I remembered the childhood sights and sounds of the Gypsy Village stage. "Ladies and gentlemen, boys and girls, direct from New York, I give you Snyder and Buckley." This vaudeville pair of old-timers would then race onto the stage, play their musical instruments, and perform slapstick comedy between the cheerful tunes. In one act they posted a large goat's head on the wall with a sign on it that read, "Bock Beer." The straight man would finish a number, approach the head, pull the horns, and get a glass of lager. The comic would follow him, pull the horns, and get a glass of milk. And they repeated the joke over and over again, making me laugh mightily every time the milk appeared.

I turned away from the park entrance, crossed the avenue, and strolled up to one of the service windows at the West End Dairy Mart. It was a little before opening and I didn't see anyone near the counter, but I thought I heard someone stirring in the back. I shouted, "Anyone home?" Mrs. Miller appeared at the window wiping her hands on her less than pristine apron. "May I help . . . Is that you, Andrew?"

"Sure is, Mrs. Miller. Long time no see."

"At least a month of Sundays."

I used one of Dad's old lines to soften the beachhead. "I've always heard a friend in need is a pest, Mrs. Miller, but I have a favor to ask of you."

"What's that, Andrew?"

"Well, you know, I've been coming here for now going on centuries to get the world's best cherry shakes. Brings back so many memories. I just really need one today."

The old woman only hesitated for a brief second before flashing a smile and responding, "Hey, anything for one of our guys on the championship team." As she unlocked the door, she added, "Come on in and chat while I whip one up."

"Thanks so much, Mrs. Miller. It really means a whole lot."

As she began pouring the cherries into the metal mixing cup, she said, "I haven't seen you around for a while."

"That's right, Mrs. Miller. I'm still away at school. Graduate school now."

"What brings you back to Louisville? Home for the summer?"

"Oh, no, I, ah, came home for my mother's funeral yesterday."

"I'm so sorry for your loss, Andrew. Was it sudden . . . unexpected?"

"No, no. Mom had been sick for a long time. We knew it would eventually happen. But it's always a shock when someone dies."

"So true. So true."

When the whirring stopped, she carefully poured the thick shake into a serving cup and handed it to me. "I hope this will make you feel better, Andrew."

I extended my hand holding three dollars and said, "Thank you, Mrs. Miller. Here, take a couple extra bucks for your trouble."

She shook her head, lightly pushed my hand back toward my chest, and responded, "No way, Andrew. With all you've been going through, this one's on me."

I spontaneously gave her a big hug, exited the shop, and headed back across the street toward the car. As I sauntered past the entrance, I could now smell the glorious mixture of fried chicken and popcorn and hear "The Happy Organ" blaring from the speakers mounted among the columns of the elegant turn-of-the-century pavilion. I wondered why, of all days, I had instinctively chosen to turn west before meeting with Catherine and returning to McGill. Perhaps it was a chance to say good-bye to a treasured past, to burn it in the memory before moving on to an uncertain future. Perhaps it was a last opportunity to offer a heartfelt, elegiac benediction to the glory and the freshness of childhood dreams. Perhaps it was a final respite before leaving safe harbor to swim with the sharks.

After finishing my shake, I took several deep breaths, eased into the car, and headed over to Catherine's house. I could feel the anticipation surging through my tightening chest. My heart rate and breathing quickened. I knew why I had become anxious. It was not about the knowing what had to be done but about the not knowing how Catherine would react. I wanted to be fair; and of all people, she deserved fairness. But fairness required honesty, and honesty meant another wave of pain for someone I would have never wanted to hurt in a thousand years.

As I drove up to the house, Catherine was sitting on the front steps reading Eliot's "Little Gidding," the last of the *Four Quartets*, which J. Alfred had referenced several times during her advanced composition course last semester. She had heard the mighty roar of Dad's failing muffler, looked up to assess the rumbling, waved, and hurried down the walkway to the car. She opened the door, slid across the seat, hugged me vigorously, and said, "It's great we have a little time alone."

After merging into the traffic, I picked up the conversation. "Is your sister staying with your father today?"

She nodded. "It's a miracle."

"Why's that?"

"Impossible getting her to stay with him two days in a row."

"You think your father will be back on his feet before the fall semester begins?"

"Yeah. He's determined to keep his promise that I'll be back at Pantheon by the beginning of September."

Like a nervous tic, I asked my questions one after another until we reached the cemetery and had begun driving up the winding road to the summit where Mom was buried. It was not difficult finding her unmarked grave. First we spotted the larger-than-life portrait statues of the Baroness and the Marquise; and then we scanned slowly to the right and located the only grave site decorated with a fresh mound of flowers.

We walked over to the grave and determined the workmen had done a good job restoring the landscape. We paused for a silent prayer and then returned to the car. As I stared out the window at the site, I confessed to Catherine, "You know, while we were standing over there just now, it was the first time I ever really felt Mom's loss."

"Perhaps the shock's beginning to wear off."

"I don't know, but when I saw that funeral spray with the word 'Mom' printed on it . . . I knew coming back to Louisville would never be the same again." I paused briefly and then started the engine. "Why don't we drive down to the large pond with the exotic white lotus?"

"Sure. Why not?"

"I like it there. Reminds me of Egypt."

"Egypt?"

"Yeah. White lotus were often depicted on the walls of Egyptian tombs and temples."

"Why's that?"

"The flower closes at sunset and sinks below the surface of the water; and then at daybreak the plant begins rising and blooms again. For Egyptians the white lotus was a natural symbol of rebirth."

"So it's really appropriate for a cemetery like this."

"Yeah. Whoever landscaped the pond area must have known the legend."

"The legend?"

"The ancient Egyptian belief that the sun god emerged from a giant lotus blossom after rising from the primordial waters of Nun."

Catherine smiled warmly. "You always come up with the most interesting stories. . . ."

As we walked arm-in-arm along the sweeping edge of the pond, Catherine returned to our deferred conversation about the European trip. I tried to figure her motive. Perhaps she had begun to detect subtle differences in my demeanor over the past few days. I knew I was different but assumed she would dismiss any perceived changes as symptoms of stress related to Mom's death and funeral. But maybe she thought a faithful recitation of the narrative would reveal any hidden secrets. And then again, perhaps it was just her way of showing she really cared by taking an interest in what her lover had been doing overseas. Whatever the motive, I realized I was now standing at the edge of the precipice staring into the vortex. As the prince at Elsinore, I knew I had to act. The readiness was all.

So I began with the transatlantic flight and then continued with the train rides, Porto, the railway station in Pinhão, José Guilherme, the Eiffel Bridge, the elegant quinta, Bianca's gracious parents, the rabelo ride up the Douro, the Tua Line, the petroglyphs, the anniversary celebration, the Vocal Arts

Collegium, the Portuguese baroque masters, mass in Viseu's twelfth-century cathedral, Lord Byron, and our unique dinner at the Café de Paris in idyllic Sintra. Catherine had listened attentively, interrupting only occasionally for clarification or more detail; but when I had concluded the description of Sintra, she noted quizzically, "You've talked a great deal about Talley and Sanders but you've ignored Bianca and Kline."

I took a deep breath and then explained, "I believe it was the day after I'd spoken with you by phone that Jeffrey got the word his first full-length play would open off-Broadway in early September. So Manhattan rehearsals were in for Jeffrey, but a trip to Europe was definitely out."

Catherine gazed into my eyes. "Anything happen?" she asked.

"Happen?"

"Yeah. Between you and . . . and Bianca?"

Checkmate. I answered quietly, "Yes, Catherine, I'm sorry."

As tears welled up in her eyes, she asked, "Why?"

So much meaning was compressed in that tiny three-letter word: Why did you do this? Why did this have to happen now? Why have I had to sacrifice so much for so many people? As she fought to regain her composure, I apologized again. "I'm sorry, Catherine. I swear I never intended to hurt you or lead you on."

She then firmly declared, "You have a choice to make, Andrew. I'd never tolerate any ongoing relationship with her."

I stared into Catherine's eyes and said gently but firmly, "I've made my choice, Catherine. I've . . . I've fallen deeply in love with her."

Catherine looked down and murmured, "What we call the

beginning is often the end, and to make an end is to make a beginning. The end is where we start from." She paused and then whispered, "Please, Andrew, just take me home."

15

cxb4!   1-0

CATHERINE NEVER LOOKED back as she walked up
the steps and disappeared into the house. And that was the last
time I ever saw her. To my surprise she never returned to Pantheon to finish her degree. I tried telephoning several times over
the years, but no one answered. I returned home to attend class
reunions in 1963, 1973, and again in 1983. I surveyed the crowds
each time, but she never appeared. I asked Knox, Anderson, and
Grimes if they'd seen her around town, and they said it was as if
she'd just vanished. Ironically, the one person among us who had
lived the most straightforward life had now become an inexplicable, invisible enigma.

So much had happened over the decades. Not long after their
first child was born, Dad and Sonya married and purchased a
larger home closer to campus in Urbana, where they subsequently
reared three highly creative children. While the eldest of my
stepbrothers enrolled at Yale, the other two attended exclusive
preparatory schools, one in Michigan and the other in Vermont.
Dad had relinquished his prized chair in physics, continued
conducting meaningful research in the university laboratory,
and by the 1980s sported the word "emeritus" among the many
professional titles preceding his name.

Since the publication of her critically acclaimed first work,

An Introduction to Musical Theory, Sonya had authored two additional books on advanced theory and was trying something new, crafting an interpretive biography of Haydn. I had recently reminded her half jokingly that she should at least give me partial credit for the idea. She smiled and assured me I would be included in the acknowledgments and that the important *Mourning Symphony* would be discussed in considerable detail.

When I visited Pantheon about ten years after graduation, I discovered I had lost two dear friends. Professor Emeritus McMasters, the local real estate tycoon and brain trust behind *The Messenger*, had died of a massive stroke. He bequeathed his substantial estate, including his extensive real estate holdings, to the university, requesting that five liberal arts scholarships be funded in perpetuity. To honor his contributions to the community, the McGill town fathers bestowed two well-deserved honors on my old landlord. They unanimously voted to change the name Courthouse Square to McMasters Square and erected a well-received bronze likeness on the courthouse lawn directly across the street from my old apartment.

During that same trip back to McGill, I also learned my invaluable mentor, J. Alfred Wagner, had passed on, dying of undetermined causes in his sleep. Since I had several hours of free time before my scheduled flight home, I decided to visit my old haunt, the rare-book collection in the main library. While browsing the exhibits in the foyer, I remembered how much time J. Alfred had spent among the rare books and manuscripts and wondered if any of his effects had found their way into the collection.

I rang the buzzer to enter the inner sanctum, checked the

card catalog, and completed a request to review their holdings of J. Alfred's material. After several minutes, a library assistant approached my table and handed me a small cardboard box containing two manila folders. I was shocked at how little there was in each. While the one folder contained several business letters from his publisher, the other held copies of brief correspondence with second-tier American poets asking permission to include their works in an upcoming contemporary anthology.

I spread the small number of pages out on the table in front of me and realized that in a hundred years these few letters would represent the sum total of Professor Wagner's life and career. How unfair. No one would ever know how invaluable he had been to all of us who now stand on his shoulders and teach professional scholarship to the next generation.

Our ongoing publication of *The Messenger* proved to be as difficult as doubling a cube, trisecting an angle, or squaring the circle. We ceased publication after only eight issues in two years. The end came not with a bang but a whimper. It was a case of simple mathematics. One after another, our inaugural contributors left Pantheon, and we just couldn't find enough high-caliber replacements with either the energy or the talent matching that of the founding authors.

Over the last decade, I have occasionally run into Donna at professional conferences and have exchanged lengthy updates with her via our Christmas greetings every year. She went on to teach advanced undergraduate and graduate courses in the American Renaissance at Poe's brief alma mater, the University of Virginia. She regularly publishes articles and serves on the executive council of the highly respected National Association of English Departments.

Since she is a warm, intelligent, attractive woman, I have always wondered why she never married. Of course, I would never broach the sensitive subject; but she has on occasion humorously alluded to her marital status in her letters, repeating her goal of "getting around to marriage one of these days." Maybe there had been too much psychological scarring to trust anyone enough to allow them unreservedly into her life. Perhaps she stands frozen between paralyzing fears—the fear of the small child in the princess dress trusting and then feeling unspeakable rejection and the fear of the aging woman at the Washington zoo avoiding the possibility of rejection but living out the rest of her days in solitude.

Bianca kept her word. She "made it right" with Jeffrey, returned to campus, and immediately buried herself in her poetry. The next two years were heaven. I knew I had made the right decision. During that sweet spot in time, we both achieved our short-term professional goals. While Bianca completed her third book of poetry, I finished my doctoral thesis and successfully defended it before a very demanding review committee.

The timing was perfect. After completing the doctorate, I was free to travel with Bianca that summer as she toured the country conducting readings to large, appreciative audiences in quaint bookstores and college auditoriums. My only complaint about the tour was admittedly rooted in mild jealousy. I realized that during the public appearances, I had become Jeffrey, standing alone in the shadows as devotees excitedly surrounded my beautiful, talented lover.

Reflecting on it now, the stark changes began the next year not long after she returned to McGill at the end of an extended tour in Europe. When I got home from shopping for our anniversary meal, I found Bianca sitting in the dark on the sofa rocking back and forth. She was holding her head in her hands, sobbing, and whispering nonsense. "I shouldn't have left her there. God will punish me."

I sat down beside her, slipped my arm around her shoulder, and pulled her in close. "Sweetheart. . . . Sweetheart, what's wrong? For God's sake, talk to me. Talk to me."

She continued rocking and repeating, "Punish me . . . punish me."

After an hour of uncontrollable crying, Bianca finally stopped rocking and rested her head on my shoulder. A sickening feeling came over me as the shock wore off and I acknowledged I had lived all this before. I stroked her arm gently and said more as a hope than as a fact, "We'll get you help. Find the best doctors. Get the latest medicines."

After several weeks of my gentle but firm insistence, Bianca finally acceded to my demands and sought help. But despite the latest counseling and medications, she began suffering tremendous mood swings. It was as if she were on a trapeze swinging between bright sunlight and the darkest night. At first, there was more light than darkness, which meant more periods of intense creativity. But over time, the trapeze arced increasingly less into the sunlight, and Bianca's productivity diminished considerably as she gradually returned to the night.

We had no idea we were at the beginning of a decade-long descent into Bianca's hell—the uncontrollable, intense fits of mania, the restlessness, the moving from city to city, the Thorazine, the Haldol, the valproic acid, the lithium, the deep depression, the shock therapy, and the shuttling back and forth between the hospitals, clinics, and home. One by one, the sycophants and wary friends disappeared. And while I would be out making a little money as an adjunct lecturer at a junior college, Bianca would stay in the house with the shades drawn, refusing to answer the door or the telephone.

Yes, I blame myself. I should have never left her alone. But we had to pay the rent and buy the food. It was my day to lecture. When I returned home from the campus, I opened the front door of our darkened house and shouted, "Sweetheart, I'm home."

No response.

I repeated a little louder, "Sweetheart, I home."

Still no response.

I switched on the lights in the living room. Bianca was not in her usual place on the couch. I shuddered, sensing something just wasn't right. I climbed the stairs and shouted again, hoping against hope, "Sweetheart, you there?"

The only response, echoes in our near-empty house.

When I reached the bedroom door, I slowly turned the handle and pushed. I switched on the light and only then did I spot the taut rope running from the center beam to the raised window. I gasped, stumbled backward out of the room, and rushed downstairs to telephone the police.

I spent the next year picking up the pieces. One of my projects was to edit Bianca's unpublished manuscripts, the product of those rare moments of unparalleled euphoria and imagination. I was on a mission to see this last book through to publication as a memorial to Bianca's genius. I had been with her during the darkest days and remained humanely loyal until the end. As her mood swings became more intense and unpredictable, I unwittingly became Beckett's tramp, believing I should do something while I had the chance. Her cries for help were ringing in my ears. I was determined to make the most of it, before it was too late. And no one can deny I kept my appointment. I was not a saint, but I followed through despite what I had learned shortly after Bianca had begun showing the early signs of illness.

During a brief trip back East for an undergraduate class reunion, I had dinner with my old friend, Manuel, who had grown up in Portugal and had presented me the prized bottle of Carvalhas Vintage Port '48. As we exchanged memories over dessert, I reached into my wallet and removed a folded piece of paper that I had carried around for all these years. I said I was curious and would love for him to translate the few lines of poetry Bianca had appended to the note she had mailed me not too long after we met.

Manuel read the lines to himself, looked up over his narrow frames, and asked if I really wanted to know the meaning. I paused, gathered my courage, and asked him to continue. He nodded and slowly began reading aloud in English:

Your life . . .

It's not my love; it's just your life.

I treasure you as I would the sunset or the moonlight.

I want the mood to last, but all I want to keep is the sense of owning it.

After Bianca's death, I worked hard over the next decade to rehabilitate my professional career. I landed a position at a respectable midwestern university as an assistant professor on the tenure track and feverishly began publishing articles ranging from "The Literature of War: A Comparative Study of Sassoon and Crane" to "Correcting the Record: An Alternative Interpretation of Ransom's *New Criticism*."

After six productive years, I became an associate professor; and then after four additional years of lecturing, publishing, serving on a plethora of committees, and playing the necessary politics, I finally achieved my goal, full professor of English with its all-important tenure. But the following year I shocked my colleagues when I announced I was resigning my university post to accept a professorship in the South. I never tried explaining why I was leaving my secure, hard-earned position. They would have never understood the powerful lure of McGill, Pantheon, and J. Alfred's old chair.

While the department head reminded me I was entitled to a larger, more comfortable office in the new Kirkwood wing, I respectfully declined and asked for space in the old tower. After settling in my new home not far from the house where Catherine and I helped build the snowman, I walked over to campus to drop off some books, supplies, and papers at my new office. After entering the ivied brick building, I checked the directory for my name at the bottom of the elegant marble staircase, methodically climbed the steps to the top floor, and then proceeded down the hallway to room 311.

I slowly turned the knob, entered respectfully, surveyed the tiny room, and whispered, "You glorious bastard. Somehow you knew I'd return." J. Alfred had left everything behind for his successors: the tall bookcases, the antique coat rack, the chairs and his monstrous carved oak desk consuming half the room. The echoes of our first conversation decades ago now ricocheted about the space: his praise for my first-semester course selection; his admonition that he would demand as much of me as he did of himself; and "the method to his madness" of the experimental composition course he had conjured up in this very room. As I turned to leave, I paused and smiled. There were still traces of Vesuvian ash lodged in the crevices of his old visitor's chair.

On the following Monday I returned to campus for conferences with the graduate students I would be mentoring for at least the next two years. But the first day on the job didn't begin auspiciously. One of the clerical staff had misplaced the personal file for my nine o'clock appointment. Everyone in the office feverishly scoured the building and concluded the folder had most likely been deposited inadvertently in the wrong mailbox and currently resided in another professor's overly stuffed briefcase somewhere between here and home.

At precisely nine o'clock, there was a sharp rap at the door. I looked up from my manuscript and shouted, "Please come in."

The knob turned and the door opened slowly. A bearded young man about my height and build entered and smiled faintly. I rose from my chair, extended my hand, and asked him to take a seat. As the polite young fellow sat there nervously staring across the desk at me, I momentarily sensed I had been transformed into J. Alfred and my first-year graduate student had become me.

I immediately apologized for the bureaucratic screw-up. "I'm sorry, Samuel, but I've temporarily misplaced your file. So in the meantime, tell me a little about yourself—a brief biography and details of your academic career to bring me back up to speed. You see, it has been several weeks since I last reviewed your file."

The graduate student smiled nervously and replied, "No problem, sir. As they say, 'Once more from the top.'"

We established a good rapport from the start. We shared a hearty laugh at the coincidences: we had grown up in the same city; we had attended the same high school; and I had had a high school classmate with his last name. In addition, from an early age we had both received classical instruction, he on the piano and I on the clarinet.

Samuel continued, "I never knew my father. When I was a teen, my mother told me that he had been recruited by one of the intelligence services; had purportedly been deployed to West Berlin as an operative; wrote several brief letters home; disappeared behind the Iron Curtain; and ultimately received recognition on the agency's wall of stars and in its Book of Honor." He paused to collect his thoughts and continued, "My mother explained that his enthusiasm for his country had influenced him to leave Pantheon early and postpone their June wedding. She also said he knew nothing about her pregnancy when he shipped out under deep cover. In fact, she confided that she really wasn't convinced as yet she was pregnant; and in any event, she didn't want to put any roadblocks in the way."

When the graduate student paused momentarily to reflect on his father, I eased in, "So tell me a little about your mother."

Samuel swallowed hard, took a deep breath, and said, "Sorry, sir. This is a bit tough for me. . . . Well, given her pregnancy, she returned home from school to live with her parents. Ah, she made a lot of sacrifices for me—working in a hotel during the day, attending nursing school at night." He paused as tears of gratitude welled up in his eyes.

"Did your mother ever marry?"

Samuel shook his head and replied, "No. She became involved with several men over the years but, to tell the truth, it was mostly because she felt I needed a father. But for some reason, none of them ever worked out."

I cleared my throat and asked, "How's she doing now?"

He looked down, shook his head, and whispered, "She died, sir, some years ago."

I swallowed hard. "I'm so sorry, Samuel. You can't imagine . . ."

"Breast cancer, sir. She fought really hard too. Literally willed herself to stay alive the last few months until she knew I had been graduated from high school."

I shook my head. "You must be very proud, Samuel."

He nodded and replied, "She was so brave."

"Yes, she faced everything life threw at her."

I took a deep breath and eased the conversation away from his personal biography to his academic achievements. He indicated he had been an excellent undergraduate English major, having graduated magna cum laude. He said one of the prime reasons he had chosen Pantheon for graduate school was his keen interest in existentialism and his knowledge that Pantheon had been at the forefront of the movement some years ago.

He lowered his head and then somewhat embarrassedly divulged, "I've delved into the cast of characters and discovered you were involved in *The Messenger*, and, ah, I was thrilled to learn you would be my graduate school adviser. . . . In fact, sir, if you agree, I'd like to interview you at some point for a paper I had in mind."

I nodded, smiled, and responded, "I'll help you as much as I can. But be warned; I was only a backroom player."

Samuel came to life then, saying, "If I were you, sir, I'd be proud to have been associated with *The Messenger*. It's legendary now—universally recognized as one of the key literary journals of the first half of the twentieth century."

I shook my head and said, "You're really too kind." After a brief pause to consult my notes, I moved the discussion along to his administrative responsibilities, the advanced composition course he would be teaching, and his own course work selection for the semester. After approximately forty-five minutes of lively discussion, I rose from my chair, extended my hand to signal our first meeting was over, and said, "I look forward to seeing you in my Introduction to Graduate Studies seminar later this week."

He smiled and replied, "Thank you, sir." He then turned and quickly exited the room.

When the door closed, I collapsed back into my chair. I was exhausted from the controlled performance of a lifetime.

Throughout the conversation, I had continually glanced from the graduate student to the framed photograph facing me on the desk. It was a picture of Catherine and me standing outside the stadium on that beautiful October day after the momentous football game. I loved the photograph. She was so young, beautiful, vibrant, and full of hope. She was wearing her beret, embracing me, and smiling broadly into the lens.

After that momentary feeling of my becoming J. Alfred and his becoming me, I quickly became convinced I was really looking at me. The young man in the photograph and the student sitting across from me were identical: the same age; the same eyes, nose, and lips; and the same striking auburn beard. I knew beyond a doubt I was sitting across the desk from our son.

Everything became much clearer. I now understood why Catherine had disappeared, never attended the reunions, and never returned to Pantheon to finish her degree. But did she know she was pregnant the day we walked along the edge of the exotic pond admiring the Egyptian lotus? Was she ever tempted to pick up the telephone or write a letter? Why did she fabricate the story about the CIA? Should I reveal who I am to Samuel or perpetually refrain from the unmasking? And if I were to remove the mask, wouldn't our son cruelly lose both of us again?

I rose from J. Alfred's chair, walked slowly toward the door, turned, and looked back at the Siege of Acre on the windowsill. I had returned the pieces to their endgame positions some years ago. Catherine's queen now stood majestically in the strong sunlight at the far end of the board, her first hopeful message intact. Had she sent this messenger today with a second note as a charitable act of consolation? A real possibility. After all, it was she who had pointed out the courage in Brahms. I switched off the lights, closed the door, and headed out into the fierce wind toward McMasters Square.